W9-CLO-749

HOLLOW GROUND

HOLLOW GROUND

A NOVEL BY **STEPHEN MARION**

ALGONQUIN BOOKS OF CHAPEL HILL 2002

Published by
Algonquin Books of Chapel Hill
Post Office Box 2225
Chapel Hill, North Carolina 27515-2225

a division of
Workman Publishing
708 Broadway
New York, New York 10003

Printed in the United States of America.
Published simultaneously in Canada by Thomas Allen & Son Limited.
Design by Anne Winslow.

Portions of this work originally appeared in different form in *Epoch* and *New Stories from the South: The Year's Best, 1998.*

Library of Congress Cataloging-in-Publication Data
Marion, Stephen, 1964–
Hollow ground : a novel / by Stephen Marion.
p. cm.
ISBN 1-56512-323-9
1. Zinc mines and mining—Fiction. 2. Illegitimate children—Fiction. 3. Fathers and sons—Fiction. 4. Teenage boys—Fiction. 5. Tennessee—Fiction. I. Title.
PS3613.A75 H65 2002
813'.6—dc21 2001055239

10 9 8 7 6 5 4 3 2 1
First Edition

IN MEMORY OF MY GRANDPARENTS

J.D. & Eloise Marion **Conley & Lena Collins**

HOLLOW GROUND

Dear Taft,

I seen them on the sidewalk before dance class. It was definitely him. I could tell by the way your mama was leaning that way. I opened the window to listen, but a train came. By my calculations they talked for a total of ninety-six cars. Ninety-six!

You know my theory, don't you? Everybody is right, Taft. He has to be the one. Has to be. He has a beard! The beard is sandy, like his hair. He has your eyes. His face is kind of widelike. It is all over town who he is. Back here after all this time.

As for me, I want to be just like your mama. You can be him. Listen. Shhhhhh. Is a train coming?

Tanya

I

ON THE NIGHT the earth collapsed, Moody Myers rode him home. Taft was thirteen years old. His eyes were shut. Wind, spring wind, entered the truck windows and flew around in the cab over him and Moody Myers. It picked up the smell of the roadside weeds and mixed with the oily odor of the squeaking seats of the truck and the ancient yellow maps and longhand papers and entry ledgers Moody always kept stacked in the floorboards and on the dash. The papers came alive but never could fly away, because they were held down with bags of lead minié balls from the Civil War and a large brass compass.

Soon, even with his eyes closed, Taft knew they had entered Alexander City, because the truck passed into the dip on the highway where the smell of entering Alexander City always lingered. It was an icy smell, even in summer. The town sat right on top of the largest zinc deposit in the world, and the mines had tapped it, and the smell came up through the exhaust tower above the highway. The smell always reminded Taft of Moody Myers, because people called the exhaust rig Moody's tower. It was his tower because he had designed it years ago for the mines. To Taft the smell was like the center of a rock, pulled up from the soul of the middle of the earth. When he smelled it, even in his sleep, he knew he was home.

Taft opened his eyes. No sign announced the name of the town. Instead a billboard said TRUCKS! TURN RIGHT 1,400 FEET. AGRICULTURAL LIMESTONE. FAST LOADING! The sign had always seemed to Taft a desperate plea, because behind it, and behind a scrim of locusts, the ancient gray lake of powdered lime the mines had drawn out of the earth stayed at least as big as the town. It had great wrinkled bluffs that changed color depending on age and weather and time of day and season. Near them, already beginning to light up like a ship, lay the zinc works. They operated twenty-four hours a day.

Moody Myers had turned off, the Ford truck's blinker keeping time louder than the new cars did, but he still stared at the road like a book he was reading. Taft had no idea what to say to him. Even if he had known something to say to Moody Myers, he would not have known what to call him. Names like Papaw or Daddy or Granddaddy did not seem appropriate. He was married to Taft's grandmother, but he was not Taft's mother's father or his grandfather. Taft didn't know exactly what he was. Moody Myers was equal, public or private, yesterday and tomorrow, in all quarters all over Alexander County.

That was the main reason Taft had chosen him to call. Moody

did not generally have questions for people about contemporary matters. He was somebody people called when an albino groundhog was shot or some odd bones washed up or it was not known what was in the background of an old photograph. Moody, Taft figured, probably would not notice that Taft was on the opposite side of the county from where he was supposed to be on a Friday afternoon after school. He would not notice that Taft had dried blood on one eyelid or that he had slid down in a fresh cowpile, which had splashed up onto his pants legs and dried in the tread of his shoes, or that he was still mostly wet from creek water and his shirt was dotted with beggarlice. He would never guess how hungry Taft was. Instead, Moody would perhaps assume that this was the continual state of thirteen-year-old boys.

It was hard to tell how old Moody himself was. He might have been very old, older than Taft's grandmother. He'd been around forever. He was small and ground down by time or work, and his beard had grown gray to a whiteness on his face. It was trimmed short, and his hair, also white but with some dark left in it, went straight back from a central point on his forehead. Taft had never seen him when he didn't have on overalls, and he always wore a pair of glasses with black plastic rims. The pockets in the bib of his overalls contained different kinds of papers and a little book and a very short pencil. Part of the middle finger on Moody's right hand was gone, cut off in the mines, so when he shook hands with Taft, which he always did, what was left of it curled into Taft's palm like a little knot.

Taft knew that for the first three years of his life he had lived with his grandmother and Moody, but he had no memory of it.

All he had was what his mother had told him, and that was not much. It was because I was poor, she said. So poor. Perhaps Moody, though, had some memory of Taft that he would not admit. Perhaps the little knot in his palm was some kind of secret handshake. Even now he was holding on to the big black steering wheel with both hands, as if he might have felt the same blustering forces in the world that Taft did, as if maybe he felt them and they didn't get any better or any less even when you got to be an old man like Moody Myers, and they weren't any more possible to talk about either.

Finally Taft said something. He said, I guess Tony is going to work about now. He said that because he figured it might catch Moody's attention, because Tony worked the nightshift in the zinc mines and Moody had been a mining engineer before he retired. He had been the one who mechanized the mines. Before him, people said, zinc was nothing here. As soon as he had said this, however, Taft realized it was ridiculous. Taft had not talked to his uncle Tony since he was six or seven, since everything happened.

Moody looked at Taft as if Tony and the zinc mines were the absolute last things on his mind. I guess he better, he said finally. Then he put his eyes back on the book of the road again.

They drove through town on the new highway. Everybody called it the new highway, but it had been built way before Taft was born. The spring sun had turned from copper to orange and red and it lay its light on the buildings of Alexander City. It was ready to sink below the world. Taft squinted at the cracked windshield. It was as if he could not see clearly enough, no matter how hard he looked.

The truck reached a crossroads.

I want you to see something down here, said Moody.

Only one problem, Taft.

Brief pause for effect.

He is married.

To somebody else, I mean.

How do I know? The register of deeds office. Where I am every day after school. Aint I lucky, T., to have a mother who helps register everybody's deeds?

He was in Vietnam. Maybe he slaughtered innocent women and children. Maybe it made him crazy. I don't know yet. But he is married and it is not happy! (I am coming to why.) Just small details now, Taft, such as the light on at the dance school at three in the morning. It was them. I mean, it was they. And the next morning, which was a Saturday, he walks into Sweeten's Jewelry Store and drops something on the counter and it is like a gold nugget.

Where did this come from? says Mr. Sweeten. He is two thousand and four hundred years old. I guess maybe he thought it came out of the zinc mines.

But, Off my finger, is the reply.

Off your finger, says Mr. Sweeten. How come this to be on your finger?

It used to be a ring.

What kind of ring did it used to be?

A wedding ring.

A wedding ring?

Mr. Sweeten thought about that. Well, he said, it don't look like one. How come it aint round like you expect a ring to be?

Because some needle-nosed pliers got ahold of it.

I see, said Mr. Sweeten. Now it's not no wedding ring no more, is it?

No.

This is when he tells his name. Mr. Sweeten asked it, God bless him. The name is Gary Solomon. Remember the name, Taft.

Solomon, says Mr. Sweeten. You any kin to them Solomons in Leadvale?

No, he says.

What about Bid Solomon? You aint Bid Solomon's boy are you? He auctioned off my daddy's farm.

Then Gary Solomon, all of a sudden, says, I got a better idea. And he takes his little gold nugget, drops it back in his pocket, and goes out the door without a word.

He mailed it, Taft! To an address in Mississippi, we hear. We should have the address by the end of the week. Check this space. Did I say he will be here Friday? He is always here Friday. (More on this later.)

See, Taft, how life is. See, it makes your mother my dance teacher (thank you, life!) and then it brings back from somewhere your mother's old boyfriend, old, old, who I know she never has stopped loving even though they both got mistakenly married. And the best thing is, we get to watch!

It will bring you back too, Taft, to me. See. See if it don't.

You wait.

The creek between the high school and the courthouse had taken most of his papers. It had hustled them over the roots of a sycamore, not the one that had tangled his feet but another farther one, before Taft could emerge and go after them. Some cows watched him splash to the bank, which was splattery and soft with the pocks of their hoofprints, and crawl along it struggling for a chance at his red notebook. *Tennessee History* had opened and gone to the bottom waving its pages like seaweed. Taft's algebra homework clung to his fingers like wet toilet paper, but Tanya's letters were all magically dry. He kept running, or half running and half crawling, along the creekbed downstream, because he knew that once loose the letters would fly as far as they could. One had gotten down to a deep pool and yet another had plastered itself upside down to a rock. By lying on his stomach in the mud and stretching his arm out as far as he possibly could, Taft was able to touch it with one finger. From behind her handwriting slanted the opposite way, but it was still her handwriting.

It was still a mile through the fields to Shelton, but Taft made it before the courthouse closed. Shelton was little. Though it was the county seat, it was smaller and much tighter than Alexander City. Anybody coming down into it from either hill saw Shelton assemble right out of the ground like the next page in a pop-up book. Here was the courthouse, columns and white cupola, and ringed around it were Bible Drug Store and Lindsey Hardware and the florist. Leave, and it all neatly folded back in again.

Taft had always thought the Alexander County Courthouse sat crooked. Someone who read the book long ago hadn't closed it right and now it jutted up too tall and narrow out of a street that slanted sharply down to the shady side. Perfect for Tanya Mayes. In the thin April sunlight men had come onto the courthouse porch to smoke. On its brick steps, worn to a sway, and beside the chalky white columns, the faces turned down to him without greeting, serious as the smells of shoe leather and tobacco and sweat, all the unreadable faces of men who served on juries, men who worked for the county, men who came to pay their taxes or to get divorced from their wives, men charged with crimes.

It was strangely level inside. The wooden floor of the courthouse popped and cracked loudly with the footsteps of everyone. It was so loud it sounded as if the floor might be on fire or about to collapse, and the sounds echoed beneath the tall ceiling. Taft thought it was strange that no one had stopped him or even seemed to notice him. He was still not dry. When he moved, his tennis shoes still squished and every joint in his body was sore where the wet clothes had rubbed against him. He was pretty sure he smelled. Several times in the fields, and once on a road, he had smelled something and he was pretty sure it was him. It is difficult to remove cowshit from the treads of tennis shoes and the weave of blue jeans. But maybe this was nothing. Maybe wet boys from the fields came into Shelton every afternoon, reeking of cowshit and carrying their warped books. This was the city in a free country. It took all comers, so Taft frowned and kept moving to show that he also had business in the county seat. In the hallway a big creaking staircase swept up one side. A black sign on it had an arrow that said, among other things, REGISTER OF DEEDS.

Women with cigarettes sat on the benches. Little children hung at their legs. A bald head with black eyeglasses poked out from the courtroom doors and called out a woman's name. Taft heard them whisper the name around him in tiny waves. A girl who looked young as the ones in his freshman class straightened up on the bench and stood, allowed herself a final draw from a cigarette, and walked in the courtroom door. Taft watched her. She moved with a cautious harmony as if there were mud puddles to step around on the oily wooden floor. When he turned back to the row of women he found them all staring at him, so he walked to the courtroom door, between the long rolls of war dead, and was tall enough to see easily through the little square windows.

Inside was a trial. Light slanted in the windows and rubbed across what seemed to be church pews. The few men and women seated in them appeared asleep. The judge sat above them with his unoccupied face, and two lawyers were poised at the bench, speaking soundlessly to him. The girl Taft had watched sat in the witness stand. Her eyes went straight ahead. Taft felt that he was watching events that had taken place before he was born. Men in uniforms or suits sat at tables before the judge, and others stood by the doors. For a second Taft imagined that the trial was about him and that the judge and the lawyers and the girl in the witness stand were trying to prove who he really was. Well, he thought, let them try.

An Essay on the Art of Kissing
by Tanya Mayes

So far I have a real good title but am awaiting the text. Maybe we can fill in more.

We interrupt this essay to bring you a special news bulletin.

He was here. Second floor of the Alexander County Courthouse, register of deeds office. Cross my heart and hope to die. Stick a needle in my eye.

We all acted like we didn't know who he is. That is the way we act with everybody we know everything about. (Except you, Taft!)

At first he just stood here with his hands in his pockets like he was thinking. Up close you can see what she sees. He has sweet eyes. I think they are blue. I was right. They are yours, Taft! Yours made over. I mean yours are his made over. He just kept standing there like he was trying to work up to talk or something. His hands stayed in his pockets. I wished I could have seen his hands. I heard he was an artist with his hands in high school. He could make anything. I wondered if maybe he had ahold of that gold nugget in there.

Finally he said, You don't have a map up here, do you? A map of the county?

We all continued to work furiously. We had not been working when he came in. We had been talking about socks. My mother volunteered to shake her head.

None whatsoever?

We blinked at him.

Then how do you tell where the roads go?

Evelyn, the register of deeds, said in her deepest, most authoritative voice, Everybody just knows where they go. Where are you from?

Here.

Well, then you ought to know where they go, oughtn't you?

I been gone, he said. I just got back.

Well, they still go pretty much the same place they did when you left.

Then my mother said, They ain't making no new places to go.

That made him smile.

What, said Evelyn, are you looking for?

Do you have a plat, he said, that shows all the cemeteries in the county?

We began to look at one another. This is another thing we do.

We, said Evelyn, probably do not have a plat that shows all the anything in the county.

If we did, said my mother, that would be morbid.

This time he didn't grin as much. And there was a kind of edge on the grin.

Where have you been gone to for so long? I said.

This was the first time he had looked at me. I sat up straighter.

Don't pay no attention to her, said my mother. Then everybody let it get real quiet.

Everywhere, he said.

But you came back, I said. It was a question the way I said it.

I came back for a funeral.

Everybody was thinking. I could feel them thinking heavy. So I said, Whose funeral?

Of course this is when my mother said, Tanya, *real loud, but in a kind of excited way that didn't have too much effect.*

Is that how come you're looking for cemeteries?

Tanya!

Temporary network trouble. Do not adjust your set, Taft.

P.S. Are you scared? You look scared. Did I scare you? I wanted to. I wish I could be. Scared, I mean. I used to love to scream. It feels so good to the throat. But I cannot be scared anymore. I have gone out in the field and cannot seem to re-create the screams of earlier days. What is it, Taft? No movies will work, no heads chopping off or scalpels, etc. Bad wrecks are on paper only. I have been downstairs several times with the lights off but there is no imagination down there, only sprouty potatoes.

See if you can scare me, Taft, because I might as well be buried for the way things are right now. That is my situation. You see where this letter came from, don't you?

The letter came from under the pasture rock. Most of Tanya's letters originated here. Several years ago his mother had been very excited about this white flat rock, as she was excited about even smaller things just before the divorce. She and Dennis, the man she had married when Taft was four, thought about moving away. They started eating different food. They tried to order a wok at the Whiteway and the clerk thought his mother had a speech impediment. Do you mean the combination type or the key, honey? he asked. They bought some antique chairs she never finished refinishing. They were building a rock garden. None of these things ever turned out. The backyard gradually forgot its rock garden, the way the house tried to forget Dennis, except for the one pasture rock, which still grew a patch of pink creeping phlox and one tulip each March. Taft liked to mow down the tulip leaves with a soft thunk.

But it was the weight of the rock that had caught his eye. Taft's mother refused to buy him the weight-lifting set, which was for sale at the Whiteway in back next to the gerbils, the turtles, and the tropical fish. So he had started his own training program with the white rock. At dusk, when motion is more fluid, Taft kneeled and lifted it twenty times. The smell of the dirt fanned out. He felt his upper arms like a physician before and after. On the seventh night, just as he was beginning to feel a difference, he hinged up the rock and there in the flat yellow elbows of roots lay a square of folded paper with a name across it.

Taft.

He reached under the rock, as if for a spider. Taft unfolded the letter, thinking it must have washed there. The paper was not like paper but more like skin from the dampness of the earth. Very little was said at first. *What are you doing to this rock?* Taft stood up and listened to the treefrogs like a million softly shaking bells. Soon the letters started counting themselves, one numeral a day. *I have to tell somebody this. It might as well be you.* Taft could not understand where she got the strength to lift the white rock. He let it drop, suddenly lighter, and stared at the back of her house.

Tanya Mayes was the skinniest girl he had ever seen. If she were a puzzle, her arms and legs could have fit each other's slots. Tanya was skinny because she was born with a hole in her heart. Nobody at school seemed to know this, but Taft did. She had an operation to sew it up when she was six. One time when they were little kids Taft heard her mother tell his mother that Tanya probably would not live a normal life span. That was the way she said it, as if Tanya were the runt kitten in the litter. But Tanya didn't seem to know, or care, that she would die. She was the only female at the new consolidated Alexander County High School who wore green eye shadow with glitter. Her hair frequently changed colors. This year she had already been suspended for dropping a bottle of red gin in the girls' bathroom.

On certain humid days one whole wing of the school still smelled of the new name by which she was called, Sloe Gin Fizz, or later just Fizz.

Fizz began to answer questions as if he had asked them. Yes, the skin of her thighs and underarms was too much like a chicken's. Her weight fluctuated as much as eight pounds between letters. She was very good at math. Marijuana grew on the roadside down toward the railroad tracks. Already one pound of it was drying at night on her windowsill. Tanya had an odd feeling in her integument. Her dad was gone all the time selling cookware and burglar alarms. In his absence, the alarms went off regularly at all times of the day and night. Tanya wore blue panties on Fridays. Her mother didn't allow anything but white panties because colored ones were not healthy and besides she did not have time to wash them separately. So Tanya did, secretly in the sink, after everyone had gone to bed. *On Friday I feel so deliciously unhealthy, Taft.* For a week he stopped reading. Still every evening the rock had an extra letter for him. At least he assumed they were his, because she had stopped addressing them to Taft D., or Taft, or T. Now the outside was blank. Taft wished he had never learned to read. He wished the ink was just ink. At last he picked one up and it said, *Well, it is about time.*

Tanya Mayes was how love was. Taft had seen it happen all around him. It came at you, uncontrollably, from the worst and most unexpected places. That poor girl, said his mother last week as she watched Tanya climb onto the roof of her house to tan closer to the sun, has got mental problems. It's April, not July.

Taft kept his back to Tanya on the roof. His mother sat crosslegged on the patio. She was tearing a white rag in pieces. The material ripped, blooming dust in the cool sunlight. Arranged around her were her chairs, her thinking chairs, the same ones she had paint-stripped after the divorce. This was a sign. After a long time Taft said, What is it?

What is what? said his mother. Her University of Tennessee sweatshirt was another sign. She had gotten it out this afternoon and put it on. The palest most ancient shade of orange possible, it rode up over the lowest knots of her backbone. Taft's mother was sinewy. In her arms and neck you could see tendons that you couldn't see in other people. When he was little Taft had assumed this was because she danced and taught dance. But in old pictures, she was the same way. Her face had a handsomeness like a man's and darker skin. She and Taft both had the same kind of coarse hair, more like the hair in a horse's tail. Tanya's skinniness was smooth and dispossessed of tendons. She presently had hair that was almost white. Her face was intimidating, but Taft could take comfort in her teeth. They were large and folded slightly in on one another as if they refused to let her face forget its childhood. There was an extra one on the top row. She probably did not know she had thin green veins at her temples. No, probably she did.

What is it that made you get the chairs out?

She stopped rubbing one chair back with steel wool and looked up. Good question, Taft, she said. To finish finally, I guess.

Finish what?

She had gone back to work. My chairs, she said.

Taft leaned against the wrought iron, which was still cold.

His mother was nineteen when Taft was born. She liked to tell people that she and Taft had grown up together. But for the first four years of his life they didn't. She left him with his grandmother and Moody until she came back from college. Taft knew she didn't have to come back. They wanted her to leave and dance. About once a year she came back from Knoxville with the *New York Times* rolled up and carried it like a log into the backyard and sat in her lawn chair all afternoon bent over it, tracing across the pages with her fingers and stopping every so often to stare up into the sky as if a rare bird had just flown from the tree.

Making a baby, she had told him again and again, does not make a father. It just makes a maker.

And, she added as if she had just thought of it, making love does not make a lover.

Taft watched the little cords of muscle in her wrists and neck and ankles as she worked. He knew why people gave advice.

I now know all details of your conception. It was not easy. (Finding out, I mean!) But I did. No deed goes unregistered, Taft. Now I am ready to write your biography. I call it, A Life of Taft. *See if you like this opening.*

Taft began life as a zygote at the 1964 Alexander County Fair. The best thing about the fair is the smell. Not the rides, because they are not scary enough, but the smell. The fair smells like straw and animals and fried onions and the dark all around with colored lights and maybe throw in some cow manure and powdered sugar and sweat. Very primordial.

His mother was fairest of the fair. Her talent was a dance rou-

tine. No, her real talent was in the car. No, they went in the weeds, because there is tall weeds not far from the fairgrounds, and you could still hear the music and smell all those smells. Need more research here about the grass. This fall I will check.

Taft didn't go up the stairs to the register of deeds office. Instead, he stood and watched his own vague reflection on the glass cases that composed the Alexander County Museum. He began to act as if he were very interested in the historical items in the glass cases, as if maybe he had come here from a great distance in order to study them and report back to the Bureau of Antiquities.

Moody Myers was caretaker of the museum. Your granddaddy knows more about Alexander County than any man alive, people said. Moody Myers, they said, has never forgotten anything in his life.

Moody, his mother said, is a good man.

As if to prove it, one whole winter when Taft was about nine she turned him over to Moody each Saturday. Moody led him out to the cow pastures to search for Civil War relics for the museum, and Taft watched him carefully. Taft imagined whole armies of bones beneath the ground, frozen in combat, his real grandfather, who died before Taft was born, struggling among them. Moody pulled the bullets out like grubs from the rooted dirt, and then Taft watched him stand and gather his thoughts in the fields, pointing in one direction and then another with his metal detector, cursing at the deceit of plow points and buried fence wire. He talked about the halo that grows around a piece of metal when it has been buried for years. Then he put on his headphones and listened to the thoughts of the dead.

In the glass cases they were all ordered, each tagged and dated with a yellowed note card. Animal skeletons assembled themselves, broken pottery bowls came back together. An old photograph was labeled STREET SCENE, ZINCTOWN, 1929. Taft leaned down to look closer. That was the name before they changed it to Alexander City. In the photograph Zinctown had headrigs and big barnlike buildings, and rows and rows of little houses, some of them with wash on the line. Moody's handwriting told what was the zinc mill and what was the changehouse, and it identified the rows of houses as Paper City. So called, said Moody's writing, due to the thinness of the walls in winter.

Taft went on to the bullet molds and heavy muzzle-loaders of the American Revolution, the glass eyes of a great stuffed owl still frozen with the instant he struck the windshield of a Gobblers Knob man, stacks of nicked coins too old to buy a drink from a machine, a brick from an ancient Egyptian city, ragged city election bills, a stone Indian pipe, a wooden canteen from the War for Southern Independence, and in the last case, practically alone, the Two Articles of Human Suffering.

One of the articles was a human vertebra. Taft bent down to consider it, a single link from a dead man's back. It was yellow and winged and had embedded within it a black Indian arrowhead. The flint had cracked the bone, and Taft could see part of the hardened sponge interior, where the marrow would have been. The second article was only a smooth rock, but the rock was sooted and slick because it had once been in the overalls pocket of a man who burned to death in the zinc mines. The human grease will not wash off, Moody had written on the card along with the dead man's name. These objects, he ended, are taken from Zinctown, Tennessee.

Taft understood. Here, he thought, is what it means to hurt and go on hurting. This is the solid place inside it all. He himself had inflicted death and suffering on a thousand insects, beheaded and impaled grasshoppers and stag beetles, poured boiling water underground to seek out the weightless bodies of ants. He had witnessed the autospasms of dismembered spider legs, the twitchkick of death in a shrew, the stench of an eyeless dog. But the world just soaked up their pain. Now a despair rose in him for absolutely no reason, not because of the cracked bone or the burnt rock or the maker or even the hole in Tanya's heart, not because he was a fool to walk here from school or because home was distant, but simply and only because it wanted him and he wanted it, an awful, beautiful pain lacing tight in his groin and belly, like going to sleep and coming awake at once.

A back door to the courtroom swung open. Frozen, Taft stared at the $10 FINE FOR SPITTING ON FLOOR notice, but his heart flew and his hands fell cold. A deputy passed, and others passed eager to leave on a Friday afternoon, each raising gooseflesh up his back to his neck, each no more than a scented wind, a spirit, brushing over him, laughing and sighing and talking, a woman in high heels and hose rasping beneath the flow of her skirt, men removing sport coats like wings, the judge with his black robe parting to reveal a glimpse of red necktie. Then all his sight disappeared. Somebody had him from behind, covering his eyes with cool moist fingers, and there was a smell of perfume and cigarette smoke.

Guess who?

Taft swallowed. Tanya, he said.

Tanya! And just who is Tanya?

When he turned around, Taft tried to focus his eyes as quickly as he could, but the cool delicious sting of female fingers was still upon them and upon the skin of his entire face. Tanya was a woman instead of a girl, standing and looking at him like a woman, and her blond hair had changed its shade. It wasn't Tanya. It was Clarice.

You don't have another girlfriend, do you, Taft? she was saying. I thought I was the only one.

Clarice was Taft's aunt. Or she was in a way. His mother called her the Girl with Six Months to Live, because she had moved in with his uncle Tony. But that had been way more than six months ago. Taft almost never saw Clarice, but when he did she acted like she saw him every day. He didn't care, though, because Clarice was a knockout. After she let him use the telephone to call Moody, and they were waiting on the courthouse porch for him to arrive, the eyes of every man who came out the door lit up with evil joy. You almost didn't know what part to look at, because they were all so good, and on top of everything else, Clarice was wild. She was so wild it didn't seem possible that she could hold down a job, but she had worked at the courthouse for a long time.

Tell me about Tanya, said Clarice. Is it serious?

Taft pretended that he was too busy watching for Moody's truck to answer. Not really, he said.

When I was your age I was married.

You were almost fourteen?

Clarice laughed. Well, I seemed that young. I guess I was seventeen.

The sound of a lawn mower in the grass somewhere near faded in and out, and he tried to picture Clarice, now leaning on the concrete rail and bumping her cloth pocketbook against her thigh, as a girl of seventeen. It wasn't hard. But now even Clarice's beauty and her girlishness had a tough side.

I thought I could do anything when I was your age, she said to him. Her voice was tired. The week was ending. You know you just missed your mama's new boyfriend. I mean her old one. What do you think about him, Taft?

MOODY PASSED THE empty Maloy Drive-In and turned off. The streets in Alexander City were still named after mine shafts. Right now they were on Number Four Street. Taft couldn't figure out what Moody could possibly want him to see here. He couldn't remember Moody ever trying to show him something that actually still existed anyway. The truck rolled to a stop at the Little League ball field. Other cars were parked around, and Taft saw a group of boys climbing the chain-link fence.

I wanted you to see this, Moody said. Then we'll go on home.

The ends of the sky had become bright pink, aging to crimson near the horizon, but on the ground people walked around in the new dark. The sun had gone below the world. Gathered behind second base, most of the people had their arms poised on their hips in an attitude of disbelief, because a patch of earth bigger than a house had fallen in.

Good gosh, said Taft.

They walked closer and all of a sudden Taft sensed with his ankles a new flimsiness of the earth. The hole went deep, breathing up the cool smell of dirt and sassafras past the rents of jagged sod. A few junked cars had already been dumped in the bottom. Boys on the other side threw in rocks, their voices swearing into the dusk that they fell on and on without ever landing. A few stray numbers, probably from last season's last game, still hung on the American Legion scoreboard.

I just heard a rumble, said a man nearby.

We aint never going to find third base.

Them mines has dug all up in under this town like a pack of groundhogs, said another. Now you look.

You, said a woman, could look all the look off of it and not never believe it.

It shook the dishes, another woman's voice said. Just barely.

For a while they watched as flashlight beams dangled in the skinned roots going down. Taft tried to see Moody's face. It looked confused and anxious, as if something, one of the calculations he kept secret in his mind, had gone completely wrong. Taft wanted to ask him a question. He could see from Moody's face that he already knew Taft wanted to ask it. Moody always waited for a question almost as if it would hurt him, as if he were a little sorry that he would know the answer.

How come this to happen? said Taft.

I can't exactly say, said Moody.

Walking back toward Moody's truck they saw the anxious faces drawing in. Three men came by carrying a cooler filled with ice and beer. They were laughing and holding out their free arms to balance it. Small campfires had begun around the field. For some reason people wanted to be here. Taft stopped for a second and turned around. Moody stopped too. Taft asked him where Zinctown used to be.

It was here, said Moody.

Where is it now?

Moody considered this for a second.

Here, he said.

2

GARY, BRENDA SAID, you know I lit the first cigarette when I was fourteen. I wanted to grow up fast, flick my ashes on old Zinctown. That's where it started. It kept me thin even if it took my breath away. I quit the day I got married and started again in the divorce. No joke. It's something how you can just go right back like you never stopped. It takes about one second. How do you reckon it looks at the dance school? All the little daughters in their little taps, and me the teacher going hack hack all afternoon. I'm cutting down if you can believe it. You don't see an ashtray in here anywhere, do you? It's step one. I have strong lungs but they crave smoke. Here, you take my lighter. You keep it away from me. No matter what I do, you keep it away from me.

She held out the lighter. It was pink.

Gary nodded. Thank you very much, he said. He put the lighter in his pocket. This sounded reasonable to him. At least the words did. He wasn't exactly certain what they meant, except that they were emerging pleasurably from Brenda's mouth, because he was halfway through his third big glass of whiskey with ice. So was Brenda. Gary still had on his suit coat and tie. He had just been to the funeral for his aunt. A lot of people he remembered were there. One of them was Brenda. Brenda was dressed a little too sexy for a funeral. The dress, which was silky green, didn't come together good at the top, as if she rarely wore it, so he could occasionally see the white freckled flesh over her breastbone, and the side of one breast before it disappeared into her bra. Seeing Brenda made Gary feel good. He felt as if he were the boy he used to be in high school, instead of what he was now. The more he drank, the more he felt like this. In high school Gary made wire sculptures and read books, and people thought he had interesting, radical ideas. He looked at Brenda when she didn't know he was looking and he still didn't see hate. Maybe it was not there. He wouldn't blame her if it was, though. Anyway, after fifteen years, it might take her longer to get good and mad than the few days he had been back.

Gary wondered if maybe Brenda still loved him, or if he still loved Brenda. Or maybe it was simply the funeral that had given him a feeling of love for all living people, or the drinking. He had not been drunk since his divorce, which had taught him forever how seamlessly love can flip right over to hate, and now the whiskey played in his brain like a church organ. It turned mere notes into chords. As Gary looked at Brenda and she spoke, numb tremors of pleasure arose in different localities of his skin. He let them. She was still beautifully lean. Brenda was lean as she could be. Her chest was flat like a girl who was still growing. Right before him, Brenda changed from a note, an individual woman, into a chord of women. Gary enjoyed this. If she stopped talking and wanted him to speak, he would smile and say, Keep on talking. You're doing real good.

Shut up, Gary, Brenda would say, as if she might hit him before she started again. He was still listening to her, to them all, even though she had stopped, when a door closed somewhere above them. The wind of it reached them in the downstairs den and lifted Brenda's attention away. He waited on the couch edge as she listened to her split-level house around them. She had one hand in the air.

Tell me where to hide, Gary whispered, but she only motioned for him to hush.

Taft? she called out, and the ceiling creaked. Then she turned back to Gary as if she had forgotten him, said, Hang on, and ran upstairs.

Sobered a little by her absence, Gary stood in Brenda's house and examined the scars on her coffee table. This had been the evening when they told everything. Everything from the past fifteen years. Women have to have such a night. To Gary it was like middle school when you went to the railroad tracks and she took off her clothes, piece by piece, and you had to too. You never touched, and it was as if whoever was the toughest naked won. Then for the rest of your life she looked at you different. Of course, tonight some things had been held back. Gary had told her about hitchhiking all over the country after Vietnam and working for seven different police departments and about knowing it was wrong the day he got married. And Brenda made him tell how he met his wife on a call to help her retrieve her belongings from the apartment of a boy who had hit her, and exactly what she looked like, but there were also huge holes in his story. As there were in hers. It didn't come up, for instance, that Gary had only stayed married forty-eight hours. It also didn't come up that Brenda's ex killed himself.

Gary had not expected a house and a subdivision neighborhood like this. Not out of Brenda Carter. He stared at her tennis shoes on the brown shag carpet, one of them turned carelessly over, the laces ragged because she wore them untied. Brenda's house smelled like candles.

This is Taft, she said, a little out of breath, standing in the doorway. Beside her, the boy was longhaired and busy thinking about other things. Gary has been wanting to meet you, son, she said, pulling him forward.

Gary shook the boy's hand and said, Hey, Taft.

Hey, said Taft. He spoke as if it caused him to lose count of something. His hand felt large for a boy his age, yet weightless as a bird wing. Gary held himself cautiously in place, concealing the dizzy heat Brenda and her whiskey had begun. He was relieved when it struck him that Taft was like a thinner male version of Brenda. The coarse hair fell in a similar way, the face softened around the same mouth and impatient blue eyes, but his stance, balancing one leg and then another on the carpet, astonished Gary as if he had come across an unsettled part of himself.

Go on now and eat your supper, said Brenda. It's late.

Taft watched them.

I wouldn't want to stand between a man and his supper, said Gary.

When Taft was gone Brenda called out, Clean up after yourself, Taft.

Gary couldn't sit down.

You don't have to look so surprised, said Brenda.

How old is he? asked Gary.

About your age.

Thirty-three?

About your age when I knew you.

Eighteen?

Fourteen. Almost. He'll be fourteen. Next month.

Gary was silent for a moment. Brenda looked at him as if she had planned that. In a minute he said, He's mine.

He is not.

You said he was fourteen years old.

Almost fourteen. I said almost, Gary.

Who else was there when you were that age?

Brenda shrugged. I forgot how arrogant you are.

I'm not arrogant.

It got silent. Gary remembered how the silence had been sometimes. Finally Brenda said, No, he's not yours. He's mine.

Gary looked into her face. Her eyes were hard and quick as bird's eyes. He remembered this too. He said, How did he get a name like Taft?

Brenda shrugged. They just kept passing it down, she said, until it got to him.

• • •

Brenda's house quieted after midnight. The silence drew in from outside, where it had risen above the whole neighborhood like a second, more certain dusk. Inside Gary's brain it was completely different. Questions and loud shouts kept coming from all the different rooms, but no matter how hard he concentrated he could not understand them through the whiskey. He kept offering to leave, and Brenda kept shrugging, but Gary was too scared to take himself up on the offer. Above them the rush of Taft's shower, his dulled movements and the creak of his bed, passed into the signal of one weak radio, and finally even that became the empty complaints of the roof beams and the foundation. Gary kept thinking he would wake up or shake his head and clear it. Brenda told small lies. She'd say she paid fifty dollars for something he knew cost thirty. Maybe she had exaggerated Taft. Maybe he was a lot younger and just looked fourteen. But Gary had seen him himself. He had shaken his hand. It was a good thing they were drunk, Gary thought. Otherwise, it might be a fight.

I got an idea, said Brenda. Why don't you, Gary Solomon, tell me what you remember about me?

Gary thought for a second. They were headed for the railroad tracks again. I remember I made a sculpture out of the heart of a walnut log. It was a woman from the back. I remember I just saw it in there before it came out.

I mean about me, said Brenda.

That was about you.

It was not.

You went away to college, he said.

See, I can't remember that. Remember more.

That's all I remember.

That's piss poor.

Gary tried to laugh. Tell me what you remember about me.

Nothing.

Remember more.

You said you were not ever coming back.

But I did.

And I said I would not be here when you did.

But you were. What else?

You're still married.

I am not.

You are too.

On paper I am. But I'm not. It will be final next month.

On paper is enough, said Brenda. On paper is on paper.

No it's not.

Yes it is.

Let's remember something else, said Gary.

I bet. Brenda laughed. Like what.

Like I had a brother.

I know you did. The one that died.

Gary watched her. She was smiling wearily. Gary liked her weary smile. He was about to tell Brenda that he had been looking for his brother's grave, but for a second there was a quick, muffling sound, which seemed to originate everywhere, and then to Gary seemed almost to have come from his insides, like a shock of adrenaline. The house creaked a little. He asked Brenda if she felt it.

What? she said.

That sound.

Brenda shrugged. The mines, she said. They shoot dynamite between shifts. Don't you remember?

I forgot, Gary said.

Well, said Brenda, remember. She stood up and Gary felt from a distance the strength in her legs. She grabbed his hand.

Let's go for a walk, she said.

Gary pretended to shake hands with her. Let's go for a sit, he said.

Brenda's eyes rolled back in disgust. She tried to pull him up from the couch. Come on Gary. We used to stay up all night. She let him drop back on the couch and seized the suit jacket he had taken off and threw it on his lap. Brenda did a kind of dance, working her feet into the tennis shoes. Gary watched her. She didn't even motion. She just left. Gary had to find his way through the garage in the dark. Out in Brenda's yard he saw her with a flashlight. He looked back at her windows. Taft was in there. Gary figured that Taft had heard them leave the house. He figured that Taft knew a lot more than might be supposed about things that went on. Ahead Brenda carried the bottle of Jack Daniel's by the neck. It was April and the grass already needed mowing. Who mowed it for her? Taft, maybe? Her flashlight swung and glinted and they passed near the brick corner of the house, huge and warm in the dark. In back the candy-striped tubes of a swing set appeared. One broken swing hung still on a chain. In the wet grass an orange Frisbee had been chewed by dogs. Brenda's shape moved out on the edge of his vision. He could not see the windbreaker or the silky green dress. He seemed to follow her by scent, his legs light and feet heavy from the whiskey.

Brenda's subdivision was new enough that all its doorbells were still lit. They came to a place where the lawns ended and the vacant fields commenced. Beyond the subdivision the songs of spring peepers rose in waves.

I saw Tony the other afternoon, Gary said.

So?

Your brother Tony.

So?

So I was just telling you that.

Brenda waited for him at a barbed-wire fence, and he wanted her to laugh or pull him by the arm then, but she only lifted the wire for him to slide through. The rust creaked. One of the barbs caught on his jacket and Gary cursed.

What about *your* brother? she said.

Gary shouldn't have brought that up. What about him? he said.

Is he why you were born?

Gary stopped. He heard Brenda stop too. I reckon so, he said. Because he died.

You still act like a little brother, she called.

What?

You do, Gary. It's in your eyes.

He felt the hill sloping down, and the soft knots of spring weeds under each step, and he saw the roof of a barn below, rusted and glassy with dew. What did she mean, a little brother? Gary stopped. Where was he? In the fields after midnight with Brenda. He had quit law enforcement and he was back in Tennessee. Here he always had to remind himself that he was grown up. You are a big badass now, Gary said. Don't forget that. It would have been a good time for another drink, but Brenda had the bottle. He remembered more. They had needed to get drunk. They had had to leave even the basement of her house for the fields, and here they were sneaking around something so huge it was too big to see. She seemed anxious to lay her hands on the hollowness inside him, and he wanted her to, and he wanted to reach his hands into her too, but he was already tired of the ache she brought back over him and afraid of the years he had not known her. And he couldn't get Taft out of his mind. He kept feeling the lightness of his handshake. All of this seemed to say that it was too late. He had waited too long. Yet on the side of the hill in the middle of the night, the air was still full of what might happen, exactly the way it used to be.

Spring is back, said Brenda. How do you like it? Trying to leap a little, she waved the bottle, a slosh of whiskey that took in the pale hill and the houses above. Her dress seemed to whirl.

La dee da, said Gary. It's the fairy Brenda.

Shut up, Gary, said Brenda.

The barn stood before them heavy with the smell of hay and oil. It still smelled of winter. On its moonlit roof a slice of tin had curled up. Brenda walked past it down a grassy rut that might once have been a road. Then she switched off the flashlight.

Brenda? he said. Trucks passed on the highway. A woven-wire fence approached him in a swell of dead weeds. Behind the fence shreds of gray tobacco canvas rotted on the ground in front of a weatherboard house.

This is where the farmer used to live, said Brenda, clicking on her flashlight from the porch.

What farmer?

From before the subdivision. They say my backyard was a pond.

It was, said Gary. It was when I left.

The gate was swung permanently open. Gary smelled moss and rotten wood. Brenda turned her flashlight on different things.

Apple tree, she said. The apple tree was slanted, as old apple trees in the dooryards of old houses always are, but it was full of thick flower buds. Her flashlight also showed him a rotten shoe on the ground. The farmer's old shoe, she said in a documentary voice, makes us feel sad.

She had already gone inside, talking to herself the whole time, before he reached the porch. This is the sink, she was saying, where the dishes were washed. Here is the window. Then she pointed the flashlight straight in his face. Here comes the farmer himself, she said. He is weary from a day in the fields.

I am not the goddamn farmer, Gary said, squinting. He tried to grab the flashlight, but Brenda jumped back and stuck out her fingers and tried to make the sound of lightning striking. She did this every time Gary used the name of God in vain. Then she offered him the bottle and they sat down on the back doorstep. I come here all the time, she said.

You bring all your gentlemen here.

You bet.

Gary drank. The bottle was slick from Brenda's hands. She pointed the flashlight in his eyes again. The farmer is about to kiss the lady hello, she said.

Gary kissed her on the mouth. Brenda kept her eyes closed for several seconds after he said, Hello lady.

Don't you try, said Brenda.

Try what?

To make up for anything. Because you can't.

Gary felt her looking at him. I'm not trying, he said.

Don't say that either. Tell me what you've been doing.

Doing?

You know, Gary. People do things.

Do they?

They do. Tell me what you do.

I been to some auctions, he said.

Auctions?

Land sales.

How come?

I might buy some land.

Brenda laughed, but she seemed interested. How come?

I don't know. My daddy sold off enough of it. I ought to get some back.

Crazy, said Brenda. What would you do with it if you got it back?

Nothing.

Then why do you want it?

I don't know.

See, you are a farmer.

Gary swirled the whiskey around. I bought a hoe, he said.

Brenda laughed. She really leaned back and laughed good. It sounded as if she had been running. Gary bought a hoe, she said.

I bought some other tools too, said Gary. It was not just a hoe.

I have a garden, she said.

A lot of things ought to be put out. It's April.

Okay, Gary. Bring your little hoe. She put the flashlight in his hand. Hold the spotlight, she said.

Gary wanted to say more. He wanted to tell Brenda that he believed that men should not be able to buy and sell land, but he didn't tell her. She might have understood. Brenda understood ideas other people couldn't. That was one of the things he used to like about her. But Gary didn't tell her. He didn't have his philosophy all worked out. Brenda had unlaced one shoe and pointed her leg straight out like a dancer. Gary watched her foot arch in the spotlight, her back straight. The tennis shoe dangled from her big toe. How long can I hold this? she asked, not talking to him in particular. She sighted down her leg to the barn and shed, a splayed outhouse, the stubbly field. Gary drank again and he imagined that the subdivision had not yet been built. This was his house. The fenced land was his. Brenda had never belonged to another man, and Taft was only a dream asleep in the pond on the hill. The beams of their house together still smelled of trees. Things like this still seemed possible here. But her leg trembled and dropped on the porch boards and she said, Not long as I used to, and he looked at the streetlights on the hill and all the possessions rotting in the yard.

I been looking for his grave, Gary said.

Whose grave?

My brother's.

You don't know where your brother is buried?

No.

How come?

Because of my daddy.

Why because of him?

He won't tell me.

Did you ask him?

No. I don't want to ask him.

Why?

Because he ought to tell me.

Brenda laughed. How very manly, she said. You can find it. There can't be that many cemeteries.

There are. There are a bunch. I can't find it.

She laughed some more. She seemed to be enjoying it. What about your mother?

She's dead.

I know she is. But she wouldn't tell you?

He wouldn't let her. He probably wouldn't.

He'd be with her, said Brenda. She breathed in. That's where a little boy would be, Gary.

He's not. I looked. There's nothing there.

Maybe you just can't see it. How come you never told me this? Back then.

Because we were kids.

But now we're not, she said, as if it made sense. And you told me. Brenda seemed happy for a second. A wave of fondness for her came over him. He thought of how he had kissed her. Her mouth was more delicate than he remembered. It was kind of like kissing a little girl. Gary didn't remember her this way. He wondered if she was just acting like this. After he had kissed her mouth, Gary had kissed along the side of her neck and he found a redolent spot in the skin there that did not smell of perfume or soap or even whiskey and cigarettes but simply of skin and maybe sweat or just salt. It seemed possible to find the taste of her bones from there. He wished he could press his face into the spot again and stay there forever.

Tell me again, said Brenda, how was it your brother died?

He was learning to shoot, said Gary, and he walked in front of a rifle.

Whose rifle?

Gary intended to say, My father's, but instead it still came out, My daddy's. He turned off the flashlight and put it in his jacket pocket and handed her the bottle. He made sure she had a hold on it before he let it go.

I remember, she said. Now I do.

He couldn't tell if she did or not. Brenda rose slowly on the creaking porch boards and she was pulling his hand again, weaker this time. What put all that on your mind? Your brother and all. That was a long time ago. It was before you were born.

I don't know.

Yes you do. When you leave somebody or somebody leaves you, you go back to things like this. You wonder what could have been. That's why you are with me. No other reason than that. But it never does work out. It never does turn out to be anything. It's impossible, Gary.

I saw a guy kill himself. That's what put it on my mind.

Who?

A guy I was over there with.

In Vietnam.

I was trying to get him to stop. We all were.

How did he do it?

He shot himself in the head.

You saw him.

He was a good boy. I think he was from Virginia. They said I told him to do it.

Gary laughed.

But you didn't.

I was trying to get him to stop. Finally all I said was, Okay. And he did it.

You can't quit just because somebody shoots himself in the head.

I know.

No you don't. Brenda was pulling on his arms with both hands.

Is that how your ex-husband did it? Gary said.

I don't remember, Gary. Not yet.

They went inside. Rain had warped the door, and the knob was loose, and they had to slide through a crack. It was a tiny house. Glass crunched on the floor. An empty cellar gaped, sending up its musty smell. Settled to the bottom of the mold and dust and rot and even the whiskey was the ancient scent of urine. Panes of moonlight lay at angles beneath the windows. Newspapers peeled themselves from the walls. Down the hallway he felt Brenda before him. He held to her hand.

Brenda stopped in a room with a window and a blanket on the floor. Gary felt as if he were watching himself. She seemed to be considering the house as if she might buy it. Then she turned the same look over Gary.

It would be difficult, she said. She shook her head. What should we do now?

I don't know.

Maybe have a cigarette.

I got the lighter, said Gary. He was holding it out, but when she reached for it he pulled it away. Then she tried to grab for it again, and the lighter fell on the floor. Gary crouched with her, patting for it in the gritty dark until they both gave up and lay down on the blanket. Brenda kept talking about this and that which had nothing to do with them. Her hair was longer than he was used to. When they took off their clothes, the air was cool enough to make them cling together simply for the body heat. She kept her forehead against the side of his neck and kissed him there, about once every four seconds. Gary felt the old house around them.

For some reason, he thought he had just the cure for their difficulties, and he reached over for the flashlight and clicked it on. He had expected it to shock her, like an animal in the headlights, and then for them both to laugh and force the labor from the air. Instead she didn't move when he put the light on her skin, her shoulder, which was freckled, the inside of one narrow thigh, not freckled, against the ragged blanket. On her belly, settled into the skin the way light falls to the bottom of water, were the old stretch marks where she had had his child. Gary put down the flashlight and kissed her on the cheek.

Impossible, she said.

3

BARE-HANDED, BID SOLOMON had already stripped a poison vine out of the cedar tree. The vine was thick and hairy and it lay on the ground coiled up in the same form the tree had given it.

Poison never did take on me, Bid said, addressing not Gary but probably the itch in the vine itself.

Bid started in on the cedar without gauging which way it would fall. His chainsaw muffled inside the cedar wood. The sour, burnt smell of the white wood came out and then all of a sudden it turned to the pure red heartwood. So fresh it was almost purple, it poured out over Bid's wrists and his coveralls and his shoes. Sawdust and the tiny cedar leaves vibrated around on the brim of his cowboy hat. Even though Bid was retired from auctioneering, he still wore his cowboy hat, the one that kept him visible in the crowds. He still carried silver dollars in one pocket.

The chain was dull. Bid hadn't troubled with chinking the tree either. Gary could see what was going to happen, but he didn't do anything. He stood back and took off one work glove and reached into his pocket and put his fingers around Brenda's lighter. It was still there from last night. Bid angled the saw. He had to push it and angle it around because the chain was so dull. Gary just watched him. Work was big to Bid. Now I'll work, he would say, as if it were a threat. Or he would say, I aint afraid to work or All I ever knowed when I was a boy was work. But Gary had never seen his father work for very long. He didn't think he could. Before Gary was born, Bid had lost one lung to tuberculosis, so one side of his chest was sunken and he leaned to that side. But he tried to make up for it. He took hold of any tool like a weapon. He always carried the blue coveralls in the trunk of his car so that in case work came up he would be ready without ruining a suit. Above him the treetop began the curious shiver of trees just before they fall, but Bid pushed harder. Then the trunk gave its death squeak, leaned back solid, and pinched the saw tight. In the sudden quiet birds were singing.

Goddamn it, said Bid. Goddamn it.

He stood there grinning at the saw, sunk tight in the wood. His grin flickered like a fire about to smother. His hands were still vibrating on their own.

I saw that coming, said Gary.

Bid was wiping his forehead with a white handkerchief. This old boy and this old girl, he said, was riding a horse. She was in the back and he was in the front. Do you know this one?

He only glanced at Gary, who did know it, before he went on.

Well, he said. Well, this old boy, he'd eat him a big bowl of beans for dinner and he was just about to blow up he was suffering so bad. But he was trying to impress this girl and he didn't want to embarrass himself in front of her, but they was a big storm coming up so he figured every time it thundered he could let off a little gas. It was thundering real big and so he just let go real good. And he told her, real innocent-like, Boy, it sure is thundering loud, aint it, honey? And she said, Yes, and I believe from the smell it has done struck a shithouse.

Bid always told that one if it was threatening a storm before an auction, but he'd scan the crowd first to determine whether to say shithouse or outhouse. Everybody would laugh, even the women, because everybody liked Bid Solomon. Gary looked up. There was no sign of rain in the sky.

Bring it, Bid was saying.

Gary looked at him. What? he said. Bring what? He hesitated exactly long enough for Bid to twist his way out of the honeysuckle and brush past him.

The crowbar, said Gary.

I *meant* the goddamn crowbar, said Bid, jamming it in the cut. Gary had to grab hold like a man about to miss his wagon. They both pulled, but at first they weren't pulling together, so Gary waited a second to let him catch up and that made Bid heave like a boy. His arms trembled, and Gary's arms trembled. In the lip of wood the iron bent. Gary listened to his father's labored breath. It had been a long time since he had stood this close to him. As they pulled, Gary eased up a second just to feel Bid's strength, and it wasn't much. In town they had told Gary that Bid had cancer. They said it was in his good lung and he went to Knoxville once a week for radiation. He drove himself, they said. Some of the people who came to the funeral for Gary's aunt told him he needed to do something.

What was he supposed to do? Bid hadn't said a word to him. When Gary's mother died, they buried her and Gary was never told. When he found out, they told him his mother had been wandering and talking to people who weren't there and it was hard on Bid and her death was a blessing. Bid told them he couldn't contact Gary because he didn't know where he was. He said he never knew where Gary was.

Gary looked at Bid. He didn't look right. It was as if his skin had taken on a new roughness and was slightly too large for his body. Even his bald head, where the skin had been tight and slick, had gone slack and rough. In back where the tendons latched onto the skull there were little folds. The blue eyes, still rigid with impatience, floated there as if they had broken free of the rest of him. Taft had gotten the same blue eyes, Gary realized.

In a minute the tree gave and slashed a path through the brush so that Aunt Una Clay's house was visible. It was a narrow white two-story with a porch along the front. It was the home place. Una Clay was the oldest of Gary's mother's sisters and, until last Friday, the last one alive. Una Clay died in the room where she was born.

She ate good, Gary, Bid had said. He brought her a hot meal each day from the senior citizens center. Right over yonder at that table, she ate a big meal. Then she straightened up, this way, and drawed a breath like they was something she had just thought of. Bid arched his backbone, popping the wooden joints of Una's chair, then relaxed. That was it, he said. She never made a sound. I got her by the pulse, and all I said was, She's gone. Who I thought I was talking to I don't know.

Trees had closed in around the foundation and the gutters, and the ground of the yard was mostly moss, but when Gary's mother was a girl growing up here, the woods had been pastures. Her name was still here. Gary knew that. It was scratched in the glass of the side window. The story, which was the first story he ever knew, was that she had typhoid, and they told her if she got better they would buy her a diamond ring. They never would have promised, she told Gary, if they ever thought I would get better. This she always said with resignation, as if they had been right after all. But they weren't, and her father had to go into town and make good. When he came back, she wouldn't believe the diamond was real until it cut her name in the glass.

Gary looked at Bid jerking the starter cord on his saw. He didn't know why he was so frantic. Maybe it was Una Clay. After the last one died, you had to clear the place out.

IN EARLY SPRING the auctions began. They posted the bills on barns, in the fields themselves. They left them in stacks on the counters of businesses. HOUSE. BARN. 107 ACRES. POND. HOUSEHOLD GOODS. ABSOLUTE AUCTION. Little pink or red ribbons, surveyor's marks, appeared tied to the twigs of trees or nailed into the ground or fastened to a barbed-wire fence. Sometimes there were letters or arrows spray-painted on the roadsides. Gary had been reading the newspaper and driving the roads looking for them. Stepping out and leaving the car running, he would try to figure how it was all cut up. On

Saturday mornings he arrived well before the crowd, handled the surfaces of tractors and hay balers still wet with dew, smelled the grease and fuel hanging in the mouths of barns. He measured the quality of grass in the hollows, the productivity of creeks and springs, the condition of outbuildings. A place needed hills for the wet seasons. In the feedlots other men's stock waited and chewed and stank. Tools were arrayed on pegs on the walls of sheds. Ax handles stood in bundles.

Sometimes it started off with a bluegrass band. The fiddle music whirled in the air like yellow jackets that had been stirred up. Then the auctioneers stood with megaphones on wagons. When Gary was a boy he thought it was the power of the megaphone that enabled his father to speak so rapidly. First they drew for silver dollars. Bid always kept a pocket of candy too. For the women there were nail files with the name of the auctioneer. Then each bull-tongue plow, each tobacco setter, each brace and bit and chicken waterer and lard squeezer went in a gibber of numbers rattling over the new grass. Dollarbid, dollarbid, dollarbid, said the auctioneers as punctuation between their sentences. Gary used to think it was his father's name rolling across the fields. Dollarbid, dollarbid. But now in each whirlwind of redistribution he was frozen. He could not raise his hand or call out. Trembling, he listened to the voices rise around him as they claimed the tools and the land. Everything went. Silently, he moved from item to item at the edge of the crowd, but he was unable to speak out, even when the white beehives were sold away to a man right next to him who shouted, Ho!

Afterward, he'd look for cemeteries. Gary had developed a

feel for their location. They could not hide from him, not even tiny ones on the crests of hills or behind the smallest church. Inside them, he was able to locate quickly the graves of children. The stones were always small. Sometimes they had lambs or a Jesus on them. Gary had usually examined several rows before he realized that he was not angry anymore. He stood for long periods watching. The ground around him rolled and sucked down like a sea.

One Saturday he got lost. Gary could not remember where Big Bend Road intersected with Squire Fox. A man was walking across the hill in front of the woods, so Gary pulled the car over and got out. The man was Moody Myers, coming toward him through the blue-green flickers of cedar trees. He was not very big, with a slim gray beard and his hair combed straight back from an ochery forehead. He had a short-handled shovel with him.

I'm lost, said Gary.

You are, said Moody.

I reckon, said Gary.

Walk on up this hill, said Moody Myers.

On the hill there was a view of the river. Its bend, so large it could only be perceived from up here, wrapped around the valley. On down, a few houseless chimney smokes bleached out below the Great Smoky Mountains, the nearest of which looked pale and hairy, giving way to the back ones that wove in and out in lightening colors of blue. It was still early in the year and quiet, but the mountains seemed stronger than Gary remembered.

I need a job, he said, looking at the mountains.

A job.

Do you know the sheriff?

I know him, said Moody.

Could you talk to him?

Moody laughed. I can, he said. You'd have to shave off your beard.

I don't care, said Gary. He touched his beard.

You aint going to stay here, are you? asked Moody.

I don't know.

Moody stared at Gary for a second as if he were reaching a conclusion.

You aint going to stay here, he said. Then he added, with an impatient gesture of his head and neck, I make it a point to come up here every March the 23rd. I still aint got it figured out.

Gary looked at his watch, but it did not tell the date. Crows hollered from the tops of trees along the foot of the hill. They were answered by other crows farther off.

I've seen it snowing or raining or warm as May, Moody Myers was saying. You don't know from one year to the next. It was twenty-two below zero the day I'm talking about. They wrote letters home to tell about it. I've read them. I've read all of the material, but I still ain't got it figured out. The Seventeenth Ohio had sharpshooters in those trees.

Moody Myers pointed, sighting along his arm like a gun barrel. Gary saw that his teeth were bad. His eyes, which had a ferocity, seemed to ease if he looked away.

There was a man in the cavalry in Longstreet's army. His name was William Williamson. You know them Williamsons south of the river. They were his people. He had been at Chickamauga and all over and he came down this hill right here and the snipers shot him right in the spine. He couldn't move and his horse drug him all the way down to that bottom where your car and the road is now.

Gary looked at the lay of the pasture. After a minute, he thought he could see where the old road used to run. Gary thought about a box of books he carried with him in the trunk of his car. He had bought them a long time ago and they were still unread. One of them was about the Civil War.

I still don't know, Moody Myers said, how come him to be here. It don't make no sense. He'd come all that way and then to die on his own doorstep almost. I've looked, and I can't find no reason for him to be here.

No, said Gary.

They went down the hill. That was a hundred and fourteen years ago, said Moody Myers. Every year another one adds on, and I still aint figured it out.

No, Gary said.

In the cedars tiny brown birds hopped. Gary wondered if the Williamsons, whoever they were, knew of this field. Did you ever run any cattle? he asked.

I done about everything at one time or another. Mostly I was in mining. I worked for the old American Zinc. Not this new company now. I never worked for them.

Gary could tell that Moody didn't want to talk about it.

You know what I been doing since I got back here? Gary said. I been looking everywhere for where they buried my little brother.

Moody looked at him odd. He was replacing his ball cap. He wouldn't be your little brother, he said. He'd be older than you are.

I think of him as my little brother.

I've found some graves, said Moody, that were lost.

You have.

You have to know how to look, said Moody.

You do.

Yes. The WPA, they took readings of every cemetery in Alexander County. And cemetery trustees, they'll have their plats. Or the inside front cover of a Holy Bible is always a good place. You can even find a lost grave with a dousing rod, because the grave of each individual, no matter how ancient, is a small disturbance in the magnetic field of the world.

Moody stopped and looked across the field. Nothing, he said, is never lost.

After the cedar was cut up and the firewood was stacked, Bid started a big fire from tree limbs and vines. Sloshing kerosene from a jug, he kicked the edges of the fire, which was sucking up the leaves and bark and dust into a single burning substance. In the wavy air, between the fire and the air, his form moved, leaning to the side to which it had always leaned. Bid had always believed there was a Bible verse that could be recited to stop blood. If you cut yourself and said it, exactly as written, the bleeding would stop. Since he was a boy, Gary had always imagined that he could say one thing, if he could just find it to say, and Bid would finally stop and face him. Maybe he could say now that he had a son of his own. That Bid had a grandson, safely past the age of James. But how could he explain? How could he say that he had shaken his son's hand for the first time last night?

It always come natural to me, said Bid. I just picked it up.

What?

They was some boys back then that could really auctioneer. First you get them in a good mood. Then you got to do it so people want to bid. So they have to. It's going. Everything's going, and they got to bid right now. *Right now.*

He stopped in midslosh, as if he were happy for a second.

I tried to get your radio show Sunday morning, said Gary.

I give it up, he said. That show was the best thing I ever done. You know who told me to start it?

Gary knew it had been the sheriff of Cocke County, but he said that he didn't know. This was how you did with Bid. If you didn't, and you said yes, you knew who it was, he would ignore that and go right on with the story.

Old Wayman Toole, said Bid. He was the sheriff of Cocke County. He said to get you a radio show and that was where the business was at. He was right too.

Every Sunday morning for thirty-three years Bid told who was sick and shut in and who was having an anniversary and who he had seen lately that he hadn't seen in a long time, and he played gospel music. He might happen to mention if a land sale was coming up. Sometimes he said something about Annie, which is what he called his wife, and when he got home he asked Annie if she heard it, and she always said yes, though she never listened. She listened to the preaching instead.

Gary had grown up knowing that his father would have

traded him for his brother James. If this was a secret, it was a secret everyone knew, which is the kind of secret that finally becomes part of the silence itself. It was as if, when Gary crossed the age at which James had died, Bid didn't know what to do with the extra time. The nerve had broken free in his eyes. Gary always had the idea that his father kept an exact plan for his son's life, but when James died he had put it away. He never would take it out again, no matter what Gary did.

Gary hoped to God that Taft did not feel that way. He didn't seem like he did, but it was hard to tell. Taft seemed like he was a good boy. Gary didn't know for certain, but he felt that Taft was so much like him. That felt good and awful too. Gary wanted to be proud of him, but he didn't deserve to. Gary wondered if it was that way with all fathers, even the ones who were there from the start.

In the fire buds juiced and popped. They finally went to the house for water. Land used to be cheap, Gary said.

It used to be so goddamn cheap, Bid agreed.

Do you still have any maps? That show the county?

Bid stepped up on the porch, feeling first with his shoe because the boards were soft and mossy. Probably at the office, he said. I was on the county court for thirty-three years. They wasn't nothing that happened that I didn't know about.

Would you care if I looked at them?

No, said Bid. Go on and look. I don't know what you think you'll find.

Gary tried to see over the top of the house, but the trees were too thick.

How big is this place? he asked.

Bid held up the space between his thumb and forefinger. About this big, he said. The rest is red cedars and rattlesnakes.

They stood on the porch a little while. It felt like Una Clay might still be inside. It was this way for a while when someone died. She might have been inside in the way a rabbit will stay frozen inside a thicket even while men are talking outside it. Gary hadn't seen her since he was a boy. Una Clay had never gone farther than Alexander City. She used to come to the Christmas dinners, but then one year, she was offended and stopped forever. Though he was no blood kin, Bid took care of her. She wasn't the only one he took care of. Every morning he made rounds at the county nursing home, distributing newspapers and popcorn. Then at noon he went to the senior citizens center and paid for the hot lunch he always took Una Clay. He kept up with how much she ate, and after she started having strokes, how much she said, as if she were a baby learning these things instead of an old woman letting them go.

Bid pushed open the door and they slid inside and he pulled it to behind them. Gary did not so much see the room as feel and smell it, the warm atmosphere of coal smoke and mothballs and newspaper and old clothing and solitary meals. The room was identical to the one in his memory. It was small. The ceiling was low and it swayed. The same paleness of light entered through the porch window and the side window, revealing the spool bed, the black cookstove, the dresser with the yellowed mirror angled such that it showed Gary's legs and his father's legs and the floor, the chair and television for watching soap operas, the black telephone with luminescent numbers, a bucket of coal and newspaper. He remembered a little porcelain eyeglasses holder with eyes on it and lettering that said HERE THEY ARE, LOOKING AT YOU!

I'm going to run us a drink of water, said Bid. We been working all morning.

Gary waited there for a second. All the family gatherings he could remember ended here. At the tail end of Christmas day or Fourth of July or Easter his mother and father brought him for Una to see, making the long drive in the snow or sun, because she refused to come to the celebrations the others had. His mother said it was because the sisters fought once in the kitchen. Una Clay went to the back room each time and brought out a box of candy to pass around, oatmeal cakes or orange slices. If it was early summer, she'd take Gary outside and let him stand under the pear tree while she knocked down pears with a tall pole that always leaned against the tree. Sometimes, when he was older, he could catch them before they hit the ground.

The pear tree was still there. Gary saw it through the window, along with the the figure of his father around the fire again. He was pushing leaves and sticks into its edges. Gary heard his voice out there. At first he thought he was calling a dog, or chasing one off, or singing, but gradually he realized he was auctioneering. Gary didn't know whether to watch or not watch, laugh or not laugh. Bid reached for a limb in the fire, and Gary saw it burn him on the hand. It set the sleeve of his blue coveralls on fire for a second, and he beat it against his leg. Gary didn't move. His father sat, or almost fell, back on a flat stump and sat there coughing and sucking on his hand.

Gary stood still. You did not help Bid. Bid coughed as if he were beating something out of himself. Gary used to go to sleep with his fingers in his ears. He looked at the glass of the window itself. His mother's name was still there. The letters *A n n* hung in one pane. There was a capital *A* and two little *n*'s. They ascended a little. She had chosen the corner of the bottom pane but not so far down as to hide anything.

I been looking for his grave, Gary said out loud to the name in the glass. He remembered telling Brenda on the porch of the old house. Now he guessed that something was wrong with Brenda to have taken him back to bed with her so soon. He took out the lighter and held it in his palm. When he looked out again, Bid had disappeared. Gary heard stomping and change rattling on the front porch.

Bid came in with a white Styrofoam box and held it out to Gary. Here, he said. You can eat this. I brought it. I been to a sale.

You have?

I told you I have.

Where was it?

Over to Choptack. Big farm. We sold everything. It was one goddamn big sale.

And they gave you this?

They had everything to eat. Everything. You eat.

Gary took the box and opened it up. There was fried chicken and cornbread and soupbeans. It was Una Clay's dinner from the senior citizens center. Gary smiled. He would never forget the greed of his father for small things. They could sell off a thousand acres, but Bid would still come home with a pair of boots that were the wrong size. Bid went back out and returned carrying two snuff glasses of water. Here, he said. Drink. Bid drank the whole glass and said, Aih, after he drank it. Then he said, This is yours.

What is mine?

This place is left to you by Una Clay.

Gary suddenly felt the mountain behind him. He remembered the glassy stands of mayapple he had seen through the trees. They meant the leaves would set soon. The summer would come. The woods would close in. The urgency Gary had seen in Bid started into him too. There had been so many times when his father had told him something would be, but it had never materialized. Or it came about in some way that was nothing like he had promised. But he believed this.

How do you know? he asked.

It's in her will.

Then Gary said, I don't know what to do. He said it before he could stop himself.

Sell, said Bid, rattling his dollars.

What?

I said sell. Bid turned to the window. Sell it off.

Gary wondered if this was water from the well that gave his mother and her sisters the typhoid. He lifted it to the light. Here was the water that put letters in the glass. But his throat was dry, and he drank.

4

SPRING OF FRESHMAN YEAR the girls began to spontaneously combust. At first it was just the new quicker metabolism of spring, exposing white knees and the backs of shoulders. Got to have air, said Scott Woody, chewing a drinking straw as he watched. At thang got to have air. He showed Taft a *Believe It or Not* book in which a man in Calcutta disappeared, leaving only his burnt shadow on a floor, and he swore Mitzi Greenlee left the singed outline of a crotch on her metal folding chair in band. Spontaneous combustion, he said proudly, working the straw around his teeth. Taft figured it was more likely Scott had done it with a butane lighter stolen from his mother.

But it was too late. Man had discovered fire. On the early bus Scott crouched behind the seats and the butane's little reptile tongue emerged to taste the soapy air around the backs of girls' necks. The winter had been long and everyone it seemed had been bored for a long, long time, since their very births, or before. Maybe this was natural. People had always used the first warm day to burn out the fence rows, scorch out the weeds that had been bothering them, and the new grass came back greener than ever. As Scott edged the flame closer and closer, incrementally so it could not be detected, Taft felt that perhaps fire could clear out the funny new mechanisms that had established all around them. The sprayed curls glowed at the tips like electric wires and then wilted into an evil smoke before Scott, giggling silently, moved toward another one. Amid the giggles and stifled exclamations Taft waited for the heads of girls he had known forever, Belinda Cupp, Angie Damron, Anna Shropshire, to snap around, each only mild and indignant at first, then half smiling, then seized with panic.

Mirrors came out and brushes. There was great alarum. Scott was smacked several times. Most of them got his shoulder, which was solid as a ham, or his neck, but one caught his cheek good and knocked his straw out. He blissfully retrieved it.

Blond, he said, sniffing the air like a hound, burns the sweetest. Red is hell to pay.

Everyone enjoyed seeing beauty burn up. Taft liked to watch the other girls' pleasure in remaining unburnt and the way they pretended to scold. They acted sick from the smoke, which was like a madness waiting to harden their faces. It was the smell of burning life, accelerated, of the human grease that would not wash off the stone from the burned man's pocket. Taft remembered it from the summer he was seven years old when they burned a tick out of his ear. It was as if something rancid lay in the very molecules of life. Scott's eyes, set in his sleek little head, hardened under the pressure of delight. He beat one uncontainable fist against his thigh to hold in the laughter. Two girls screamed forcefully enough to suggest that terror exists and they tried to hide behind Taft, and Scott winked as if to say he had set the girls on fire for his best buddy.

Fire one up, Taft, whispered Scott, pressing the hot lighter into his palm.

The bus rode over the same swells as yesterday with old deaf Mr. Frazier scraping gears. He hadn't heard a thing. Taft, however, could imagine the principal's office filled with girls missing a curl or a part of the collar. He just sat there letting the spring fields go by in their twenty shades of green. Out on the fourlane he gripped the lighter and concentrated on the gristle and pop of gum in the mouths of the three girls in the seat ahead of him. He listened to them giggle and bump in an air of banana flavor until he had discovered the smallest muscles working in the hollowness directly behind their ears, almost obscured by the downy hair that grew along the neck.

Burning out the tick that summer got his ear infected. All through July he had a fever and a blue nerve of pain inside. When his mother laid her hands on his forehead and then his temples, and when she put him in the bathtub with ice, she kept repeating Dennis's name, like a swear word. By the time Taft finally got better Dennis was gone.

But they were together the night she found the tick in his ear. While they were picking blackberries it went in, perhaps crawling first around the rim and then into the tunnel itself. Dennis struck the matches. The two of them held Taft on the sink and crouched down and shined a flashlight in his ear. Taft saw down his mother's shirt to the center of her chest where the ribs knitted together. They tried at least eight or nine matches before Dennis unfolded a paper clip, heated the wire with a match until it was red, and stuck it in Taft's ear. He smashed Taft's head against the counter so hard he couldn't breathe, but what he remembered most was the sound. The flesh inside his ear sighed and bubbled a little as it burned, and he was screaming, but it sounded as if he were screaming from within the fire itself, which was burning him up. The other thing he remembered was Dennis laughing, and his yes sound, the little high-pitched affirmation he made as if he had just read something of interest and was beginning a note in the margin, when he held up the tick. Dennis had adopted Taft, and Taft still had his last name. Defaro. He hated it. Taft wished that he could have stayed a bastard.

Do it, Taft, said Scott. Do it. He had on a yellow short-sleeved T-shirt, even though there had been frost that morning. Scott had sworn off coats due to the length of the winter. His drinking straw was almost chewed up in his mouth, and Taft thought Scott with his crabbed arms and sleek head looked almost like a tick, in the way they will clutch in their mouths the smallest flake of skin.

Tanya Mayes raised both arms and laid the backs of her hands against her neck and flipped the whole length of her hair over the back of the seat. The scent of the hair washed across Taft's face. It was unburnt, all of it. Then she slid down in the seat and laid her head back guillotine fashion, plenty far enough for him to see the front hairline and the forehead with its green veins and almost the eyebrows and the tops of her barely opaque eyelids. It stayed that way for several miles, though she did swallow once or twice, and her eyelids shifted in a way which he guessed meant the opening and closing of her eyes. Taft tried draining the butane into his fist and then lighting it for an empty whoosh of flame, but she didn't flinch. Just as everyone became bored with the standoff and comment was imminent, a window five seats back slapped down and Scott's voice was audible somewhere out in the wind. When everyone turned only the ass of his blue jeans, with a blue comb in the pocket, and his legs were visible.

Seven o'clock and all's hell! he screamed into the streaming air.

Get that fool head back in here, shouted Mr. Frazier's angled face in the safety mirror, but he did not stop Scott from squirming back in to assume his lookout position in the last seat next to the dusty back window. Mr. Frazier knew what was next. Everyone on the early bus knew. Even Tanya had retrieved her hair. Scott began to check his big digital wristwatch.

Two after seven and here he comes, said Scott. And goddamn it, he's flying.

A wave of bodies rose against the left windows, mostly boys scattering notes and rolls of gym clothes, but Tanya got up too. She climbed up on the seat Taft was in and arched herself over him to get closer to the window and she was so near him the ends of her hair brushed his cheek. Taft looked down. He stared at Scott's thick *Guinness Book of World Records* splayed on the floor. It had fallen open to that picture of the world's fattest twins riding motorcycles. But he couldn't resist Tanya's stomach rising and dropping with each breath, so he went ahead and looked up. Of course he could see up her shirt, which was not tucked in. It was sort of dark inside her shirt, but the light came through it too, like a bedroom window in the morning, and he saw her ribs where they came together and then went out like the boards in a little boat. The surprising thing was the downy hair, downy but dark, that extended up around her navel, and even higher, almost the way a man's did. Taft couldn't believe it was there, but then she shifted a little and he couldn't look up without her knowing, so he turned to the window just as his uncle Tony flashed alongside again, throttle flat out on his motorcycle, shirt whipping like a parachutist's, his body sharpened into the racing position as if he dared the bike to run faster.

Godamighty, said Scott, chewing harder on the plastic straw.

Tony downshifted, flexing as if to shrug the huge yellow bus aside, and his front wheel rose in the air and hung weightlessly as he flew past. That was his uncle. Sit down, Mr. Frazier was saying as the long moan of approval died and the highway slid by empty. Sit down. Taft tried to freeze in his mind the blurred metal and bare arms of his uncle, but Tony was like the antipodes in poems at school, a man who worked the night shift in a mine thousands of feet below Taft's bedroom, whose day was over when Taft's began. Their orbits crossed only for a split second each morning, but when they did Taft always felt his family zoom out from him, taking in fourth and sixteenth and thirty-second cousins he would never meet, the most distant dead ancestors, all whipping past him now behind a motorcycle escort. It had been six or seven summers since Taft last saw his uncle. Then, back in February, he had watched a black Trans

Am dodge and rev and flirt with the bus. Taft was surprised and pleased and scared when he saw at the wheel this uncle his mother said was a bad influence. He wasn't much changed. Prison, or the years themselves, hadn't done anything to him that he couldn't handle, Taft gathered by the way one wrist lay propped on the steering wheel. A silver keychain swung from the ignition. Tony never turned his head from the road, as if he knew Taft was there, seeing. At supper that night Taft mentioned it to his mother and she stopped with the fork almost to her mouth, at once perplexed and unconcerned, then went on eating her salmon pattie.

Ignore it, she said. Then she added, in a stern voice, Do not get in the car with him, Taft. He drinks.

But come the end of March the Trans Am became an old red Corvette, the kind even before the Stingray, and by then Tony just shot by in a wind that rocked the bus, his face pointed straight ahead and bored solid. Taft was careful not to be caught looking or to participate in the great insuck of air all the boys made together as the car flew by, but he thought he caught maybe a minor slowing of the Corvette after it passed or perhaps the quickest glance by its driver into the rearview mirror. The rest of the day Tony was only a soothed look in Scott's eye or a certain knowing punch in the arm, yet each morning just as Taft had stopped believing it the Corvette or the motorcycle overtook him again.

Tony was a scaler. That was the most dangerous job in the mines. His name was Taft too, except no one called him that. Taft's mother made it a point that the name was old in the family, so Tony wasn't the reason for Taft's name. She reminded Taft of his grandmother when she talked about people in the family as if they were parts of a story. But he knew what she was doing. She was tapping around the place where everything was closed off to see if the seal was still strong. So no matter what she asked, Taft said he did not remember. He had answered this way so many times it had become a kind of truth. Still, she always wanted to know what he did remember, and he had to be careful that it was always the same things. His grandmother's old house, mainly, certain of its rooms, the only memories he had of living with her when he was little. She would punctuate his sentences with You were seven years old and You were a child and You were so little. But you remember the people. You remember Lucy. With the red hair. Before Taft could say that she had been Tony's wife, she always interrupted him by saying the same thing, that Lucy was ignorant, so ignorant.

One day, she always said, you'll know. I can't stop that.

Of course he already knew. He knew what happened when they took him swimming in the river. Lucy swam on her back all the way across and called to Taft, and he thought she looked thin and still as the herons they saw in the shade. Dennis sat on a rock with a book and stared across. Lucy always asked him what he was reading, and he never would tell her, and she splashed him with water from the river. She always had something she needed help with over there, and Taft had to stay in water below his waist. On those afternoons he felt as if he were near a new place in which he did not know the territory. It did not surprise him at all to see Lucy's body, naked, and Dennis working on it in some way that was not surprising either but somehow infinitely understandable. Her swimsuit, which was green, hung from one ankle like the skin of an insect, inside out, with white patches inside it. The thing Taft remembered most was the cavalier attitude Dennis took, as if he had simply eaten the last part of the chocolate and was mildly sorry. For a long time afterward this all stayed in some part of Taft's brain where he didn't go. He didn't even connect it, somehow, with their separation and divorce. It arose, instead, much later with the craving to see, not to touch but to see, a woman's body.

So goddamn ignorant, his mother said. That was Taft's cue to skip to the cellar, the final ritual of their Sunday afternoons and the one that never failed to divert her thinking. We always went to the cellar, Taft said, this in the big frame house whose rooms he still can remember, the single bulb above the dirt stairs, clicking on and waving the light, and all of them looking down together into his grandmother's freezer, shining with white and silver bundles all packed and hard. They always let Taft carry the gift they would take home, the package of frozen strawberries or corn or fatback, up the steps toward the little door where bachelor buttons hung drying.

His mother listened as if she were being touched somewhere she most wanted to be, but Taft distrusted her pleasure because they both knew the same secret, that their inside worlds were equal, and they both knew that Taft was the reason everyone had split up. He was the reason his mother left Dennis and Lucy left Tony and their lives became the way they are instead of the way they were. Because he saw what he saw. It was not just divorces either. Divorces are not the end of anything, Taft knew. After his mother divorced Dennis, he killed himself because that was all he had left to hurt her with. Tony hurt Lucy too. He beat her until she was almost dead and they had to remake her ear from some skin on the back of her leg, and they found him guilty of raping her too, even though he told them he did not remember that part. He said he remembered beating her, but as far as he was concerned that was all he had done.

Now Tony's motor dredged into the mornings, raising a thicket of arms and necks and hair in the bus windows. My brother, Taft's mother told him, will always be trying to run away from what he did. But it never seemed that way to Taft. It seemed to him that Tony was running straight toward it. Sometimes after he caught up with the bus he swerved the Corvette over so close that the little steel feelers at the wheels nearly touched the yellow metal. It was the kind of flirtation, Taft knew, that preceded a fight, to which he was being beckoned as deliciously as a lover.

What, Taft's grandmother told his mother, is the matter with your brother I surely do not know. He's got his salvation right under his nose. That Clarice cooks and mows the grass and he's afraid to marry her. That girl could make a living off a slick rock, but that's what he is. Afraid. Then she told the story of how Clarice came over there one day when she didn't know them from Adam. She said she had seen Tony's picture in her high school annual and did he still live there? Taft's grandmother pointed down the hill toward the trailer Tony had pulled in, but they talked for a long time. A lot has happened since the yearbook, she said, but Clarice said she didn't care. Half the things they tell are not true, she said. Taft's grandmother loved Clarice. She thought she had been sent down here for a reason. Her husband had left her too, one year ago, and she had just been looking at the annual and wondering.

A picture in a book, his grandmother said. That's how come her to be down here.

This morning, when the bus crested the hill over town and the swollen city water tower glided past on the right, Taft felt a new and secret joy. It existed outside him in the lay of houses and the stores and arcs of streetlights, the empty rows of speaker stands at the Maloy Drive-In where killdeer ran, and in the zinc works and the sea of pulverized limestone. It had been seeking him out for a long time, and now he was beginning to understand. He understood the water inside the water tower, the ordered peopling of the bus hull as it plowed through the air, the weightless butane in his hand which gave the fire its reckless shape. Taft drew breath to speak, to confirm it with Tanya Mayes, who had felt it coming too, and the bus tires sang and gathered speed inside him, only to flop over the railroad tracks at the bottom of the hill and shudder him back. At times Taft had to protect the joy with his body and hands like a candle flame, but it would always flicker back to life. Today the bus made it through the one red light on caution.

Taft guessed he was crazy. He was crazy to hope for a design that pulled people in and out of one another's lives. They all left trails indistinct as old cowpaths, their pattern too large to see from the ground. Mr. James at school was crazy too. He was the kind of person that people referred to as a bird. That Mr. James is a bird, aint he? they said. Taft did not want to be a bird, so he was careful not to walk like Mr. James or give that same crazy grin, but sometimes he felt he was doing it inside where no one could see. It began in winter, when Mr. James taught the Civil War in striped polyester pants that reached only to his ankles and did not match his shirt, which had a leather drawstring instead of buttons. The girls delighted in the six hairs they counted on his chest, calling him Old Number Six, but then a whole goatee sprouted on his chin and he started wearing steel-toed boots and work clothes like a farmer. His wiry red hair grew out in a cloud too large for his head and when he stooped over to slam desk drawers or stomp paper airplanes a freckled bald spot appeared. The freckles seemed embedded like glitter inside a clear rubber ball, and Taft thought Mr. James's brain must have been freckled too. He slapped the blackboard. He read aloud long navigational passages from *The Journals of Lewis and Clark,* pausing once in a while as if he were finding his bearings on the Missouri River. He seemed to quit bathing, and the other teachers picked and spoke over their cottage cheese at lunch, letting him alone at his own table. Mr. James was given to shouting or simply reading the social page of the *Alexander County Plain Talk* aloud, but on dark days, when the clouds hung low and black as bowels, rumbling over the wet and brilliant fields, Mr. James's mood turned to the Cuban missile crisis.

I was in Washington, D.C., he began, and books closed all over the room with little soft pops because the whole class knew what was coming. I was in college. John Kennedy was president. Spy planes photographed Soviet missile silos in Cuba. Do you know where Cuba is? Cuba is no ways from Florida. No ways. Cuba is not far from you right now. You can't see it out the window, but you don't have to. Imagine the state of Tennessee, and then going south the state of Georgia, and then the panhandle of Florida, and then right there it is. Cuba.

Taft looked out the window, and beyond the outline of Tanya Mayes chewing her fingernails a thin flock of wet grackles rose and settled, rose and settled, picking at the grass. Mr. James turned off the lights. He paced through the rows, fixing his eyes on the cinderblock wall. Scott grabbed his zipper. Here's a Cuban missile, he whispered.

We were on the edge, Mr. James was saying. Close as we've ever come. The streets were quiet. Maybe some of you were being born. I went out in the car. Empty fields around the city had opened up. Just opened up. A barn had split apart. You could see right down into the missile silos. You could see in these holes just the tip of a missile. I remember thinking they were pointed at Russia. I had never really thought before which direction Russia was. Does anyone know?

No one did. A few heads shook slowly. Taft watched the muddy Holsteins stand on a hill in the rain. He thought of Tony, blasting away the rock inside the earth and milling out its zinc. Zinc was what civilization used to keep all its iron and steel from rusting and seizing up. It probably kept the missiles from rusting fast in their silos. Zinc was one pure thing, existing in a little square on the periodic table and in great quantity in the hollow ground below Alexander City. The air explodes, Mr. James was saying. There is nothing but a flash of light. No sound, just a huge silent wind.

When the bell finally rang the chairs and aisles emptied, and Mr. James stood amid the rush of books and voices as if he had forgotten class would ever end. Khruschev, he said into the din as if it were, See you later.

Mr. James is a Communist, said the boys in the hall, notebook paper goatees plastered to their chins. During his morning wait in the cafeteria, Taft always saw Mr. James ride by the windows on his one-speed bicycle. There he goes, said Scott riding his imaginary bicycle, hands outstretched, legs pumping, eyes closed, paper goatee thrust into the wind. Taft weighed each symptom of Mr. James's insanity, afraid they would match his own. He took baths to wash off all that had touched him and was careful never to read while he ate. He tried not to think of the opening fields, the end of the world.

Read us one of your poems, Sputnik, called Scott.

Mr. James was out in the hall watching the janitor put in a lightbulb.

Scott cleared his throat. I quoth. Between your thighs, your pussy lies.

I know why he's crazy, said Angela Noe, and the rows of faces turned to her, a girl with LOVE ME on her notebook about whom everything seemed bleached, her hair and eyebrows so white the roots were pink. Taft always imagined that she loved the milk from her father's dairy. I know the reason, she said.

I'd say you do, Scott said.

I do, said Angela. His grandmother is dying. She raised him. He was a illigiterated baby. It aint that he's sorry. He's waiting on her money and she's got a lot. She's a-laying in the nursing home right now.

Goddamn, said Scott. Sputnik a rich bastard. No wonder he don't care about nothing.

That afternoon on his way to gym class Taft rounded a corner in the hallway and Sputnik was there all at once, tall and unshaven and taking long absent strides, an old book held open before him, his head aloft and oblivious as a pharaoh's, and without ever looking he reached down and slapped Taft on the back and said, Hello, Comrade Taft.

So when they lined up for battleball, the little gymnasium huge with whistles and shouts and the smell of sweat like a chaotic church, Taft quivered in his shorts and blue shirt. It was as if he were not really there, had already been put out, whipped across the thigh with a ball that sought him out hard and helpless as a bullet. The big white hand of Sputnik kept landing on his shoulder. Taft gripped the cold knobs of his kneecaps. Here were his skinny legs, newly hairy, his ribs inside their damp cool shirt with its number and little white Alexander County elk on the front, his arms small and angled. He could not believe this was all he was. Other people saw. The balls whizzed past, booming against the concrete walls, and girls flashed by like shrieking deer. Taft ran among them, faking and dodging past the incomings, and suddenly he ran flat into Tanya Mayes. It was like hitting a soft wall. There was a dull explosion that smelled of soap, and her hair spread across his face like spiderweb, and some hard point, an elbow or even a chin, jabbed his throat, another larger soft part against his mouth. Then he was on the cold wooden floor, and her face looked down at him through a tunnel of hair. Taft, it was saying. Taft Defaro. But he was too numb to answer, and just then Shoebox Wright, who had failed three grades and was known for his strange rectangular head, bore down on him with a fierce throw. Taft saw the white ball speeding toward him like doom, the eyes of everyone following its flight execution style, and then Tanya Mayes stuck out her foot. She lifted it with unspeakable grace, rising easily as the very first step of a dance or the selflessness of someone catching open a door for him. It was not a perfect leg, no, but more beautiful in its imperfection, not a description of a leg in a handwritten note but a leg covered with wonderful markless baby skin and its skinny sockless ankle before him level and still as a hub. The ball slapped on it so hard it was almost obscene, so hard he was afraid the bones inside it had splintered, but Tanya just spun around and walked off the floor without so much as a glance at anyone. Then he was lifted by the arms, and Taft hung there in disbelief as Scott shouted directly in his ear, Get off your ass, and he felt in his arms the smooth round ball. Taft stood on the big flat floor, Scott yelling for him to fire fire fire, and at last he cocked his arm to throw.

BEFORE LONG THE newly hot afternoons had grasshoppers popping out of the grass like new thoughts. The week of cheerleader tryouts came, when girls did splits and cartwheels and handsprings in the grass. They emerged in number to cheer on the flowering trees and children bicycling past and the women kneeling in rock gardens. Mrs. Mayes's wash hung on the line, the white sheets and underclothes sunlucid enough to reveal a wasp caught inside, the short row of Tanya's blue jeans dark with water and swollen at the hips. Tanya herself leapt and chanted below the redwood deck. Taft marveled at the way her limbs snapped in unison.

Ready! Okay!

Taft was digging ants in the garden while his mother and Gary tried to crank the old rototiller. With the same foothold on the greasy engine Dennis had used, Gary jerked the cord and it recoiled again and again without starting as if he were a film someone kept running backward. Taft's mother stood over him resting her hands on her hips. She was smiling at Tanya across the yard.

Spark plug, Gary panted.

We are the best. We can whip all the rest.

Oh, Gary, she said. Let me try it.

Ants wound up Taft's legs and buried their tiny mandibles like nerves, but it did not feel as good as it used to. The clods still turned up their egg chambers, networks of tunnels, but he lacked the interest. What was wrong with him? He had decided a long time ago to have no feeling for anything except nature. Nothing else existed, after all. The world man had made up, it was false. In second grade he had traced the diagram of a worker ant from *The Amazing Insect World* and memorized the simple and compound eyes, the tough knot of thorax, the scent trail of formic acid. Taft had decided never to believe in anything else, but now there was a slipping in his brain.

The rototiller cranked suddenly with great force, drowning out Tanya's cheers, and Taft saw Gary lean over it and grip the shivering handles as if it were a horse he distrusted. It set off bucking and whirling the dirt, dragging him along, the tines clanking on rocks. Tanya thrust out her fists and waved them. They were small fists, not very dangerous-looking, and then she fell into a split, and he saw her legs in a straight white line on the grass, her arms raised and the open hands flickering at the top. Taft wanted to know everything he could. He wanted to know exactly how food nourished her and how her bones fit into their sockets and exactly how many cells her body contained. He wanted to measure her sleep patterns. There had been no letters for three weeks. Each night he waited until after dusk to check the rock, and each night it was empty.

Far across the garden Gary seized the rototiller back into line. The rows he laid off were crooked, and Taft's mother followed him dropping purple seeds from a bag. Taft had watched these spring tryouts before. People tried to make their own world, but it would all rust down despite the zinc. Tanya would never make cheerleader. The neat rows of peppers and broccoli and peas and tomatoes, the hilled potatoes and sentry mounds of cucumber and squash and cantaloupe would last until early June. His mother would hoe and stake and clap away the dogs and crows. She would wash the first lettuce and radishes carefully in the sink and bring out her wooden bowls. Then the weeds would catch her. The johnsongrass and bindweed and poke would take over. In high summer the garden was a hot wasteland Taft loved. He and Scott had tommietoe fights, perhaps glimpsing an okra bloom among the tall weeds or sliding on a waspy melon rind. To celebrate victory, nature put up a passion vine, waving at the edge of the garden. Taft ate the seeds of its green apricots.

Unknowing, Gary hoed at the tough spring clods like a runner who uses it all in the first mile. You don't know what's waiting for you, Taft thought. But then he heard Gary call out to her, and his mother's first name, Brenda, hung over the newly opened dirt for the longest time. In Gary's voice the name sounded wrong and right, like a word repeated until the meaning blurs. She rose with dirt on her knees, her face asking, Yes? Gary's back arched over the potato ditch, the shoulders working, an elbow rising with one thick vein coiled round it. Taft watched them confer, his mother's hip swaying slightly toward Gary. She had on a straw hat which speckled her face with sunlight. He saw Gary watch her hands as they cut seed potatoes, the silver knife pushing through each grainy body careful to leave an eye to each slice, and he thought of Tanya's fists.

Gary had spent an hour looking at the bird nests and the insects and strange rocks in Taft's room and Taft could not stop talking and explaining, but afterward he wondered if Gary had been interested because he couldn't find anything else in which to be interested. Taft felt a little sorry for him, and he did not want to feel sorry for his father. Gary told a bunch of stories about being a cop in New Orleans and in Hattiesburg, Mississippi. He said it was well known that if something crazy was going to happen, it would happen on his shift. Right now, though, Gary wasn't a cop anymore. He was driving a school bus. Taft watched him lean on his hoe, blowing softly on his palms.

I bet, he said to Taft, that you think we're crazy. Don't you?

No, said Taft.

Then you're wrong.

That night, as the worker ants took their tunnels deeper into the jar, his mother announced that they would go to church on Sunday. It was Friday night. Gary was gone, but he had left his hoe next to the back door. He had also left Taft a book, *Strange Lives of Familiar Insects,* that he had found in a box of books he bought in New Orleans. The dishwasher went on groaning and spraying, smelling of hot soap, and Taft did not answer.

Taft.

What.

Did you hear me?

I heard you.

Well, what do you think?

About what?

Will you go with me?

I thought you meant Gary was taking you.

I want to go with my son.

Your son hasn't been to church since he was little.

That's not true.

It is.

Well, she said, and her face recomposed itself in that childish expression of mock hope and excitement that burned him inside. Can we give it a try?

I don't really guess I believe in it that much, said Taft.

The dishwasher had opened in a great boil of steam. It left her face glistening as she walked over, barefoot and dangling a towel. When he looked up in the lamplight from his ants to her reddened face, dirty at the neck from gardening, he was struck with shame that she was not just a hot vapor trying to madden him but an actual person.

Then what do you believe in? she asked.

Taft didn't say anything. Then he thought he would. Nature, he said. I believe in nature.

She looked at him a second longer and then said, Oh. Who made nature?

Nature, said Taft.

Oh. Then who made you?

You.

Oh. She seemed to like that.

And Gary.

Taft looked into her face hard as he possibly could, but nothing changed.

Well, she said finally, something had to make nature. And love. What made love?

Taft shrugged. We just think there's love, he said.

The rest of the night she was different. Taft felt bad. The shaky look of happiness on her face had been so easy to kill. He had never thought himself able to do that. Why couldn't she just say who Gary was? Taft stared at the ants. He wondered if there were already tunnels away from the glass, where he couldn't see. His mother stayed outside a long time. Finally he went outside and she was on the doorstep in the dark.

There used to be lightning bugs when I was a kid, she told him.

It's too early, Taft said.

5

PRESENT? said Coach Jenkins.

Bible brought?

Yes, said Taft.

Way to go, said Coach Jenkins. Bible read daily?

No.

Lesson studied?

Yes, he lied.

Ministry to others?

None.

All right, Defaro, let's get that Bible open every once in a while.

Taft nodded and Coach Jenkins went on with the Sunday school roll, the paint-dusty window open where they sat in a circle of folding chairs, the coach urging them into lessons on Moses and the Israelites in a voice hoarse from spring practice.

Then it was a plague of frogs, he said palming his worn leather Bible, his glance skating across Taft to the other boys as if he were sketching a pick and roll. Every species of frog. Big. Little. Brown. Green and greasy. Did you ever see that movie where all them frogs take over?

No, said Scott. He usually sat still in church with his hands folded, looking up with reverent interest as if someone were about to hit him.

I did, said Kenny Grimes, twirling his clip-on tie like a chain. That's where that big old frog comes out of a woman's mouth.

That was gross, Tex Beason said.

Well, she was done dead, said Kenny.

Taft had not been to church since he was little. But nothing, absolutely nothing, had changed. John Luster giggled in the chair beside him. He was small for his age, but he had been saved since he was seven and he did a great deal of what the coach called ministry to others, so much that everyone called him John the Baptized. John the Baptized had an aunt and uncle who were missionaries, and each Christmas they returned from Rhodesia, showing up at school with slides and zebra skins and an elephant's foot trash can.

That's how it was like in Egypt, the coach was saying. Frogs hopping all over creation. You couldn't do nothing for them. You would go to bed at night and there would be about fifty frogs laying under the sheets. Of course then the river ran blood.

I never seen that one, Kenny said.

There was an old sanctuary beside the Alexander City First Baptist Church. Between Sunday school and the service Scott and John Luster and Taft slipped through an unlocked door into it, the old part of the church where no one worshiped anymore. Their stiff dress shoes padded along the carpeted aisles where ragged hymnals still lay in the pews below a great steadiness of old light. They stole up the rounded steps, where a red velvet curtain hid the dry baptistry, and they delivered sermons. Scott gripped the wooden pulpit and signaled for quiet in the empty choir bed where organ pipes hung like plumbing in a great basement. He panned his own face slowly beyond Taft and John Luster to the rows of pews, arranged like the gills of a dark mushroom, arcing back and back to the opaque windows teeming with sporey dust, the vast hood of the balcony gaping aslant at him, a little life in the center, an animalcule smaller than an ant.

Yes, said Scott, his voice flopping out in the emptiness. This morning I would like to address a subject of concern to us all. Scott reached into his back pocket and removed his wallet and began to unfold a paper from therein. The topic is . . . The topic today is titties.

He had unfolded a magazine page closely pertaining to his topic.

John the Baptized began to giggle and wheeze. True to his saintly nature, his appreciation for the profane was exponential.

Taft had clicked on the switch on the old organ and it built up a low thrum that seemed to come from the center of the earth. The keys made no sound, but he made a silent clicking flourish on them anyway.

Now, said Scott, perhaps in the midst of your busy day you do not pause to consider the importance of titties. Woe unto you then for you are one dumb son of a bitch.

Amen, Brother Scott! said Taft.

John the Baptized giggled.

Why do we hide titties? asked Scott. We should not conceal them. They need light, fresh air. They need the eyes of men upon them.

Scott paused for thought and swallowed. Today, he said, we form a sacred bond which we shall call the Tittie Society. Please come forward if you are ready to join me this morning. If you are ready to make this public statement of your belief in the importance of titties.

All came forward.

Now let us sing, he continued. Just one more verse.

First, said Taft, a Bible drill.

Swords ready! shouted John the Baptized, like a reflex.

The verse is Judas 12:12, said Taft, pretending to read a card. Judas 12:12. Draw swords.

Swords drawn, they answered.

Charge!

The thin pages rustled. Scott had an old hymnbook instead of a Bible. John the Baptized, who could name all the books of the Bible so quickly the names blurred into one long name, tried to protest that there was no book of Judas in the Bible, Old or New Testament, but Scott called out Victory! and tried to wrestle Taft from his organ bench. He was always wanting to wrestle.

Judas 12:12, quoted Scott. I quoth, Plug ye all the women ye can.

But just then the first chords of the real organ pushed through the walls like huge blunt fingers and the voice of the congregation rose, and Taft was running with Scott and John the Baptized back up the aisle, sliding out in the corners in their hard shoes, each pushing the others past the portrait of church founder, Thales Butler, whose glassy eyes were sworn to follow you down the hall, back at last into the new part of the church, smelling of aftershave and disinfectant and choir robes, and they slid through the swinging doors, the real congregation before them already in the midst of the second chorus of the Ode to Joy, the real hymnals in their hands like bouquets they offered, the arms of the song leader signing in the air, drawing music from them below the huge ceiling, the calm face of the pastor barely moving over the familiar words. They split up. Taft walked into the forest in the pews. Singing people glared down at him. He found his mother in a pew with Mrs. Mayes. They pretended not to notice him sliding past.

Hymnals thumped softly closed. Throats were cleared. Taft and his mother sat together in the great rustle of everyone sitting, and she placed the hymnal back in its wooden sleeve on the pew and smoothed her dress over her legs. It was a new dress. Her arms were bare to the shoulders, because it was spring and the dogwoods were blooming, and she had on pink lipstick. Around came the deacons with their collection plates. They waited patiently at the end of each pew for their thick brown pans to float from hand to hand. Taft passed the heavy plate to his mother, threading himself to everyone like a bead, and she dropped in an offering. His mother's offering wasn't in an offering envelope like the others. It was just some wadded-up dollars.

During the prayer he located Tanya Mayes with some other

girls near the front. She bowed her head and he saw a thin silver necklace through the hair over her neck. Just before she closed her eyes Taft's mother picked a long hair off Mrs. Mayes's skirt. Taft imagined it was Tanya's. His mother flicked the hair away blindly, and the two women did not even exchange a look. The prayer voice went on. His mother's eyes twitched as if she were dreaming. Beside her Mrs. Mayes tapped one white painted fingernail on her bulletin. Her black-blond hair was cut short with false sideburns, and she wore big white plastic earrings. In her pew Tanya turned to whisper, her eyes still shut, and he saw in her ear a tiny version of her mother's earring. Taft shut his eyes. This was a prayer.

He had thought it might seem shorter, or that maybe even some of it might make sense now that he was older, but the sermon seemed just as long and torturous as it had when he was six. Taft looked around and even the adults had hunkered in defensively as if for a long onslaught. His back hurt. At last, the pastor finished with a long dim prayer, which ended like dawn over the church, and the choir stood in their pale blue robes and the song leader motioned as if he were lifting a baby congregation to its feet, and they all sang. The pastor, a short tightened man with his hands clasped, walked down on the steps in front of his pulpit and waited. Taft knew he was waiting for souls.

When you are ready to make this public gesture of your belief in Jesus Christ, he said, I will be waiting here this morning. Then he restarted the great machine of the hymn and all the gears of its voices again began to work and turn together. Taft's mother stood beside him, singing. She sang inside the same hymn as Mrs. Mayes and Tanya and the pastor and the song leader and Scott Woody and even John the Baptized, but she seemed out of place. She looked more like she was going on a date than going to church. Taft liked that. He didn't want his mother ever to be like the others. When he was a child he had always been afraid that she would leave again, the way she had when he was a baby, but now he was more afraid that she would give up. Taft was not about to see them give up and offer their souls to the church. It was the bastard part of him, he guessed, that made him feel this way. The pastor balanced along one of the steps. He smiled.

One more chorus, he pronounced. Will you come?

Taft didn't.

Outside under the dry sting of the sun everyone was happy. They were all greeting one another and waving and even the most hateful old women wore something close to grins. Maybe this was why people went to church, to revel in the sudden freedom of it being over at last. His mother said hello to people she did not know. Taft wondered why she did this. They didn't really want her there. Taft looked up at the church steeple, which had a metal needle at the top, and it was crooked.

Look, he said, pointing.

What? said his mother. She wasn't really looking.

The steeple is crooked.

No it's not.

Yes it is.

She had one hand shading her eyes. Several others looked up.

No it's not, she said.

In the car as they went home the steeple appeared between buildings and between trees and from different angles. It was very crooked.

Taft spent the afternoon killing ants on the driveway. He bounced them to death with a tennis ball. They were large red ants, running their shadows over the concrete, and the great sphere fell pop, pop, pop, and the crushed bodies flew into the air like explosion victims, the ball gathering heads and antennae and spiky legs into its green fur. In an instant they gave up their ant souls. If a steeple pointed at God, Taft thought, wouldn't it point a little crooked? Wouldn't that be just like man? He kept thinking of the lie Scott Woody had told.

Chalk up another big one, said Mr. Butane on the phone.

Another what? said Taft.

Another *F*, son.

You made an *F*?

An *F, U, C, K.* I didn't mention it at church. What with John the Baptized right there.

A pause followed, in which Taft imagined Scott sprawled on his bed breathing into the telephone, blacklight posters glowing on his dark walls like velvet windows to a neighborhood of off-color jungle tigers and chopper-mounted skeletons, and tacked over one wall a huge American flag from his father's casket. Scott lived a block away, but he called at least every odd day, usually to tell lies about his dead father. Taft squatted on the floor in the hall, his mother stepping over him with laundry, and Scott would say, We had a swimming pool at our other house, or He kept a live grenade on his desk. He brought it back with him. I still got it here somewhere.

This is number three, said Scott.

Congratulations, said Taft.

She was a good one. She looked like a cross between Stacy Berry and Karen Byrd.

Mules, said Taft.

Mules, my ass, said Scott.

I mean mules are hybrids like that.

I wouldn't know about that. Never Taft did I fuck no mule.

I mean hybrids. Hybrids don't reproduce.

The hell they don't. This one did. Her mama works at the Food City bakery with mine. We had to go over there to get a hairdo magazine. It was way out of the county. We did it right there in her bedroom.

It was quiet again. He added for proof, She had a bunch of stuffed animals.

What about your mother?

She was talking in the other room. She was going good. Right when I got it in, this girl let out a big old groan and her mother hollered out, Christine, are you all right in yonder, and she said, Yes mama. Yes.

Is that how come you to be so quiet at church?

I was giving thanks. If this keeps up I'm about to run out of rubbers. I wish now I hadn't wasted some of them on car antennas. Taft?

What.

Taft.

What?

You got some catching up to do, buddy.

Taft remembered when he was ten years old and applying his coaster brake as Scott Woody's front yard slid by with Scott in the middle of it perched on a box. He had just moved into a little house with a carport. Taft. Taft Defaro. Come over here, Taft. Guess what. I got a hummingbird in my pocket. I caught him. Taft said, How, and Scott said, I caught him off a bush. I feel him Taft. I feel him in there afluttering now. I got him caught. And in the wrestling of hybrid Christine amid a zoo of stuffed animals, ruby-throated hummingbirds freed themselves from the dark pockets of Scott Woody to whip around the room, looking at them as she gulped the answer to her mother.

Taft had some catching up to do. Even Mr. James, the crazy one, had laid a hand on Taft's shoulder and asked, Taft, do the girls call you? He had heard his mother's friends ask, Does he like girls? Taft didn't understand. He did not like girls, he coveted every particle of their flesh. It lay on him like an indescribable burden. It was nothing to be talked about in so light a manner. There were weeks when Taft had thought that the only way he could satisfy his need for female flesh was to be it himself, to be female and to love his own body, and that worried him until he realized that it could never work because no one would long for the body he inhabited. Inside him everything had changed. But he was still the same outside.

Across the yard, wide as the savannas in social studies, Tanya's house suffered in the Sunday quiet, its big foundation holding without flinch the sting on her ankle, and Taft looked up again to the big world and there was Tony's Corvette with his elbow out the window, and for one second Taft felt the motion of the early bus swinging him past his uncle again, but the whole subdivision was still except for Tony's hand, waving for him to come over. It was time to die. Taft hadn't thought it would come so soon. But that was probably what everyone thought, and then one day sure enough. Taft wanted it, though. He wanted to stop thinking and leave at once, go on and face death. The passenger door flipped open. Tony opened it as if his sister's son traveled with him every day, and Taft threw his tennis ball back toward the house and never saw it land.

Hey, Tony said.

Taft looked at him. He was smaller up close, but he still had his jaw set. Hey, he answered back.

You want to go somewhere?

Taft nodded one nod.

Then come on. I got something for you to see.

That was all Tony said. Taft wondered what the last thing he would see would turn out to be. It seemed that his whole life comprised being shown things anyway. He thought of Moody at the sunken baseball diamond and even his mother smiling as she showed him Gary, but nobody had any explanations. Taft looked at his uncle. Tony always kept his black hair neatly cut, and it always seemed to be wet around the edges, as if he had just taken a shower. He smelled strongly of aftershave.

Taft looked around and he didn't see a can of beer anywhere. Tony only drank beer, but even if he was drinking he gave the impression that he had it under control. Everything was in balance. He was actual. There were no two worlds to Tony. He was one. The motion of the car was miraculous, hurling away behind its loud engine, each new gear flattening Taft against the seat, air whirring around the doors, the tires surging and whining with each upshift as they wound out of the subdivision and out onto the highway. The name of the highway was 11W. Bloody 11W. Taft had never really thought much about the name people had given it or about the wrecks that happened here at night, but now he did. It was the open highway, coiling in through the farms and the woods, punctuated with roadside markets offering HOT DOGS NIGHT CRAWLERS COLD BEER GO VOLS. The inside of the car smelled of metal tools and old clothes and stale cigarettes and sweat with a little gasoline. Tony's boot worked the clutch, and Taft sank back in the sudden freedom of death, of being in someone else's singular world, away from the driveway complicated with ants. He was flying into the coming dusk on a dangerous road with this uncle who did not even glance at the big arched speedometer, registering eighty-five, and who perhaps figured it was nothing unusual for Taft to leave this way without telling his mother. Taft decided not to show that his life meant anything to him. Let it be something he might give up any time he took the notion.

I guess you can drive, can't you, said Tony.

Taft answered but his voice drowned inside the car. Tony watched him shake his head.

You need to learn. I could drive when I was eight years old.

Taft nodded, but he could not imagine making the fast engine work.

Use your palm, Tony said. It wants to go to the right gear. You just let it.

Does this top come off?

One night we'll take her off, said Tony. You need to learn. You might need to drive me somewhere.

Tony rolled down his window and Taft rolled his down too. Fence posts and honey locusts and red clay banks sang past, and the air was warm and sweet with silage. His stomach floating in the dips and over the tops of hills, Taft thought he felt the world steer toward him, rippling with grace and little acts of courtship like the sacrifice of Tanya's leg and the very press of his back against the hard car seat.

Are you still scaling? Taft asked.

Tony didn't seem to hear him. After a long time he said, I might not be. If we go on strike.

Are you going on strike?

Tony shrugged.

What does a scaler do? Taft asked.

Ride a big lift, said Tony. It's a hundred twenty-three feet tall. He looked up. You've got a metal pole and you scale rock off the ceiling. To keep it from falling on somebody.

How do you keep it from falling on *you*?

You can hear it working. You better respect it when you hear it working.

He hit the brakes, and they slid up into a gravel spot beside the road and it was quiet all of a sudden. Taft suddenly realized the distance they had covered was irreversible. They had gone through Alexander City and Shelton and even crossed the river. It would take him all night to walk it. Tony headed up a steep gravel driveway. Taft couldn't see where it led. When he got out and followed he was not much shorter than Tony, maybe an inch or an inch and a half. Tony spat and they walked on up past a coal pile and toward a stand of cedars. Beneath the cedars was an old white two-story house and Clarice's big station wagon with Clarice herself sitting on the tailgate. The station wagon had a big piece of wooden furniture, like a cabinet, tied to the top of it. Clarice was looking through some boxes.

It's Taft, said Clarice. She looked surprised. Hey, Taft.

Hey, said Taft.

Where did you find him? she asked Tony.

Where do you think I found him? said Tony.

You better take him back.

I aint taking him back. Am I, Taft?

No, said Taft.

Tony laughed. Taft hadn't thought he could do anything, no matter how funny, that might make his uncle laugh. And the laugh was sort of goofy, like his mother's, but louder and longer than it had to be.

You know what we're doing today? Clarice asked.

Is it illegal?

She looked embarrassed. Taft hadn't thought he could embarrass Clarice either.

No, it aint illegal. You know who lives here?

I sure don't, said Taft.

Gary Solomon. She motioned to the boxes. He's moving in. But he aint got that much to move. We're helping. You want to help us, Taft?

Go on in there, Taft, said Tony. He's inside.

How do you all know Gary Solomon? Taft asked them.

Tony just looked at him. After a second he said, How do *you* know him? Clarice slapped Tony hard on the shoulder and said, He's a friend. Tony was still grinning.

Taft went up to the porch. It was cooler there and the porch boards were soft and mossy. A rain barrel, filled with thickened water, sat at the corner of the house. Off to the side some trees had been freshly cut. Black carpenter ants were crossing and recrossing the porch boards. It was impossible to see through the screen door, so Taft waited a second and then stooped down and cupped his hands to the screen. The inside smelled of coal smoke and soup beans through the cool filter of the screen. In a second Taft realized Mr. James's face with its jutting goatee was staring straight into his eyes. Mr. James was seated crosslegged on the floor directly in front of the screen door. He had a box of books in front of him and one was open. Before Taft could jump back Mr. James stood on his knees and cupped his own hands to Taft's hands with only the screen between them and peered into Taft's face.

I can see a long way in there, said Mr. James. His breath smelled like smoke and onions.

What are you doing here? said Taft.

Nothing, said Mr. James, opening the screen door. Reading Gary's books. Join me.

Somehow, Taft was not surprised to see Mr. James. He might as well be here too. Everyone else was. Maybe even Tanya was here. Taft looked around.

Hey, Taft, said Tony. He was untying the ropes atop the station wagon. Look at that thing on his chin. Do you not think it looks exactly like the hair on the tip of a bull's dick? Now tell me the truth.

Something, said Mr. James, loudly, has to be on the tip of a bull's dick. It might as well be hair.

Exactly like it, said Taft. That made Tony laugh again. Taft liked the feeling of making Tony laugh.

You look better without it, added Clarice.

How, said Mr. James, would you like to have a pop quiz?

Hey, Taft, said Tony, tell Gary to get over here if he wants to unload this big son of a bitch.

It'll never go, said Mr. James. I can see from here that it will never, ever go.

Where is Gary? Taft asked him.

He shrugged. Out back.

Taft cut around the corner of the house and went to the back. In back the outhouse had gone crooked and another building was completely collapsed under the moss, but you couldn't see much farther because the wilderness began almost immediately. Right up next to the back porch lay a pile of pink and yellow ribbons and a few fresh wooden stakes, some of which had numbers penciled on their flanks. A ways off there was a thrashing in the leaves such as a squirrel might have made, and the top of one smaller tree was moving. In a minute Gary burst out of the underbrush with an armload of ribbons and some more wooden stakes. Taft could hear briars ripping at his clothing. Gary was taking long hurried strides and breathing hard. He dropped one of the yellow ribbons and kneeled to pick it up carefully. Then he took them all and pitched them in the pile he had started next to the house.

Taft, said Gary. He was trying to get his breath. Little leaves and tiny pieces of bark were stuck in his beard and in the sweat on his face. He was wearing heavy boots and he had briar scratches up his wrists. How did you get here?

Tony, said Taft.

Oh. Gary looked up through the leaves at the sky. He was still trying to get his breath.

What are you doing? said Taft.

Cleaning up.

Cleaning up what?

Some little mistakes.

Who made them?

Somebody, said Gary. Somebody who misjudged me.

Oh.

Somebody who misjudged me completely.

Taft motioned. Is this your house?

It is now. Gary had his breath back. Now it is.

Whose was it?

It was my grandmother's. On my mother's side.

Are you going to live in it?

I thought I might.

It needs work.

Taft noticed the way Gary was looking at him. I'll show it to you, said Gary. I'd like to show it to you if you want to see it. You could stay with me a night or two. I used to stay out here when I was a boy.

I notice you've got black carpenter ants out here, said Taft. All we have is the red ones.

Gary looked at Taft almost as if he were glad to know that.

Tony said for you to come help him.

Wait just a minute. Gary opened the back door and reached in and brought out a milk jug. He said, Clear us a place in the dirt over there. Use that shovel.

Taft got the shovel and started to scrape a place in the dirt, which was black.

Make us a ring of dirt, said Gary. He took all the ribbons and the stakes and piled them up in the ring and poured kerosene on them and took out a book of matches. Get back a little, he said, and the ribbons burned in the fire. Gary didn't smile or frown but he seemed to be thinking.

Did you write down all those survey calls? said Gary.

What survey calls?

These. He pointed at the fire.

No.

Good. I hate damn surveyors.

How come?

Because they draw little lines all over everything where there aint no lines.

Gary stood up and took the shovel out of Taft's hands and dug a little and started to cover up the fire, which protested and started to smoke. Cover up the rest of it, said Gary. Like this. Then he went around the corner of the house toward the front. Taft tried to hurry, but he wanted to get the fire out good. Taft felt as if something had been accomplished, something like conspiracy. He propped up the shovel and ran back toward the front of the house.

They had the big wooden cabinet off the top of the car and onto the front porch. Tony had the front and Gary had the back. It was very heavy and their arms were shivering a little. Tony was cussing. Clarice was standing back with one hand shading her eyes from the sun, and Mr. James was leaning against one porch post smoking a tiny stone pipe. He opened his mouth and let the smoke out.

It will not go, he said. It will not go.

Shut up, Marvin, said Clarice.

Shut the fucking hell up, Marvin, said Tony.

I will, said Mr. James, but it won't.

Arrest him, said Tony.

I can't arrest him, said Gary.

You're a goddamn big lawman, aint you? Do you see what he's smoking? Arrest his ass.

I aint arresting nobody, said Gary. I just started back. It aint worth the paperwork.

You are one hell of a cop then, said Tony. He laughed too loudly again.

What have they got? Taft asked Clarice.

Clarice was just about as tall as Taft. She looked at him, but she kept shading her eyes. Taft watched her chest rise and fall with her breath. Her beauty wasn't as fearsome up close. She only smelled like clean clothes. It's a corner cupboard, she said. It was Gary's mother's. She whispered. He stoled it. From his daddy's house in town. He stoled it. It was on the back porch.

It came out, said Gary. It has to go in.

Not necessarily, said Mr. James.

I thought, said Tony, that I told you to shut the fuck up.

You told him to shut the fucking hell up, said Taft.

They all looked at him for a second. Tony was the only one who laughed.

Tony, said Clarice. You see what I'm talking about.

Lift your end up, said Gary. Taft could see by the way he said it that he had not approved of what Taft said. He decided not to say anything else.

Wait! said Clarice. Wait. I almost forgot. She was searching through Gary's boxes again. She grabbed something and ran up on the porch and got down on her knees and crawled under the corner cupboard while Gary and Tony held it up. The scissors, she said. When you move in, the first thing you take inside has got to be the scissors. Otherwise it's bad luck. Taft heard the scissors drop in the center of the floor and Clarice came crawling back out. Tony tried to catch her between his legs, but she wiggled out.

Help them, Taft, she said, motioning. They need help. Help them, Taft.

Taft went up and tried to get hold of the cupboard next to Gary but there wasn't much room to get hold of it. They were trying to go in at an angle, but the door frame was a little warped.

When he gets it turned, Gary said to Taft, push. He made it sound as if they really needed help. Tony was watching them from the other end. Up close, Taft could see the way Tony looked at Gary. He looked at him a different way, with a peculiar respect, as if Gary were a bolt he could not untighten. Taft wondered if it was because Gary was a lawman and Tony used to be a criminal, if because of this they understood each other.

Mr. James took another draw on his pipe. Never, he said. It will never go.

6

THE GIRL WAS LUCY KERR. It took Gary a minute to figure this out. After his headlights crossed the ragweedy yard and hit the side of a mobile home where a girl was standing on the porch, he felt a tinge of familiarity. It was a good idea, when you were on patrol by yourself at four o'clock in the morning, to examine any and all tinges of familiarity. Sometimes they were hard to pin down. Though he had only been working for the sheriff's department two weeks, it might have been that he had been out here on this end of Choptack already, maybe on a domestic or a busted mailbox. Other times such a feeling of familiarity was only a ghost, arising from lack of sleep or the smell of the air. But this time it was the girl. Lanky and redheaded, Lucy Kerr had gone to school with Gary. He hadn't seen her since then, but now she was back, standing in the beam of his headlights on the porch of a mobile home.

Gary keyed the radio and said he was out of the car, but no answer came back. He knew why. This was a dead spot. The road ran right along the foot of English Mountain and the radio could not penetrate. Normally he would have driven up the road until he could get out on the radio, but tonight he decided not to. Lucy Kerr, Gary said, looking at her in his headlights. Or Lucy Something Else. You aint here.

Of course she was. Tonight was odd. It was haying time. In every field it seemed hay was down, not windrowed or baled yet, just down. It smelled of oily rope. There were parties. Gary had hauled in four drunks already. One of them was a woman who reared back in the seat and kicked out his side-window glass. It took her four kicks. Gary looked back through the cage and suddenly wind was blowing inside and she was trying to wiggle her way out feet first. Her face had a persistence on it like that of a woman trying to fit into a new dress. Even when Gary pulled over and stopped she kept on wiggling. She had gotten her legs through and most of her hips and the legs were swinging and kicking viciously enough to make him step back. Gary stood there on the road and looked at his patrol car and its pair of legs. He wasn't surprised. Nothing ever could be simple. It always had to mushroom into a state of affairs known as a clusterfuck. Gary was an experienced clusterfucker. After all, he had been a very small part of the supreme clusterfuck of the twentieth century in Vietnam.

If it hadn't been for the heat lightning, the red silent kind common to haying season, he would never have found her shoes. Waiting for the kicking to ease, Gary walked up the ditch line and they blinked into sight. He had put them in the seat beside him, and sure enough, after he dropped her at the jail, he forgot about them. She was in the drunk tank and her nice blue shoes were riding around in Choptack. Gary tried the radio again. It was all empty. Tonight was perfect too for radio skip. Since just after dusk, some sheriff's department in Texas had been breaking through. At first it was only a syllable or a word, but after midnight whole sentences came through about Texas. It was all quiet, though, in the dead spot under the mountain. He decided to watch Lucy Kerr for a few seconds. There was never any harm in waiting to do something. The harm always came in doing it too quickly.

This is the house, he heard her voice say. It sounded just like high school. I'm the one that called. She pecked on his window. Are you coming or not?

Gary stepped out with his flashlight and checked the trailer's underside for the circle eyes of dogs. Then he put the flashlight on Lucy Kerr. Do you live here? he asked. He knew she didn't, but it was a good idea to see what she would say.

Her face squinted at him, fitting right into what he remembered, full of brown freckles, but a side tooth was missing. My daddy lives here, she said. I got to thinking and I couldn't sleep. I just got to thinking. I never seen the light. He always does turn on the light. Now he won't answer.

Gary couldn't tell if she had forgotten him or remembered him so well she felt no need to mention it. She had forgotten him, he guessed. People forget things. It was his own fault that he never could. She kept talking, telling him again and again about the light, so he looked her over good. Nothing about her was attractive. Nothing. She had just swollen into a big girl, not a woman. She was almost as tall as Gary, and she had long red hair, unstyled and down to her waist, even past it, like women at the Pentecostal church. Her face seemed pasted onto her head at a jaunty angle, and she had on a frilly yellow Sunday dress.

Gary made her stop talking. Where do you live? he asked.

She pointed silently.

Gary was still thinking about the odd cast in her voice when she said daddy, as if it were a daddy longlegs or some other insect. He saw immediately that she was snakebit. That was what he called people who had had enough bad things happen to them to make them start doing bad things to themselves. In law enforcement, you got used to seeing it. He asked if she had a key.

I don't have no use for no key. You took your time in coming. I got to thinking and I couldn't sleep. Did you not ever get to thinking? I can't sleep with something laying on my mind like that. I know I'm crazy.

She grinned with one side of her mouth, the side which had all its teeth. Gary saw that she was going to talk a lot. It made him nervous. He put his flashlight back on the yellow dress and shoes. What would we do, he said, without crazy people? Were you going somewhere?

She used the eyes on him. I had this laid out for church tomorrow. Did you not ever see a woman dressed up?

No.

Then take a good look.

Lord, said the sheriff on Gary's portable radio. I forget how dark it does get at night. On these curves back here a man likes to meets hisself coming the other way.

Lucy looked at Gary shyly, as if the sheriff's voice might have come from inside him. Gary could see ideas working in her eyes so he started knocking on the door with his fist before she could ask. The sheriff had been carrying on this way all evening. It was his wedding anniversary. At first Sylvia, the dispatcher, had answered back when he commented on the lightning or the mist over the river, but now she had stopped and just let him go on. The sheriff's voice was clear even in the dead spot. Gary wondered if they could hear him in Texas.

He's drunk, aint he? Lucy said.

Oh law no, said Gary.

The windows rattled for a second after he quit knocking. The day had been hot, but the night air smelled like the deepest roots of a tree. Lucy backed away to the porch edge as if her father would surely spring out now that the law was here. Then she came right up behind Gary and said with a closeness that stopped him, I done done that. He won't answer.

Gary let out a long breath, and he pulled up his belt and adjusted it until it stopped creaking. What do you want me to do?

I don't know. You're the law. Get in I guess.

Are you telling me to get in?

I aint going.

Gary looked at her. He could tell she had said that before. When is the last time you saw your daddy?

Lucy thought. She thought in the manner of a little boy trying to well up his mouth to spit off a bridge. Tuesday, she said after counting the fingers on one hand.

Gary rattled the door, as if that would help. This is Sunday morning, he said. Did you talk to him?

No.

What was he doing when you saw him?

Going to get his beer. He always goes to get his beer.

Reckon he's just passed out?

He don't pass out.

When is the last time you talked to him?

She thought again. Then she said, Fourteen.

Fourteen what?

Fourteen year old.

Gary looked at her. That aint going to help, he said.

Lucy shrugged.

Well, said Gary, I hate to mess up a man's door if he's just passed out.

Lucy shrugged and shifted her weight and her panty hose made a zip sound inside the yellow dress. Find you a window, she said.

Gary had to go around to the side to locate one at chest level. It was open but there was a screen. Fourteen, he said aloud, fumbling with the screen. After he got the screen off and set it down atop some stiff ragweed and leaned half his body inside the trailer, Gary knew Mr. Kerr was dead. He balanced there with his legs hanging out and his torso inside and he cursed Lucy aloud. This was exactly why he had quit law enforcement. There is a feeling when you pierce the air for the first time inside a building where someone is dead. It isn't exactly a smell or a taste or even a different temperature, but Gary had learned to sense it. Nobody wants to be the first to find the dead either, because then there is a bond between him and you, a bond that can never be broken. He had seen this with killings and accidents and suicides, how the one who found the body always sticks around a long time, too long, after the shift is over, telling the story of how he found it and what he was doing when he did. People said they went into law enforcement to help others, but that was not so. They did it to confirm something they always suspected, that the world was one fucked-up place. But at some point, Gary wondered, how much confirmation did you need?

Gary pushed himself the rest of the way in, but inside it felt like pushing an animal up a chute. The animal did not want to go. He swung his flashlight around in a dusty yellow stillness, and the light named things. Beer cans. Rat poison. Boot. Rags. Another room. Even though he tried not to think at all, but simply to be ready, unsnapping the snap on his holster, he thought, Where would *I* be? If I was an old man who had never heard of me, who was about to die alone in an old trailer with a yard full of ragweed, where would *I* be?

Mr. Kerr, he said, louder.

Oh Lord, said the sheriff's voice on the radio. Oh Lord, borned of a woman, full of trouble. That was the sheriff's favorite phrase. Borned of a woman, full of trouble.

Well? said Lucy's voice. What? What?

Right back here, the sheriff said, is where I growed up. He was back now to childhood. Gary had known he would be. Liquor is good to deliver you there. Right here is where the old lane used to be. This is where I growed up. I watched them build this road when I was a boy. They swung the sledge heads on a rope. Hah, they'd say, and that steel would go, Ping! *Hah!* Ping! *Hah!* Ping!

Lucy's voice came through the open window. Well? she said,

closer. The trailer seemed to list like a little boat. The floor was so soft and creaky Gary was afraid it would collapse.

Will you shut up and wait a minute? he said. Gary stopped and stood on the soft floor in the trailer in Choptack and collected himself. He put his hand on his throat and felt the knob when he swallowed. The air inside the trailer smelled like someone had built a fire from unwashed clothes and then pissed the fire out. That was how these houses always smelled. It had been so in Mississippi and New Orleans and Chattanooga and it was so here. Law enforcement did not vary from one place to another. Suddenly Gary realized the smell in the trailer was like that in the old house where he and Brenda went to make love. In the language they had developed on Brenda's couch, they referred to making love as going to the old house. They would kiss, and Brenda would ask if he was ready to go. Go where? Gary always said, pretending, and she always gave him a mock angry look. Gary wished they could stay in Brenda's house. He wished he could watch her brush her teeth or get up in the morning and sit on her side of the bed. But in the daylight she wouldn't kiss him or let him touch her, even if they were alone. She was snakebit, he guessed.

Mr. Kerr? he said.

Borned of a woman, the sheriff sang out, full of trouble.

Gary kept going. One bedroom, the size of a closet, was empty. So was the toilet. At the other bedroom the door moved back heavily. There was a white mattress on the floor with some sheets. Mr. Kerr hung from the back of the door. He was naked, the electric cord sunk in his neck the way Gary had seen vines do with trees, but somehow his haired skin seemed like a kind of clothing. The first thing Gary felt was relief. Relief that Mr. Kerr was dead and not him. He moved his flashlight beam over the body. The shiny blue head was a couple of sizes too big. So were the legs from the thighs down. A hernia had swollen up the testicles like the throat of a bullfrog, and for some reason Gary remembered the boys in high school staggering around, holding lunch bananas out from their crotches. Bring on the women, they called. Bring on the women, right now! Mr. Kerr was a little short man. He had been born little and short enough to hang himself on the bedroom door of a trailer. God, Gary said. He stood there for a long time. It was as if he had forgotten where the door was. Then he remembered that the old man's body hung against the only door. Gary took the doorknob, next to the dead man's kneecap, and opened the weighted door slowly enough not to have to hear the scuff of flesh against it again.

In the hall he ran into something and a numb heat shot up his spine through his neck across the back of his skull. In a second he had hold of its wrist, a little cool bone in his palm, and then he had its mate, and he was about to shove it up against the wall when he realized from the length of the hair it was Lucy. He held on to her longer than he had to, pushing against her with his whole body. It might have been the need that arises in the presence of the dead to cling to something alive.

Then one of her hands came free and smacked across his nose. The radio hissed and flopped against his hip. Lucy seemed to convulse and leap as a child will, and by the time she fell backward they had reached the front door and her head hit the frame. There was her face again, and Gary thought, I knocked her tooth out.

You hurt me, she said, bending over her folded arms as if she had a stomachache.

I was trying to help you.

You hurt my head, said Lucy, as if she had just discovered it. You hurt my head.

Come out to the car.

It was barely light enough to see that slugs had crossed the porch. The dew had risen thicker and colder than rain, and it soaked through Gary's pants. Holding her head, Lucy picked through the weeds as if they were briars. He let her in the front seat.

Feel, said Lucy as he picked up on the radio to call the ambulance. Feel what you done to my head. I'm going to report this.

Gary said the numbers for a dead person, a suicide, and the numbers for an ambulance, and his traffic got out this time, because Sylvia the dispatcher said okay. Gary sat there for a second looking at the silent radio and waiting to tell Lucy about her daddy. He was completely in control of her life, but he didn't want to be.

Feel, Lucy was saying. Really, feel.

Gary looked at her.

I was trying to keep you from seeing, he said.

Seeing what? She withdrew her head with a look of angry satisfaction. Are they dirty books in yonder?

Your daddy is dead. He hung himself.

Lucy stiffened in the seat. Her head almost touched the roof. Gary had done it wrong. He waited for her to cry. Once a woman started crying, you had something entirely different on your hands. But Lucy didn't cry. She had a look on her face as if it were too good to be true.

He aint dead, she said.

Gary nodded that he was.

He aint neither. She was looking through the windshield at the wall of the trailer as if there should be some sign. You don't know.

Gary took out his metal clipboard and opened it to a blank offense report.

The law aint worth nothing in this county, said Lucy.

I need to fill out a report, said Gary.

I don't want you to do nothing.

I have to put your name on the report.

I know that.

I know your first name.

Good.

What's your married name?

Burton.

Lucy Burton. You and me were in school.

She picked a fescue seed off the wet hem of her dress. I don't remember that far back.

My name is Gary Solomon.

I know it, said Lucy as if he had just done something absurd. I know who you are.

I didn't think you did.

Don't think I won't remember who you are. She swiveled toward him. Or what you done.

You were married to Tony Carter, said Gary.

Lucy looked at him as if she did not comprehend. You never married, she said.

Yes I did.

It never was in the paper.

I was down in Mississippi.

We're not good enough for you here.

I was working, said Gary. I got divorced.

Lucy turned back to the windshield. Oh, she said. Then she said, in the way answers are given when the game is already over, You're the one that's dating that Brenda again. You won't last long. None of them do. She'll do you every crazy way. She made that one kill himself.

Gary closed her up in the car and went back inside to look for a note. You always have to look for the note. People like a reason. He wondered if Brenda's ex-husband had left a note. He had not asked her. There was no note this time. When Gary came back out, Lucy was still in the same position, staring at the trailer as if it had just been painted purple. The ambulance was busy so two boys from the rescue squad came. The boys must have been nineteen, and they backed up the ambulance as if they had arrived to load a refrigerator. Goosing and shoving each other, they followed Gary to the front door. Both wore white coveralls with green crosses on the back. One unfolded a body bag. They had their two-way radio turned up on the public address so they could listen to the sheriff as if he were a ballgame.

I got called to a little church back here when I was first elected, the sheriff said. Back here in Choptack. His voice had tenor in the open air, but the liquor had begun to tremble around its edges.

He aint far from here, said one of the boys, the one with a

thin sandy mustache and moony eyes. You can tell by the sound. We done got him spotted once tonight.

They aint no way he'll win the next election, said the other. People are tired of it.

Come in the door and such preaching as you never heard was going on, the sheriff said. Hellfire and damnation and everything. Everybody just sitting up, listening.

He paused for a second. Maybe he was laughing.

I said to a man there in the back row, What do you mean calling me all the way out here for nothing? And he looked at me and said, Sheriff, that up yonder aint our preacher. I got to looking, and sure enough it was old Eddie Ball, higher than a cat on dope. It took me and three others to pull him out of there.

Radio static.

We had to wait on the prayer.

The two boys laughed as hard as they could. It was harder than they had to. That's our law, right yonder, said the blond boy, pointing into the dark toward the sheriff. He kept laughing. He had a too-handy laugh and perpetual squint-eyed smile from smoking too much pot.

That girl, Gary said, just lost her daddy.

They glanced at his patrol car. Lucy was watching them as if she were looking through a keyhole.

She don't seem to care a whole hell of a lot, said the boy.

They went into the room. Mr. Kerr was still there. Beard had come out on the blue face in little silver stitches.

So this is daddy, said the blond boy. Hi, daddy.

One thing is for sure, said the blond boy, widening his eyes. I'm proud I didn't have to find the bloated son of a bitch.

You can just take me on back now, Lucy said after he finished the report. On the road to her house, Gary watched the rim of English Mountain harden and fur with trees as the stars began to go out. Her house was another trailer with the doorbell lit. It sat a little crooked, as if it had just landed in the middle of a field. Gary stopped with his arm across the wheel.

That aint no way to die, she said. It aint no way. Did he even leave a note? said Lucy.

Gary looked at her.

Didn't he leave no note?

No, he said.

Well, said Lucy, apparently even more pleased. He knowed the reason.

Gary didn't say anything.

It eat him up, I guess. I guess it did finally.

Gary moved his face into something like a tightened smile.

It aint got nothing to do with me, she said.

No, said Gary.

One thing is for sure. You don't know what you'll do. You just don't never know. Things come back on you. You remember that.

Lucy got out of the car and swung the door shut. You remember that, she said through the glass. Gary watched her walk toward the door. He watched her take out her keys and hunt for the lock and then open the door and go inside. She did it, he guessed, the same way she always did. The door closed and the trailer was intact again. Gary stared at it for a minute, and then drove away.

Tired, I'd say tired, the sheriff said. The daylight anymore just wears me out to see it coming.

Ahead on the road a car flashed its lights a couple of times. Gary slowed up and the sheriff's car slid alongside his and there was the sheriff's face with its gray hair and mustache and one elbow out the window. It seemed to have materialized out of radio waves. Gary rolled his window down too.

Gary Solomon, the sheriff said, grinning. Think the sun will hurt the rhubarb?

They sat in the road for a few seconds with their engines idling. The sheriff seemed far, far inside himself. The red end of his cigarette moved slowly from the steering wheel to light up his face. The smoke came out as he spoke. Who's dead out here?

Gary said that it was a Mr. Kerr. He read the whole name off his report.

Kerr, the sheriff said. Oh yeah. He nodded. Did you tell his girls?

I told one of them.

I guess she was glad to hear it.

It seemed like it, said Gary. Why is that?

The sheriff turned and looked up the road. Good reasons, he said. How'd he do it?

Hung himself.

The sheriff considered that a second. What with?

Extension cord.

He shook his head slowly for a long enough time. You could tell him anything, good news or bad, and his first reaction was gravity. Goddamn it, he said, I never can find one when I need it.

Gary smiled. Maybe you don't need it bad enough.

You may be right, said the sheriff. You may be right. His car idled a little faster. They're just about all dead now. Just about every one of them is. The old people. I started once to count everybody I knowed that's dead, but I stopped.

Good thing.

The sheriff winked and put his car back in gear. Gary did too, but the sheriff put up his hand. Hey, Gary, he said.

What.

You know how come they call it Choptack back here?

Gary said he did not.

Because if you chop a tree under that mountain, when the ax goes chop, you hear the mountain answer tack.

He drove off slowly and Gary sat there and watched his taillights rise and then drop out of sight. Then he went on himself. Beneath the mountain the barns already had edges, and now dimension. Names passed on the sides of mailboxes. Behind their mailboxes and gravel lanes all the farmhouses seemed abandoned. Not a soul stepped off a porch or flung out dishwater. The clotheslines were empty. Gary kept seeing items from Mr. Kerr's trailer. He saw a pile of cigarette butts in a glass ashtray and he saw some chickenbones in a box. In one closet the stock of a little rifle was visible. Gary thought about Mr. Kerr's body, riding back out of Choptack just like he himself was. The body, he thought, got lighter as it died. The soul just drains right out. He had seen this happen with the boy who shot himself in Vietnam. It just slipped right away from him and it was gone. Gary saw the stock of the little rifle again, and he realized it was not in Mr. Kerr's trailer. It was somewhere else in his memory.

Gary told them on the radio that he was off-duty. He wished he could see Brenda, but she was sleeping. Taft was sleeping too, up in his room. He would have liked to pull up and wake them both. If you were the one who found a body, you wanted to go home afterward and be with your people and take a good shower and be in a clean place. But they wouldn't understand. Taft hardly knew him. And Gary would have told them what he had seen, and he didn't want to do that either.

Before he came back to Alexander City, Gary had thought about killing himself. Not the way Mr. Kerr had done it, but some other, better way. It was a quick thought, but it lasted a long time. It made him come home.

Gary passed the green rock monster, which somebody had painted beside the road on a boulder that looked like an open mouth. He turned at the light and went down into the town and turned again at the city pool. He stopped at the railroad tracks downtown. Sure enough, a train was passing, its reflection warping in all the empty storefronts on Main Street. The train was just as loud as when Gary was a boy. The empty parking meters leaned different ways along the street, and sometimes bricks fell off the tops of the buildings onto the sidewalk. No one moved them. Gary let the train pass, and then he got out and walked up the empty street to the old real estate office. It was on the second floor from the street, up a set of stairs that still smelled of cigars and shoe leather, of commerce. The office had probably been closed ten years, but Gary knew his father still came here. The key was still over the door facing.

Gary remembered the creak of the office door opening. Inside were two big windows and a couple of desks. Nobody worked at them now, but there were still various papers. Gary stood in the office, and the longer he stood and thought the more he became aware of the stock of the little rifle visible in the corner of a closet. Around it lay stacks of rolled-up papers, each containing somebody's farm. Gary put his hands on his hips and looked at the little rifle for a minute.

Why did he keep that? he said aloud. Why in the hell did he keep that?

Then he sat down on the floor crosslegged and reached out and took the little rifle with his hands. The other side of the stock had two flowers carved into it.

He had to, Gary thought. Gary didn't know much about it, but he had been told that his mother was hanging out clothes on the morning James died and she ran over to where he fell and picked him up. He was eight years old. She rocked him for a long time on her lap and she kept asking if he was all right and she told his father he said, Yes. For the rest of her life she thought he said, Yes. She didn't understand how he could die after saying that. Now Gary closed his eyes and he was asking James the question himself, but he was Taft. Taft said, Yes, but Gary felt him zipping away. Gary put the rifle stock on the floor and looked down the barrel. It was just a hole. He couldn't see far down it. Then he rested his forehead against the muzzle and felt along the forearm and the receiver until he found the trigger guard and the trigger. The muzzle made the coolest ring against his forehead.

He felt that ring as he walked back down the steps and drove home and undressed and even when he lay down to sleep. As he slept the ring was there again like another eye in his head and no matter how hard he slept the eye still saw.

7

IT WAS LATE JULY before Gary knew for certain that Bid was dying. Nobody had told him, but he knew it. Bid had made sure Gary had enough firewood for the winter. Mostly cedar, it was stacked up on the dry side of the house. Bid had cut some trees Gary didn't want cut, and he had worked after dark a couple of times, but Gary realized that he had done it because he knew his time was running out.

Gary tried to locate somewhere in his mind what his father's death would mean to him, but he was unable to find it. He tried to understand it in the way he understood his mother's death, but he could not. He only knew that Bid was dying. On the last day they cut wood, his father left without saying anything. He ran all the gasoline out of his saw, and instead of placing it back in the trunk of his car he left it on top of the woodpile. Both he and Gary knew the stack was big enough for the winter.

Gary was sorry that they had finished before Brenda let Taft stay with him for a couple of days. He knew now that Taft would never see Bid alive. Gary knew what his father would do. He would not go to the hospital until he was about to die. He would not go early and then not die and have to come back home. He would go and he would die. Gary would have to be careful, or Bid would die without him.

The day Gary picked Taft up, Brenda refused to come. She had never been out to Gary's place. He told her about it and talked about all he wanted to do with it, but she wouldn't come. As Taft got into the car, Gary could tell that Brenda was already lonely. When he drove Taft away, he felt as if he had stolen him from her. But he tried not to let on with Taft.

Gary showed him how the barn was constructed. It had been built by Gary's grandfather, who died before Gary was born. Saplings had grown up in the front and honeysuckle and fox grapes had climbed the saplings, but once Gary and Taft pushed inside it was cooler and the smell of a barn was still present. It was dark inside. Neat, Taft said, looking up into the loft where dirtdaubers dangled in a bluish light as if on threads. On the dirt floor cowshit had aged into a substance like weightless concrete. Tools were still hanging on the back wall.

Gary began to feel excited too. He found a brush hook and the blade was still sharp. He took it down. All that afternoon Gary and Taft slashed at the brush around the barn. They cut some sumac and the smell of its pith was like peanut butter. They cut some other weeds, the smell of which reminded him of fish, and they even went after the saplings with a hatchet. There was nothing they could do with one big old wild rose. Gary got blisters first and before he realized it they broke and watered and bled. He started to tell Taft to watch out about getting blisters, but he couldn't tell Taft something like that. I should have gone into town for some gloves, he said. Taft looked up. His bangs were plastered down with sweat. It's all right, Taft said.

It was close to dark when they quit so Gary couldn't see exactly all they had done, but he felt as if it were considerable. They went back to the house, holding sticks in front of them for spiderwebs. Gary drove Taft to town and they got footlong hot dogs and ate them in the car. They drank three or four Pepsis each, they were so thirsty. The girl who brought the hot dogs looked at them and said, You been working, and Gary said, We have.

As they ate Gary told Taft about what he'd like to do with the farm. If I could get maybe one field clear, he said, I could have some cattle. Maybe goats first. They could eat the brush.

Taft nodded. He had found a velvet ant and gotten it in a bottle. The bottle was between them on the seat and the red-and-black velvet ant kept trying to climb the glass sides only to tipple back.

You could have a pond, Taft said. If you dammed the spring.

Gary liked that idea. It could have fish, he said. I'd like to have bees too sometime. I could sell the honey. There are a bunch of sourwood trees in there. I saw them blooming.

Bees are a lot like ants, said Taft.

I've got a big cedar log, Gary said. I'll show it to you. I'd like to make something out of it.

Like what?

I don't know yet. You have to work with it a little while to know. That's what I used to do when I was in high school. I used to draw too. But I don't have any tools. I'd need some tools to work with.

There might be some in the barn, said Taft.

That night Gary made Taft sleep on the bed and he took a sleeping bag and unrolled it on the floor. He was more interested in Taft's sleeping than in his own sleep. He lay in the sleeping bag wondering what they could do tomorrow. He didn't want any more work, because while they were eating the hot dogs he had seen Taft's hands and they were covered with broken blisters. They would dry out, though, maybe before he took Taft back to Brenda, if he didn't aggravate them with more work. But Gary wished he had told Taft to wash his hands so they wouldn't get infected. He should have remembered that. Gary stayed awake a long time. He wanted to go on through to the next day with this same feeling from today, and he knew if he slept it might change. The change would slip not just into his mind but throughout his body, beginning with the lungs where he breathed, until it had filled him, because Gary knew he was not deserving.

In the morning the window was filled with the green light of the pear leaves. Taft had already awakened and noticed the letters scratched in the window glass. My mother wrote that, Gary said, sitting up. He had to clear his throat and say it again. He told Taft the story about her diamond ring. Taft went over and felt the letters. Telling the story made Gary remember something else. He was grateful that he remembered it, because it gave him a plan, and Gary didn't want Taft to know that he didn't have a plan. What he remembered was his grandfather's peach orchard. Gary had heard his mother and Una Clay tell about taking a wagon up the mountain to the peach orchard on the side of the mountain. He wished he could ask his mother where it was. There must have been a road, because they took the wagon.

I know what we can do, Gary said.

What? said Taft.

There used to be a peach orchard. It was up on the mountain. I wonder if it's still there.

We could find out, said Taft.

They might not be there anymore, Gary said. Peaches are bad to split in the trunk or they grow so that the wind will break them. Without somebody watching over them, they don't last long.

We could eat the peaches, said Taft.

We got to eat breakfast first, Gary said. He told Taft to pick up a stick for spiderwebs before he went to the outhouse. Gary wasn't really worried about spiderwebs, but it was his way of telling Taft about the outhouse.

The spiderwebs are bad already, said Gary. It's an early sign of fall.

The outhouse was not a pleasant memory. It was hot in the summer and it smelled and it usually contained a dirtdauber or two, which you could never be sure wasn't a wasp. Now Taft, Gary thought, would have that memory too.

Gary decided to make biscuits to go with the sausage. He had learned how to make them from his mother. It's simple, he told Taft. He showed him how to use a fork to cut some shortening into his flour and he put in just enough buttermilk to make it cling together. Gary saw Taft looking around at Una Clay's kitchen, which had once been a back porch. The old white stove smelled of meals it had cooked a long time ago.

As soon as the sausage and biscuits were done they each ate a couple. Gary took out some milk to go with them.

They're good, said Taft. He looked surprised.

You bet they're good, said Gary. We're going to take some with us. That's how come I made extra.

They'll taste good, said Taft.

I remember my mother used to make breakfast for supper, said Gary. She would make it at all times of the day, especially if I felt bad. She said it was the healthiest meal of the day, no matter when you made it.

When did she die? Taft asked.

Five years ago. Six this November.

When he was done eating Gary took an old shoulder bag and put in the rest of the sausage biscuits, wrapped up in aluminum foil, and some Fig Newtons and two apples. Taft had found a wooden cane Gary had leaning next to the door.

Where did this come from? he asked.

That's my short-timer's cane, Gary said.

What's that?

A tour of duty was thirteen months, but you got to come back out of the jungle after twelve months. So you got a short-timer's cane. You'd take it and walk around like you were really something.

The cane was smooth wood with a black thorny vine wrapped around it.

Gary looked at Taft and he realized that Brenda had told him some things about him. He wondered what else Taft had been told. Most of it was not good, he figured. For a second he started to tell Taft about how he had had a small file of things he carried in his mind while he was in Vietnam. They were things from home. He could take them out and for a second they gave him pleasure. But he had brought home a bigger file and its items came out at the opposite time, when he didn't want them to.

Gary remembered how his mother and her sisters talked about a big spring that was clear and tasted a little bit like pine, so he took a cup. He got out an old sheath knife and had Taft put it on his belt. He went ahead and put on his gun. That seemed to quicken Taft up. It was as if they were going on a real expedition.

For snakes, he told Taft. My aunt killed some big ones. Rattlesnakes. She was real big on snake killing.

Rattlesnakes? said Taft.

Gary went to a drawer where Una Clay had kept her snake relics and took out some pictures and a rattle with nine links. He shook it. In one of the pictures Una had killed a rattlesnake and hung it over the clothesline, and in the middle it was as big around as Gary's leg. Its pattern was all worked together like a design that had taken a great deal of time in forming.

Did she shoot it? Taft asked.

She never shot a gun in her life, said Gary. He said it proudly, the way Bid had always said it. She used a hoe to chop off their heads.

She must have been quick, said Taft. I hope we see one.

They went out the back door and the heat and the light were already full. All the high summer grinding and clicking and chattering of the insects had begun. Gary looked into the woods. He hadn't acted like it, but he hoped they would see a rattlesnake too, so they could kill it together. He looked over some of the trees and he could see the top of the mountain. It was unassailably yellow-green with heat. Maybe it would be cooler in the woods. It would be cedars for the first half mile at the foot of the mountain. They would drop their itchy leaves down into the sweat beneath their collars.

Gary looked at Taft. He had on tennis shoes and jeans.

You need a hat, Gary said. He ran back inside and got hats for both of them.

You got a hat, he said.

Great, said Taft, with mock disdain.

To the mountain, said Gary.

Upward, Taft said. Onward.

For the first thousand yards behind the house the honeysuckle was heavy and the trees were small. When they got separated in the cedar thicket Gary hollered out and slapped the side of a tree.

It's just a rattlesnake, he said. I'll be all right.

Taft laughed. Strangle it, he said. Bullets are too expensive.

Naw, said Gary, my hands are full. I'll just spit in his eye and get him in a leg lock.

I got one too, said Taft.

Tie him in a knot, Taft.

That would make him too hard to skin, said Taft.

Oh. Gary stopped. He was laughing. Get him by the tail and

pop him like a whip. Gary took off his hat and shook off the little cedar leaves.

Somebody's done moved into this cedar thicket, Gary said, pointing to the back of a house.

Taft laughed. It's us, he said.

They had come out where they started. At first the back of the house looked like the back of somebody else's house.

Hellfire, said Gary.

This could be a sign.

Take off your knife, Gary said. It's got a compass on the sheath.

Gary and Taft looked at the compass, which had a very jittery needle.

The mountain is south, Gary said. Don't forget that.

South, said Taft.

Birds flushed out of the branches. In places they had to crawl. Gradually they entered a low place at the foot of the mountain. They followed a little creek for a while. The creek had several sunny spots and in one some blue dragonflies were perched on weed stems. They were bluer than neon. Is there anything about blue dragonflies in that book I gave you? Gary asked.

Probably, said Taft.

You know who we need?

Who?

Moody Myers. If anybody could find the old road, he could. He probably knows where it is.

Almost by accident, Gary found the road. He had to urinate, so he went behind some trees and suddenly he saw it winding up ahead of him. It had some saplings in it but it was still a road.

Hey, Taft, Gary said. I found the road.

They looked at each other. Upward, said Taft. Onward.

The cicadas had been going all morning. Their sound was like the sound of heat. They seemed to be grinding it out. Farther up the road the trees were big straight poplars, and the road turned back on itself and at times in sunny places was tall with weeds. Gary held his arms up high. They had gone a long ways, Gary guessed halfway up the mountain, before they stopped. It was extremely quiet. For a while the road had been spongy, so Gary knew there was a spring close by. He realized they were inside what had once been a clearing. It was flatter, and the trees had closed in, but he could see the rock foundation of a house. Behind it there was a pipe, and the springwater was coming out of it and splashing in a little clear pool. Scattered around the foundation were the milky white disks of ceramic from the lids of old Mason jars. Taft picked one up. Not much else was left of the house.

This is it, said Gary. He held his cup under the spring and drank. He swallowed and swallowed and he could feel Taft waiting for him to say what it was.

This is the peach orchard, Gary said, out of breath.

What is?

Gary sat down on a foundation rock close to the spring and opened up their lunch.

Stop, said Taft.

Stop what?

We don't need that. We can eat peaches.

Very funny, said Gary. Here, have a freestone. He handed Taft a sausage biscuit.

They sat on the rocks and ate. If it had not been summer, they could have had a view off the mountain. They could have seen for miles, probably. All of a sudden they stopped knowing what to say. One minute it had been easy, and then there was nothing.

Finally Gary touched his face and said, I shaved off my beard.

How come? said Taft.

I had to. The sheriff wouldn't let me keep it.

Oh.

Your mother didn't say a word. I don't think she even noticed.

She cried, Taft said.

She what?

She cried after you left.

In front of you?

No. But I could tell.

Gary stood up. Did she tell you I volunteered? he said. I bet she told you I didn't get drafted.

Taft nodded.

She told you the truth, Gary said. I volunteered for tunnel-rat work too.

What was a tunnel rat?

We'd go down in these tunnels the VC made and blow them up. Gary laughed. But we got an extra eighty-seven dollars a month. It was interesting, Taft. They had big rooms and even hospitals down in there. And you could see every dent in the ground where they had dug them out with a handpick. I think that was when I knew we were all in trouble. When I saw those little pick marks.

Did you know?

Know what?

About me.

Gary looked around. I knew, he said.

Gary waited for Taft to ask why he left. He had no idea in the world what he would say. He guessed he would just hear it when he said it. But Taft didn't ask. Gary waited, but he just kept eating, and Gary realized that Taft had lost any need of knowing.

I thought there might at least be some peach saplings, Gary said at last. We can look in a minute. You'd think there might be saplings.

But Taft was already looking. He found a couple of the jar lid disks that were still perfect and put them in his pocket, but they didn't find so much as a peach pit. At least there was not some pitiful piece of the orchard remaining. Gary sat back down on the rock to eat his Fig Newtons.

Snake! Taft called out. He was about forty feet away, behind some trees.

It is not, Gary said, but he stood up.

Yes it is, said Taft.

Gary went over and saw right away that it was not a rattlesnake. The color of the leaves, the snake was only about two feet long and coiled loosely up. When it saw Gary approach it raised its head and spread out its neck like a little cobra. Gary laughed.

It's a spreadhead, he said.

A what?

A spreadhead.

Taft laughed too. There's no such name, he said.

For a second Gary didn't even know where he'd gotten the word either. But in a minute it came to him. It was from his father. Bid used to talk about finding spreadheads when he was a boy. Gary hadn't really believed it. He thought it was a lie, like the snakes that chased you or coiled up in a hoop and rolled where they wanted to go. Gary and Taft leaned over the spreadhead as closely as they dared, watching its black tongue dart out. The closer they got, the more it spread out its neck. Suddenly Gary felt a stab of terror. He wasn't afraid of the snake. But it was exactly the same kind of fear he used to feel in Vietnam when something was not right. It was the kind of feeling wild animals live under all the time.

Let's catch him, Taft said.

Gary couldn't say anything. He was looking all around the woods for what had scared him. There was nothing but sunlight in the tree limbs. Finally, he said, We better leave him alone.

Gary didn't remember much about walking back down the mountain. Taft still made some jokes, and Gary thought he made some too. He hoped he did. But it was quiet for longer and longer times, so quiet that their strides were most of the sound. It was late afternoon when they made it back.

Taft, Gary said, opening the door for him, I got to go into town for a few minutes. I'll be right back.

Taft nodded and sat down on the edge of the porch and started whittling with the sheath knife as Gary got in the car and started down the lane toward the road. In a minute he stopped and backed up. Taft looked up when he got out of the car.

Be careful with that knife, Gary said.

8

GARY PARKED IN THE LOT of the little hospital on the edge of Alexander City and went inside and said his father's name to the woman at the desk.

At the end of the hall, Bid's door was closed, but Gary didn't knock. He just walked in. For a second, he thought his father was already dead. Bid was flat on the bed and it looked like he had gotten longer and meatier. His jaw was wide open. They had oxygen taped to his lip, and his temples and his eyes were sunken down to the skull. But he was breathing. It seemed like a long time before a breath actually came, and it was a little like a snore, and Gary suddenly remembered all the times he had heard his father snoring, but it was different too, as if the air were going to a different place.

Daddy, Gary said, but Bid didn't open his eyes. He could see them moving, though, beneath the lids, which had grown thin, so thin it seemed that maybe he could see through them. Gary said, Daddy, again, and this time all he heard was his own voice. It didn't have pity or compassion. It was more like Bid had fallen asleep on the couch and Gary needed to wake him up. His father's ears were big and plastered to the sides of his head, and their tunnels were lightly furred like the inside of an iris flower. Bid's arms, which had been big, were wrinkled at the elbows and the skin where his muscle had been was slack and white. Gary was ashamed. Seeing your father dying on the bed made a mockery of strength. It made a mockery of everything.

Gary picked one of the chairs in the room and sat down. He sat there through the rest of the afternoon, with the sunlight growing stronger in the window curtains, and gradually he began to know the sounds of the hospital around him, the little bells and the voices and the feet and carts going past. He started out telling Bid about the spreadhead and the peach orchard, but gradually he quit. He studied the empty bed that was in the room with Bid and the painting on the wall and the silent television set and the telephone. Every hour or so a nurse came in and Gary smiled at her and she smiled at him.

By evening it was a different nurse and the window curtain was orange with light. They adjusted Bid and lifted his arm. They put Vaseline on his lips. Most of all Gary knew the breathing. It came out of the head, never the chest, and Gary saw it was nothing but will. Will was all that was keeping him alive, one breath and another in a little room while the sun went down.

Gary leaned down and began to find beggarlice on his jeans

and in the laces of his boots. For an instant, he smelled the way Brenda smelled when he held her on the blanket in the little house. Gary had never wanted a woman so much as he wanted her then. He wanted her so much that he tried to recall the way she smelled, but he couldn't exactly.

He sat in the hospital room with his father all night. It was amazing how long in coming the darkness was in East Tennessee in high summer. It was exactly the kind of dusk Gary had longed for while he was in Vietnam. There, the darkness was absolute, so absolute that the night was composed entirely of sounds, and there were millions of them. Sometimes little airplanes, called smokeys, came over and dropped flares that lit up the mountains like a false day, but they would fade out, and the complete darkness would resume. At the end Gary went fifty-three days without taking off his boots. They were too slow to lace up. When he finally saw his feet again, they had started to rot like long skinny white roots.

Here the evening light was like a kindness, sticking to everything like moisture that never fully dries out. It stuck even beyond dusk into the night on certain things. And it stayed in the sky until late. It was forever before it was fully out, and perhaps by then you were asleep. Gary didn't turn on any lights, but he didn't sleep. Early in the morning the breathing changed. It grew higher and thinner and shallower and more hurtful, and finally shrill. It was pitiful. It got so Gary did not think he could bear to hear it. He wanted to cry or put his fingers in his ears, but he could not. It filled the room, but it could not fill up Bid's body. You might think a lot would go through a man's head while he stays up listening to his father's breath, but Gary found that it was not true. There seemed to be great spans between breaths, in which there was no thought, and then during each breath there was not thought but only feeling. Toward the last, for what seemed like an hour or two or more, the breath seemed only to exhale. It was high and whining and it seemed only to want to push out and out farther and to take nothing in. Gary did not so much hear it stop as realize it. When he realized it, his first thought was that Bid had awakened, but he was wrong.

Gary went out and found the nurse at her station. She was eating a peanut butter cracker. When he said his father had stopped breathing she didn't say anything, but looked at him as if he might accuse her of stopping it, and stood up. They went back into the room and there was still no breathing, and she turned on a light and Gary could see it had gone out of Bid. Whatever it is that goes out had gone. The nurse picked up his arm and stared off at the wall. Her mouth was still moving softly around the cracker. Watching the nurse lay down his father's arm Gary felt something leave him too. It had left Bid, and now it was leaving him.

What do I need to do? Gary asked the nurse.

The nurse looked at him. She had brown eyes. There's a preacher, she said. I can call him.

Okay, Gary said.

The preacher came almost immediately. The first thing he said was, Let's have us a prayer together. During the prayer, which went on for a few minutes, Gary opened his eyes slightly and looked at the preacher as he prayed. His face was hard and creased in the forehead and the cheeks. His hands were rough. He looked like a man who had worked hard and things had still gone bad. He was wearing a blue knit shirt. Gary didn't listen to a word of the prayer, but he knew to open his eyes when he heard, In Jesus' name, amen.

So, you are the boy, the preacher said. You been gone a long time, aint you?

Gary nodded.

Your daddy was a fine man, said the preacher. He come to me when the doctors told him about his cancer. He come and said he was just about eat up with it and they wasn't much they could do. He said he hadn't been to church in a long time, since he was a boy, but that he had been baptized and saved when he was nine year old. In the river. I tell you we don't never know what we are going to have to go through in this world.

No, said Gary.

The preacher looked at Bid. He had his pride, he said. He told me that when it got so bad in his bowels and everything he couldn't stand it no more, so he finally just got him an old rag and stuck it up inside of him so he could have some peace. This here life is a trial. It's going to take it out of every one of us sooner or later.

Can you call the funeral home for me? Gary asked.

Yes sir. The preacher picked up the telephone beside the bed and dialed a number. He told them what had happened and they must have said okay.

Mr. Solomon done had his arrangements all made, the preacher said.

Ask them about a grave plot.

He done has that.

Ask them where it is.

The preacher gave an odd look. It's right up here in town.

I need to see where it is, said Gary.

He wants to see where it's at, said the preacher. Beside his mother. It's beside of your mother. You'll have to meet them up there this morning. They'll lay it off.

After the preacher had hung up the phone he stood awkwardly for a few seconds and then he asked if there was anything else he could do for Gary.

No, Gary said. I appreciate it.

You let us know, said the preacher, if they is anything we can do.

He left. Gary walked over to the bed and looked at his father again. He was not surprised that Bid had not told him any of the things the preacher had said. Bid had always been able to tell strangers things his family never knew. Strangers thought he was the friendliest man they ever met.

You were right, Gary told Bid, about the spreadhead.

There was a man smoking on the front steps of the hospital when Gary went out. They nodded to one another. Out on the new highway the sun had come up behind the zinc works and the headframe was black against the light. The cliffs of limestone were the color of the moon. It didn't take long for the day to take hold. Gary felt giddy. But all of a sudden he remembered Taft. Gary had left him alone all night.

Goddamn it, Gary said.

He drove out through Shelton and crossed the blue bridge over the river and by the time he pulled in the lane it was bright daylight and the jarflies had already started. Gary ran into the house but it was empty. He looked in all the rooms. He even ran a little ways through the cedars where they had started up the mountain yesterday. Gary stood behind the house and panic flickered all over his skin like bee wings. His stomach was light.

Goddamn it, he said.

Gary's first reaction was to call Brenda, but what if Taft was there with her? Or what if he wasn't? Gary ran back into the house and the screen door slammed behind him. Taft's clothes, which he had brought in a paper bag, were gone. Gary ran back to the car and drove back toward Alexander City. On the way he looked frantically behind some barns and one steep hill.

Goddamn, Gary said, louder, when there was no one there. My dad was dying, he said. It was as if he were talking to Brenda. My dad was dying, Brenda, he said.

But Brenda wouldn't give a damn. He had lost Taft. Gary drove around in Alexander City as if that would help. No one he knew was around. He drove past the cemetery, which lay on the side of a hill above downtown, and there was a man working. Gary pulled over, sliding in the gravel, and slammed the door and started toward him.

Goddamn, Gary said, under his breath. A path, going crooked at a slant, beginning wide and thinning down, had been cut through the weeds. Waves of black-and-yellow grasshoppers kicked off from each step, sometimes clinging to his pants. The weeds were high, some high enough to obscure the names on the stones. The man was swinging a scythe. He was cutting the weeds. It was swinging so smoothly there almost seemed to be no swing to it.

When he got close enough Gary saw the man was Moody Myers. After each stroke he waddled backward one small step.

Gary slowed down and tried to approach him carefully, as if he might run away. The weeds left a ringing sound in the blade, and they fell without falling, the edge sharp enough to leave them standing in a flattened shock. Moody Myers had his back to Gary, and his neck was creased and dark, the breath coming up from him in quick little sighs. Gary waited a minute to say something. He felt the empty country around him.

I appreciate this, Gary said.

What, said Moody, the weeds?

You doing this.

Moody ran a sleeve over his forehead. Okay.

My daddy died this morning, Gary said.

Moody looked at a sweatbee on his arm. He seemed to shake his head, almost imperceptibly, as if it were a kind of tremor. Is that right, he said.

He died about four o'clock, said Gary.

Moody was quiet for a minute. Finally he said, Well, I knew I was working for some reason. I just didn't know what it was.

Gary was shaking, even though he was sweaty. A gallon milk jug, half full of drinking water, sat on a headstone. Other sweat-bees were drinking in the moisture on its sides. They lit and dabbed their tiny pink tongues. Gary stared at the jug. He was the last one. His mother was dead. His father was dead. Even his brother, whom he had never met, was dead. They were all together. Gary was alone on the side of the hill in the sun.

I got Taft, Moody said. He's here.

Gary said quickly, I didn't forget about him. I was coming back. But he wanted to fall down on his knees. Instead he said, Where is he?

I think he's with Johnny.

Johnny who?

Johnny Sartain. I told Taft to help him. He can't half see. They're here somewhere. You can find them.

Moody went back to work. Gary went over to the side where his mother was buried, and they were standing in the weeds. He saw Taft. Gary had planned for them to open the box of books last night. He thought there was one in there about snakes. Taft was stomping down some weeds for Johnny Sartain, whom Gary remembered from high school. Johnny had a big wide paper unrolled and he was trying to look at it. He was cemetery superintendent.

Hello, Gary Solomon, he said when Gary reached them. Is that you? He reached out his hand, but it was clear to Gary that he couldn't really see him. He was reaching the hand out into the air.

Hey, Johnny, said Gary. I believe I know this other guy.

Taft looked at him. The top of his hair had some copper in it in the sun.

I hate to see you under this circumstances, said Johnny. He was squinting. He was big and brown. But that's what's going to happen to all of us. Even me and you are not that young no more, Gary.

I know it, said Gary.

Johnny was carrying a hammer and four cedar pegs. This is your mother right here, am I right? he said.

My mother, said Gary. He thought Taft was watching him as if he had caused an accident. Gary looked at his mother's stone.

They will be some letters in the ground, Johnny told Taft.

On marble blocks. See if you can find some *S*'s. I hate this about the weeds, Gary. This is a shame. A bunch of us is getting together to do something about it but we just aint got it done yet.

How come it to be like this? Gary asked.

Because the mines is on strike. They still own this ground from back when it was a company town. When we went on strike, they quit mowing.

Quit mowing, said Gary.

Aint that a sight? Johnny said to Taft. To think the company owns the ground they bury you in.

Taft shook his head. He was down on his knees looking. Here's one, he said. Right here is an *S*.

He spread back the grass with his fingers and Gary saw a perfect *S* cut in a little marble block, no more than three inches square. Part of the body of the letter was filled with chaff and grass seed.

No, said Johnny. That would be his brother right there. It will be one over. One more over.

My brother, said Gary.

Keep going, said Johnny.

You had a brother? Taft said.

I did, said Gary. He died before I was born.

He don't have a stone yet, said Johnny. They is not a stone there, is they? Do you see a stone?

Taft started to look but Gary said, No. There's none.

I thought not, Johnny said. But he's right here. He's right here with your mother. I know he is. Step off one more and here. Johnny held out his cedar stakes and his hammer. It was an old mule-ear hammer. The stakes had been sharpened on the ends.

Goddamn, Gary said. He saw Taft sneak a glance at him that was so filled with confusion that he wanted to break down and cry. Instead, he helped him square it up the best he could and Taft drove in the stakes. A couple of times he missed the stake.

Use the side of the hammer, said Gary.

They'll square it up, said Johnny. You don't have to worry about it being square. They know how to do it when they dig.

Before Taft could finish he dropped the hammer and reached carefully into the weeds. Gary had to finish the stake. When he looked up Taft had a praying mantis as long and lean as a butter knife on his wrist. It was greenish brown.

Look at that, said Gary.

What? said Johnny.

He's got a big walking stick on his arm.

It's a praying mantis, said Taft.

Look at him turn his head, said Gary.

He'll bite the fire out of you, said Johnny.

Gary tried to laugh. No it won't, he said. Taft is an animalist.

The praying mantis lifted off Taft's arm and flew down the hill. Gary felt it sailing away forever on its rattly wings. It hurt to see it keeping aloft, farther and farther down. It crossed above Moody Myers, who had nearly reached them with his path. He had stopped for a second to rest. They saw him absently reach out and pull a morning glory vine off a stone. Its purple flowers had already closed up for the day.

Wonder, Johnny said, if somebody will do this for us?

Surely, said Moody, going back to the weeds. Surely they will.

9

THE NEXT MORNING when Taft awoke someone was kneeling in front of his bookshelf. It was Tony. Tony had lifted a wren egg from the mossy nest on Taft's bottom shelf and he was holding it up.

I thought I was going to have to wake you up, he said.

At first Taft couldn't speak. Finally he said, What's going on? in a voice he thought sounded like a girl's.

Get dressed, said Tony. We need you down at the river.

Taft didn't really want to dress in front of Tony. He glimpsed around his room to see if there was anything of which Tony might not approve. Taft wondered how Tony had gotten in. Where was his mother? It was barely daylight.

Hurry up, said Tony. He was lifting the ant formicary, which Taft had made from a sawed-up yardstick and two glass panes from an old birdfeeder.

Is this just dirt? he asked.

It's ants, said Taft. He was afraid that if Tony tilted it he would mess up the whole thing.

I hope they don't get loose, said Tony.

Once Taft was dressed they went down the hall, and his mother's coffee cup was sitting on the table with her book. Through the patio door Taft saw her on the grass doing her exercises. She was nearly upside down, with her legs forming a wide, still V. Tony stood at the door for a minute and watched her.

What does she think she's doing? he said.

Stretching, said Taft. He said it as if he didn't understand what she was doing either.

Tony shook his head. His Corvette was nudged in the ditch a little ways up the street. They had to roll the windows down to see better because the fog had stuck to the glass. It was so foggy in Alexander City the zinc works had disappeared. The little metal shack the strikers had set up was barely visible. They had a fire going. Tony slowed down and blew his horn as they passed. Out toward Shelton, they couldn't see the road ten feet ahead, but Tony still drove fast. It was like flying through the clouds. Tony cut off on three or four roads Taft didn't know and all at once they were down along the river. At least he thought they were. No river was visible in the fog, but the trees changed to sycamores and musclewoods and the air had the smell of the nearness of water.

When they coasted to a stop Taft heard voices interspersed with crackly static.

We got to walk from here, Tony said. After they had gone a

little ways and were close enough to hear the water, he called out, I got him.

Good, said a voice.

Taft saw that the voice went with a gray-mustached man. Wearing a sport coat with a gold badge on the pocket, he was standing on the riverbank smoking a cigarette. He took a draw and flipped it away, still burning.

Taft knew it was the sheriff. He had seen him in the newspaper. The sheriff reached out and shook Taft's hand and then just stood there and finally Taft said, What are we doing?

The sheriff looked surprised. He gave a little jerk of his head and they followed him down closer to the water, close enough to feel its size and movement. Ahead of him, the sheriff and Tony clung to the wet trunks of trees or to vines, and they would pat each to show Taft where to get ahold. On the bank, wedged in some tree roots, a little boat sat half in and half out of the water. The sheriff and Tony just looked at it.

Ever seen this boat before? the sheriff asked. He was staring at Taft.

It's Moody's, said Taft.

The sheriff looked at Tony for a second and then back at Taft. You were the last one to see him, he said.

Where is he? Taft said.

The sheriff turned back to Tony. That's what I'm trying to find out, he said.

He didn't come back last night, Tony said. Then we found his boat.

Taft couldn't believe it. They had made a mistake. The sheriff had kneeled down close to the boat and stuck his hand into the river. He pulled up a stringer run through the gills of three catfish. They flopped and rattled the chain.

Looka there, the sheriff said.

Above them on the road and in the trees a commotion of voices shouting and engines revving had started. Taft turned around but he couldn't see anything. Then on the river a boat magically appeared. It had one man crouched in the bow and another steering the motor. The boat was plowing against the current and the man in front reached around to get the other man's attention and pointed directly at Taft and Tony and the sheriff.

Puss, the sheriff said as the outboard shut off and the boat coasted silently toward the bank. Foggy, aint it?

The boat hit gravel and Puss, who was wearing white coveralls with a green cross and the word CAPTAIN printed across the back, stepped out, testing the ground first to see if it was solid.

For every fog in August, he said, pausing to take a draw of air, they'll be a snow this January.

The other man, who was more of a boy, handed Puss a little dolly with an air bottle on it. It had a clear plastic mask and Puss loosened a knob on the bottle and put the mask over his nose. In between draws he took a bite from a ham biscuit.

I always heard that, the sheriff said.

This here, said Puss, is a deep one. Wait and see.

How come they call him Puss? Taft asked Tony when Puss wasn't listening.

I think because he always has been kind of a puss, said Tony.

You mean a sourpuss?

I guess. Or just kind of a puss.

Puss had a big wide whiskery face that looked like it did not appreciate any foolishness. In a few minutes more boats came, out of the fog and down from the bank on trailers. About a dozen rescue-squad men set about adjusting chains and tuning their outboard motors. Everybody seemed to know Tony. One was looking out into the fog.

I can't even see the other side, he said, cupping open his mouth to receive a chew of tobacco. It's like the ocean.

Another one pushed him. When did you ever see the ocean? he said.

Shoving back the arms of the younger ones who tried to help him, Puss had already tied his boat on a sapling. He wheeled his little dolly in the mud.

First Bid Solomon and now this, a skinny squad man said cheerfully. You never do know, do you?

What in the world does Bid Solomon dying have to do with this? said Puss.

Both of them are dead, the squad man said.

Shit, said Puss. He shook his head. Lot of people is dead, aint they, sheriff? he said. Me and the sheriff been around a lot longer than you have. They aint no use analyzing. Puss started to say more, but all he got out was, It all, and then he stopped, gulping. He had to take a draw from his mask, but they all waited on him. In between a squad man holding what looked like a huge fishing tackle box asked what happened to Bid Solomon.

Eat up with cancer, another one answered.

It all comes in threes, Puss said. He paused again. I was just wondering what would be next.

Something always is, said the skinny squad man.

Bring the hooks, Puss said, pointing to a white truck that had been driven onto the riverbank. Two squad men hoisted them out and, slipping in the sandy mud and holding their free arms high, dropped them at Puss's feet with a sound like the crash of cymbals in a marching band. He kneeled and began untangling a clutch of hooks so wicked and sharp Taft could nearly feel them in his skin.

The sheriff motioned for Taft to come over to Moody's boat. He had climbed in and was sitting on the bench paging through a small notebook.

This is all in the world that was in here, the sheriff said, holding it up. He handed the little notebook to Taft and Taft began to look through the pages. They had handwriting and diagrams on both sides of every page. The handwriting was tiny and sometimes it ran vertically up the margin if it ran out of room at the bottom.

What did you all do yesterday? the sheriff asked.

Went to the graveyard, Taft said. Moody cut some weeds.

What did you do after that?

He took me home.

Didn't he say nothing about going out on the river?

No, said Taft.

Well, said the sheriff. He's been going. He's been going for a long time.

He could have run off, said a squad man who was nearby.

He could be on a island, another one said. Sometimes people are on the islands.

Why, said Puss, you couldn't run him off.

He come up to my farm to hunt with his metal detector, the sheriff said. He never did bother nothing. You don't know what he found, do you?

No, said Taft.

Moody Myers was brought on, Puss said. Not many people know that, but he was. He come here with the mines.

Where did he come from? the sheriff asked.

Puss didn't seem to hear. All the mining was grassroots before he come, he said. He was the one figured out how to pull the air out from underground. Now you got Euclids and diesel loaders and what have you underground. Now we're down two thousand feet and more. He done all that. I don't know when people are going to wake up.

Wake up? the sheriff said. He was examining the sides of Moody's boat as if for fingerprints.

Look at your ball field, Puss said. He had to stop for air. What happened to it?

We've had more waterlines to sink and break this summer than we ever did, said a squad man with a beard. They just blow up like geysers.

What is it? the sheriff said.

We're sinking, said Puss. All I can say is, We gone.

He said We gone as one word. Wegone.

Ah, said the sheriff, we ain't gone yet, Puss.

I heard the bank is going to close, said the bearded squad man. Because of the safe. They say it has done sunk nineteen inches and has been clocked at an inch every forty-eight hours.

Shit, said Puss. He was twitching and had to take a draw of air. They is a river, he said, pointing into the fog. A river bigger than this one underground. I remember in '58 when we first started that mine we hit a big fault that was wide enough to run a Uke through. Goes all the way from Chattanooga to Virginia. One day we'll all be riding that river. We gone, sheriff. I'm telling you, we gone.

Is that why the church steeple is crooked? Taft asked.

They all looked at him as if he were not supposed to speak, but the sheriff seemed interested. I heard they can't decide if it is or not. They is one bunch in the church that says it is and one bunch that swears it aint. It's about to cause a split.

It's crooked, said Puss. You know it is.

I done heard they aint a casket left under the cemetery, the skinny squad man said. I heard they got them all stacked up in a room down in the mines.

Now that one aint true, Puss said. That one right there aint. He looked up toward the sun, which was just beginning to burn the fog. You can't hardly find a man this time of the year, he said. I dread it, I tell you. They get bloated up in all of that moss. You can't hardly tell a dead man from a tree log or a rock or what have you. It's all growed up. I've had snakes to fall on me.

Puss, the sheriff said, you ought to take them three catfish home with you tonight.

This here boy, said Puss, gesturing toward Taft, knows something he aint telling us. Aint that right, boy? For instance, what did he eat?

You mean what did Moody eat? asked Taft.

You heard me.

Taft didn't know at first if he meant what Moody ate in general, but he decided he meant the day he disappeared.

I don't know, Taft said. I didn't see him eat. He drank a lot of water.

God, I hope he eat, said Puss. When they don't eat they lay on the bottom forever.

Puss, the sheriff said. Did you hear me? Them fish are still breathing.

You know I can't eat fish, sheriff. I got a descending colon.

The sheriff lifted the three catfish up from the water suddenly and their tail fins slapped and they made a croaking sound.

He said, Eat me, the sheriff said. Clean me and eat me, Puss baby.

Them fish are nobody's now, said a squad man. You ought to just turn them loose.

Nobody can't eat fish, the sheriff said. I hate to see a good mess of fish go to waste.

The boy can take them, Puss said. Give them to the boy.

That's right, said the sheriff. He handed the stringer to Taft. It was heavy. Taft had the notebook in one hand and the stringer in the other. The sheriff started back up the bank toward his car just as the outboard motors fired in a boil of blue smoke. Over the noise Puss shouted to the sheriff to have Jack fix them all cheese sandwiches for dinner. The sun had begun to melt in a blinding place on the surface of the green water. Taft and Tony followed the sheriff up the bank, and the boats all went out into the fog that would become snow.

We'll find him, the sheriff said, turning around. I can promise you that.

10

SCOTT WOODY'S EYES grew large as if this represented the biggest opportunity in world history.

Dragging the damn river, he said. Goddamn! I wisht we could be there to watch it.

He might not be dead, said Taft. He might just be missing.

Oh he's dead all right, said Scott. Goddamn it, he's dead. You can count on that.

They were both light-headed from trying to spit all the time. At a certain age a boy no longer swallowed his saliva. Men spat. Taft's afternoon bus driver for instance sent out a lizard's tongue of tobacco juice every odd stop. Quids dried on the hot roads. Some men could hold spittle on their lips and then blow it with a soft pop for long distances. Scott had begun spitting through a gap in his front teeth. It was practice for when he started chewing, which might be any day soon as he decided on the brand. Red Man or Levi Garrett or Taylor's Pride.

Go ahead, Taft, he said, sighting his BB gun at the Tolliver's mailbox. Swallow. You'd be sick up the gills by now.

The tin mailbox thunked and Scott recocked.

How fast do you think one would go? he said.

What?

A damn body in the river.

About the same speed as the current, said Taft.

Scott rolled his eyes. I mean, dumbass, how fast would it rot?

I don't know, Taft said.

Pretty damn fast I think, said Scott. Hot as it is right now.

Taft still didn't believe Moody was dead. It had to be some kind of experiment. He was surprised when his mother took it so seriously. Taft had watched her run from one place to another in the house before she finally left for his grandmother's. She had a sidelong look in her eyes the way scared animals do. The last thing she told him as she started the car was that she would be back to take him to church tonight for his baptism.

Do *not* worry, she said.

As if he could. Taft had better plans. He stood in the driveway feeling the kind of sudden freedom that involved what he had begun to think of as Tanyatic potentiality.

I don't think he's dead, he told Scott.

Scott didn't look at him. He fired at the mailbox again and missed. They found his boat, he said.

I know. But he could be somewhere.

Like where.

Anywhere.

He told you something, said Scott.

No.

Your uncle did. The one with the Vette.

No. He couldn't tell me anything. The sheriff took him to jail.

Scott couldn't believe it. He stopped in midshot. Taft had wanted not to tell him. But he had been unable to resist.

In jail, said Scott. Goddamn! For what?

Probation violation.

What the hell is probation violation?

He didn't do what he was supposed to do.

Scott crossed his eyes. That is usually why you go to jail, Defaro.

He didn't check in when he was supposed to or something, so they violated him.

Ouch, said Scott. They violated him. There is more to it than that. He looked into the sky. With him there is. This is all connected. Every damn part of it is. Scott began counting on his fingers. You been to the funeral for one granddaddy that is dead that you never even met. You got another one that is a floater, and uncle is in the big house. Something is going on here. Damn if it aint. Did you not notice this all started after you went up in church Sunday?

Taft looked at him.

Something aint right about you, Defaro.

Scott loved conspiracy. He had pictures of the dead JFK and UFOs, and he did not believe in coincidence whatsoever. Taft didn't subscribe to his theories. But he did wish he had never gone up in church. After the service two weeks ago Taft had asked the minister if he could just show up on a Sunday evening and be baptized, and the minister smiled a big broad smile and said, No sir, Mr. Defaro, you must first make your decision in public! He said In public! real loud so that a bunch of people heard. So Taft went. He went the next Sunday during the second chorus of Amazing Grace. Sure enough, the next morning, by the grace of God, Tanya's letters resumed.

Me again!

Taft, I am so excited for you. I have a lot to tell that I have been saving up, so listen. Yes, the second time you are born is more embarrassing than the first. But you are almost as naked! They have these big white robes, the same kind fat women wear, except with a hem full of lead weights.

I asked, What are these for?

To keep your beautiful white robe from floating up in the water, they said. Now we couldn't have that, now could we?

On the way to Ogle's for Cokes Scott fired at bumblebees and especially large leaves or just for punctuation in the conversation. Mr. Ogle was a barber, and when he replaced the Coke machine in his shop he brought the old one home and set it up in his garage. It had Cokes for fifteen cents. They always went into the Ogle's big backyard to drink them.

Scott aimed his gun way up and pulled the trigger. For an instant, high in the air, the BB appeared, coppery and round, then was sucked away. Taft saw that he was shooting at Little Ogle's kite, but it was way out of range. Mr. Ogle was big, so they called him Big Ogle. That made people start calling his son

Little Ogle. Little Ogle was freckly and wispy tall with soft red hair. His kite had settled deep in the sky, looking down at them with a couple of evil eyeholes. How Little Ogle got it off the ground in August, when there was no wind anywhere, nobody knew. It could have been before dawn, Taft imagined, in the breeze that came out of the mountains then, mysterious as dew. Other people's kites got stuck in the trees and power lines in March. Little Ogle's seemed to have gotten stuck in the very air.

Thermal winds boys, Little Ogle said, watching the string twitch his freckly arm, that is the secret. They're up there. High thermal winds.

You ought not to be flying that thing of a Sunday, said Scott. He was sockless with his black Converse untied. It aint respectful. Fire two. He always shot with a bucking motion, as if his gun had a recoil. That was practice too, for a future shotgun.

Damn ten-gauge goose gun will lay you on your fucking ass, he said. Wonder what it feels like to get shot? Dad knew. He got it by a machine gun.

How come? said Ogle.

Because he was in combat, dumbass, at the time.

You could ask him then, Ogle said. He had eyes the color of fish's eyes.

No can do, Ogle. He's MIA.

Oh, said Ogle. I reckon.

You could shoot yourself, said Taft, and tell us what it feels like.

Scott looked at him as if that was exactly what he was talking about. Then he pointed the gun at Taft's head and gave a long-range squint. If I shot you right now, he said, you'd be going to hell because you aint been baptized.

He will be, Little Ogle said. Tonight.

Tonight is a long ways off, said Scott.

But Ogle had gone back to watching his kite. The little hole at the end of Scott's barrel reminded Taft of how useless other people are. He thought of how long blindness is and how Scott would enjoy apologizing for it.

Shall we devote a chapter of A Life of Taft *to friend Scott Woody? I think not. Suffice it to point out that upon being caught beating his meat, he told his mother he had sneezed on himself.*

Hell also had no duration it was so long. The coach, his Sunday school teacher, had made them imagine how long forever is. Taft's mind kept skipping. Well, boys, the coach concluded, it's way longer than that.

I wouldn't die if you shot me, said Taft. That gun wouldn't kill nobody.

What we need, said Little Ogle, is one of them weather balloons. We'd blow that thing up and set it loose. They rise on up into the atmosphere, and it's got a tag on it with your name so anybody can send it back to you when it lands. Taft has the catalog. Don't you, Taft?

Shit, said Scott, lowering the gun so a thousand BBs rattled inside. How do you expect us to blow up a goddamn giant balloon? I can see the three of us huffing on a weather balloon till we bust our balls.

Vacuum cleaner, Ogle said, would blow it up.

Vacuum cleaner, hell. Vacuum cleaner don't blow. They suck, like you. Scott paused, surprised at his own wit. Did you ever see a motherfucking vacuum cleaner that blows, Taft? God Ogle, I can't believe how dumb your ass is.

He never could. Scott liked to remind Little Ogle that twenty-seven years old was too old for kite flying. He was always asking him questions too, like what is a hundred times a hundred, and did his tonsils get pregnant. See, Scott would say, I told you that rubber would work. But usually Little Ogle recognized the tone of nonsense, and he stood looking down at his feet as if someone had cautioned him never to pay any mind. Oh, Scott Woody, he always replied, the devil roosted on your bedpost last night.

Little Ogle smelled vaguely of his own short red haircut, and his fingernails stayed long. Mr. Ogle had tried teaching him to cut hair at his barbershop, but it didn't work out. Still, when no one else was around, especially in early March when the kite first went up, he had thoughts on several projects, all of which Taft would listen at, nodding as the wind passed over them. It was probably wrong, Taft figured, to let his wrong ideas go like that, but wrong ideas were finer and more subtle than right ones. Scott said he disliked Little Ogle because he sat down to piss instead of standing up like a man, but he was still good for a Sunday afternoon. Scott and Taft finished their Cokes in small bottles the color of pond water, and they all lay on the grass below the kite.

Taft's granddad is in the river, said Scott.

Is that right? said Ogle. How come him to be in the river, Taft?

Because he's dead, Ogle, Scott said.

Oh, said Little Ogle.

They're dragging right now. Scott was sucking on a wild onion.

I guess they are, said Ogle. He moved the string a little, and the kite flapped. Taft liked that he never tired of it. He wished there was anything besides Tanya that he himself could never tire of.

Over yonder, boys, Ogle said, pointing with his chin. At all them buzzards.

Beyond the subdivision's edge, above where the dairy pasture sank toward the railroad, a tall funnel of them had collected. It spread out when he looked. Each rode its own circle, all the black wings leaning in and in without a flap, like blades peeling something hard and invisible from the air. Taft held up his Coke bottle, and they all fit inside, the highest ones barely flecks. The one rule at Ogle's was to put the bottles back. He saw what city the bottle was from and was about to announce it when Scott fired off toward the buzzards.

Goddamn, he said, shooting once into the ground for punctuation. I know where you and me are headed, Taft.

Chattanooga, said Taft.

I took my lead weights out, Taft! It wasn't hard, utilizing skills acquired in Home Economics I and II. Too bad you were not there, but this was before your mother felt the need of God. (I liked her better without Him!) Otherwise we could have been baptized together. Nobody knew. I did it while they were checking the temperature of the water. They were like those things you fish with. Heavy. When they had me go down the steps to the pool I had them all in one hand so I cast them upon the waters.

Down, down into them, Taft, I went, just like you will tonight. It clings all over you and the whole place smells like a pool or a bathtub, but you can see out over all the heads of the people watching you.

It didn't come up as far as I was hoping, but maybe far enough. I had on my bikini, which I chose exactly so it would show through (good and black!), and I am pretty sure the robe came up at least to my waist, maybe beyond. You know that glass panel for the water? This is what it's for. The view. There are times, Taft, when it is so good to be a girl.

I was smiling so big. But everybody thought it was an accident! They felt so sorry for me. We found the weights, they said. They were on the bottom of the pool. Poor Tanya! We saw her tail on her baptism day. And her panties, black! Of course, they mentioned not a word to my face. Now I wish I had taken off the bikini for the full effect. You know! Total immersion.

They broke the bottles on one rail. Scott's was Atlanta. At first it skidded and clinked on the oily rocks without breaking, but Scott ran after it and sent it against the rail. He started shooting at the larger pieces. Taft's broke more easily. He looked at the silver rail for a second in regret, and Scott saw him.

Him flying that kite on a Sunday, Scott said, and they went on down the tracks toward the buzzard column. In no time it started. The railroad tracks smelled like a telephone pole, but rot began to occur at certain places like a bad thought. Scott went stiff as a bird dog, the way he did when he farted. Whoa! he said. Take a whiff of Jif! They continued, without talking, until they reached the one long bend in the rails, and by then it had a uniformity. Its curiosity was gone. The railroad cut was filled with rot, touchable as sunlight, denser and wider than Taft had ever felt.

They stopped. Scott laid down his gun and raised both arms. He began to squirm out of his shirt. The stub of an old railway flare, corroded like a battery, lay at his feet.

This has to be what it was like in the war, said Scott.

Which war?

WWII, the big one.

Scott had been reading a book about Hitler and the bunker. Most of the books he read were about conspiracy and war dogs and combat. He said the books Taft read were pussy. A lot of things were pussy to Scott. There were pussy cars and pussy shoes. Pussy was fine in its place, he said, take it from him, but there was no need in the whole world being pussified. Scott had the shirt wrapped around his face with only one eye visible. He stood still a second, breathing and staring at Taft, as if he were testing out his makeshift gas mask.

What are you doing? said Taft.

Protection, son. Something done crawled up inside this world and died. Scott cocked and fired as a gesture toward the buzzards, much closer now but still as silent. We go up this bank, across that field, and into those woods, and there she is. He shot toward each as he named them.

Why? said Taft.

Why not? said Scott.

Because it stinks.

Taft, you know what they say, son. Once you get past the smell, you got it licked.

Taft balanced on one rail, burning through his tennis shoes. So far up on one of the telephone wires that it almost could not be seen was a tiny singing bird, making a noise such as the wire itself might make. Taft wondered how it could sing amid the heavy rot. Now all they could see of the subdivision was the black dot of Little Ogle's kite. Stay with us, boys, he had said. Where you headed?

Going to see a man about a dog, said Scott.

Don't go, said Little Ogle. We can all lay down and pretty soon them buzzards will come after us. I done it before. Didn't we, Taft? We laid down until they got in the trees right over us, and then we got up.

Scott laughed. God Ogle, he had said, you are so intelligent. Now Scott's face, what was visible through the shirt, had turned whiter. He was breathing calmly, waiting. In his one visible eye the pupil was tiny and round as the hole in the end of the gun. Only the heat waves that didn't exist could move.

I bet he done it himself, said Scott, the shirt muffling his voice.

Who did what?

Your old granddad. He jumped in that river.

Taft didn't say anything.

Old man like that, couldn't take no more. It runs in your family. Scott thought for a second. Then he propped the gun between his knees and leaned down as if the barrel were a drinking fountain. His mouth was open under the shirt. Bang, he said, is how Adolf Hitler done it. Except this would be a Luger.

Taft stared at him.

How would you do it? said Scott.

What?

It, stupid. It. Scott gestured. He enjoyed dissecting misfortune. He liked to shoot a watermelon in somebody's garden and then dig into the pink like a surgeon after the BB. Taft realized he was not expected to answer, just think. He was glad. Scott had scrambled up the red clay bank out of the railroad bed, his crack showing over the top of his pants. At the top he clawed the air as if brushing aside a jungle. Godamighty, Taft, it aint far now, he called, sighting up the hill with his gun. He motioned for Taft as if he were at a great distance. Taft got dirt in his shoes going up. Sumacs broke off in his hands, but he could not smell the sticky brown pith for the rot in the air. On top he saw the silver tracks going on until they joined. A woven-wire fence yawed back and forth with Scott's weight. He had already pitched his gun across in a cornfield that stretched up the hill toward some trees.

It's nothing but a dead cow, Taft said, but Scott didn't even turn around. He only said, *Defaro,* with caution in his muffled voice.

The air of the field was drunk with rot and a million slithering corn leaves. Each cornstalk had purpled near the dirt, where little bird-toed roots held it up. Their pointed ears had black tassles on the ends. The decay seemed to incite Scott. Going up the rows, he fired his gun every few steps as if he were testing. Taft heard BBs go tearing off through the green leaves. He tried pulling the collar of his shirt over his nose, but it didn't work. He had to take the whole thing off and wrap it around his face, corn blades slicing like paper across his ribs. The sun itched his shoulders. Immediately he had drawn all his own smell out of the shirt, and rot came back so strong it had a dry taste when he inhaled. It caused Scott to whoop. Rich! he called out. Grade A pasteurized! From ahead in the leaves he began to whistle and hoot in a low voice, respectful and soft as the one he used over dirty magazines.

Books, he called them. This summer he had built up a library of books, which he produced at each convocation of the Tittie Society. The first one he had found tossed out on the roadside, but others he had traded for or purchased himself. At first they were phenomenal. Big, giant titties, the likes of which no one had ever seen. And crotches with every color of hair, some even with none. Soon, however, they knew all the pictures by heart.

Now titties like that, he told Taft, they aint asking what they can do for you. No sir, they want to know what you can do for them.

The library left them with a feeling that they had to go search for something, but there was nowhere to search. One night after dark Scott had an idea. For a time Tanya's house didn't have any curtains. Her mother had taken them all down. A few of the windows had sheets over them, but most had nothing.

When it gets dark and they is light on inside, Scott pronounced, you can see it all.

They hid in Ogle's garden for at least an hour, and every time the lights came on in Tanya's bedroom Scott hit Taft on the leg. He had a pair of army binoculars. The okra was extremely itchy.

They weren't going to see any titties, Scott had said. Tanya was pretty much flat-chested. Taft was glad she was. Maybe the rest of the world would leave her alone and he could have her forever.

But most of the time girls would get so hot at night they'd fuck themselves with something, said Scott. There was this one girl one time who fucked herself with a Coke bottle until it pulled out her intestines. Now that would be something to see, wouldn't it?

What city was it from? Taft asked.

Ha ha ha, Defaro, said Scott. Very funny.

Sometimes Taft wondered which world was real. In the books everything depended on fucking, but outside it didn't seem that way. People didn't make much of a big deal about it. Even Scott seemed to have a knowing disdain the majority of the time. Yet the world was this way with physics and biology too, and Taft knew they ruled everything.

After about an hour Tanya's light came on again and they saw her come in and sit down on the edge of the bed.

She's got on her pajamas, whispered Scott. But you can't see nothing. She'll be taking them off in a minute.

They were close enough for Taft to see that she was writing. He knew she was writing to him. Unless she wrote to someone else too. Taft felt something hot pour into his stomach. What if he didn't get a letter tomorrow? He hoped that Tanya had already taken a bath. It was late. Probably she had. He didn't want Scott to see her naked. For some reason, even he didn't want to. She kept on writing. She wrote and wrote and wrote. Then she put down her writing tools all of a sudden and lay down on the bed all curled up. Scott jumped as if he had a fish on the line. Whoa, whoa, whoa, he said. Even without the binoculars Taft was the first to know what she was doing. She was crying. He could tell by the way her body moved.

Look at her go, said Scott.

Taft wanted to hit him in the face or tackle him on the ground. He wished he could find a weapon.

Then Scott lowered his glasses. Well, goddamn it, he said.

Strangely, they could hear her crying. It was pitiful, deeper than you would expect from a girl, more like an animal that was hurt. Scott stood up, popping his knees, and said Well, he had to go, and they started sneaking out of the garden. But at the edge in some tall johnsongrass lay a man's body. They almost tripped over it. They jumped back and hid and gradually they saw it was Mr. Mayes. Taft recognized him by the shape of the bald spot on his head. He was lying facedown in the johnsongrass, and he was crying too. His arms were stretched out and his hands were trying to grip the dirt. It was his crying they had heard, not Tanya's, but the two of them were crying together, on the same night. This was the first they knew of Tanya's parents' divorce.

Son of a bitch, said Scott. Will you look at that.

Your mother's ex had sense enough to take himself out of the picture. I dreamed the other night that my daddy did it. We found him in the morning lying in the yard and I was so happy. I didn't want to wake up.

I don't think my baptism took, Taft.

I don't feel different. I mean, I don't feel baptized. I want to, though. But it seems like it went away soon as my hair dried. It might have stayed as long as the water was in my ears. Maybe if you baptized me, Taft. You hold your hand up in the air and lay me back in the water. But don't forget to hold my nose!

In the field it felt as if they had to shout above the smell. Shit, Scott shouted, I hope I don't never die this time of year. It must be hell to be dead right now.

It's not that great, said Taft, to be alive. He had always conceived of dying as the very last day of school. It lay continually and half sweetly in the distant future. Then one day, sure enough, you are stacking books and washing the blackboard.

Scott had stopped. He looked back over his shoulder, the shirt quivering with his breath. I'd of waited, he said, if I was your old granddad. This is one hell of a time to die. Middle of goddamn August. It's got to smell like this in heaven with all them dead people.

There's no smell in heaven, said Taft.

Scott shook his head, the shirt falling down across a smirk. Huhuh no sir, he said. Look in the Bible. The body is what goes to heaven. And does the body smell? You tell *me.*

Scott had taken up a stance in the corn row with aplomb in his eyes. Taft began to feel tainted by him. The only thing he had ever admired about Scott Woody was that he didn't believe in anything. Now this, from a boy whose only comment in the back of Taft's annual was *Plug a lot of women.*

I'd not have drownded myself neither, said Scott. That was his dumbest move. A body that aint buried can't rest. That's in the Bible too if you just know where to look.

People were always finding such minds in the Bible. Digging in his thumb where he hoped it would turn up Psalms, all Taft ever located were lists of names begetting names and a color photo of the typical tomb. There was nothing to help him understand. Where was the real information?

He's not my grandfather, Taft said. Moody Myers is not any kin to me.

Scott wheeled around. We're all brothers under the skin Defaro.

Taft wished he had stayed with Little Ogle. But the bottles were already broken. At the edge of the cornfield a woods began, its trees old and spaced widely apart. Scott fired once in the air to signal their crossing. Now the buzzards hung patiently above them. From a distance Taft had assumed they turned around a center, but they swung out wider than he expected, looping across the pasture, their shadows intersecting one another on the ground. The air they rode seemed rough, hoisting them up or down suddenly, making them adjust their wings. Taft saw their heads, which were the color of wine birthmarks, turn to look at him. He thought of Little Ogle's high thermal winds, flying the buzzards like kites. That is the secret, he had said. To them, Taft figured, the rot smelled good, if they were constricted by senses at all. Nothing could be profane.

The dead cow was in the bottom of a gully. A pile of gray dirt, Taft thought, was all it had ever been. Thousands of maggots, so many they made him think of a mass of living cells, struggled upward, all of them working on Sunday, only to break off in thick fringes and roll back. Whole sections of the cow would move unnaturally. Taft saw that the head of a calf had emerged a little from the cow's back end before they both died. They had died of birth. The calf had gotten out just far enough to see. Scott shot into it twice and there was no effect.

After a few seconds he waved Taft along. Cow skeletons, sometimes overgrown with weeds or emerging from clay banks, lay under the trees. They went around kicking at them, not sure yet whether to pick them up by hand. The bones were so clean they excited a kind of greed in Taft, such as he might have for the information in a book. Scott took up a jaw and used it as a sickle for the weeds. Taft hooked his finger into the eye socket of a skull, its nose ragged. He wondered if the rattle inside could be the dried up brain or just some leaves.

THAT EVENING HE was looking for a place to display it in his room when Tanya called. They talked for two and a half hours. A lot of the time she giggled. For the first few seconds after he picked up the telephone he almost didn't know who it was, she was giggling so much.

He told her everything. They talked a lot about what they hated. Tanya hated her parents and their divorce and the hole in her heart, and she hated that they were not both older so they could be together. Taft hated having Dennis's last name and he hated the way Gary and his mother acted. Why can't they just get back together? Tanya asked, and Taft said he thought too many things had happened and that really they should just give up and quit torturing themselves, and Tanya said that wasn't easy, was it? And Taft said no it wasn't. Talking to Tanya was an unbelievable luxury. It was as if the world had finally allowed them something, and they made a secret plan of conspiracy. They made their own church and their own religion. Taft's mother came home five minutes after they hung up.

I baptize you, said the minister, in the name of Tanya.

And the sound of the water when the minister ducked him

beneath was like her giggling. He tried to look straight out at her when he came up, but his eyes were blurry and stinging. Dripping, he climbed back up the concrete stairs in his white robe, the lead weights popping on each step. A woman was waiting for him at the top with towels.

On the way home, his mother told him that Gary had asked her to marry him. He came over to mama's today, she said.

What did you say? Taft asked.

I think what I said was, Shit.

It was silent for a minute. You said shit? said Taft. He started to laugh.

She was laughing too. Shit is not exactly what you dream of saying when a man asks you to marry him, she said. But her laughter began to break down around the edges and she was crying.

Taft rolled down his window so he wouldn't hear her. The clean night air came in. Taft waited a long time before he said, Why did you say that, Mama?

Because he will mess up, she said.

Mess up?

Yes.

Everybody messes up, said Taft.

Not like Gary.

Taft shook his head. She had stopped crying, but he leaned even further into the night wind. It felt cool, as if it had come up from a secret spring. Now almost nothing of the afternoon remained, except a metallic taste in his mouth. It came from the moment when he and Scott had gotten in the shade and his whole body had turned cold and the trees and the pasture all went white. He hadn't puked much, mostly the Coke, but it burned his throat and his nostrils coming out. Even through the puke he could still smell the awful flesh of the air.

Ah, Defaro, Scott had said. Don't puke your guts out. He was leaning against a tree, mildly watching. Look at me, Taft. Look at me. It don't bother me no more. I can't smell it no more.

Then he stepped back, filling his lungs with air. I swear it, Taft. I don't smell nothing. Look. He raised his arms. Look here, Defaro. Oh how sweet. Nothing.

11

WHEN HE WENT BACK to town for a loaf of bread and a stick of bologna or to find a spark plug for the little boat, everybody wanted to know what he had seen. They waited, but Gary never had time to talk. He always had to get back. He was not the one counting the days. They did that. Nine, they told him. Nineteen. Twenty-one.

The sheriff let him have the boat. Turned over inside his barn, it was covered with red clay dust and pigeonshit, and the outboard was an ancient one. At first Gary wasn't sure. He had intended to have a stone made for his brother's grave. He had been to three different marble cutters before he realized he did not know the dates. The last one had asked him, and Gary didn't know.

See, it was before I was born, Gary told the marble cutter.

The marble cutter, whose britches were covered with white dust, looked at him as if of course it was.

Gary didn't know where he could find the dates between which James had lived. He knew some anniversary rolled around and struck his mother on the same day each spring so that she could not leave the house and could barely move, but he didn't know if that was the day of James's birth or the day he died. Gary had not been inside Bid's house since he died. He knew people thought that was strange. After somebody died you were supposed to go in and go through everything and clean out the house, but Gary had not. Someone had been calling him. It was a lawyer from town. The lawyer had left notes at the sheriff's office too, but Gary never called him back. He never answered Una Clay's telephone when it rang either. It would ring at odd times. The ring was very loud because Una Clay's telephone was the old thick black kind. Sometimes on about the ninth ring Gary would get afraid that it could be Brenda. Once he picked it up, but it was too late and the dial tone was back. After he picked it up, though, Gary was sure it had not been Brenda. It was the lawyer.

The first couple of days after Moody disappeared Gary went to the courthouse and spent a long time looking in the glass cases of the museum. The objects seemed to be arranged in a puzzle he could not figure out. It wasn't that he was glad Moody had disappeared, but he was glad for the opportunity. Bid's death had not done to him what it was supposed to do. Out on the river he felt as if he had found a true vocation. The river turned and turned back through the country. It had thick fogs in the mornings, worse in some places than others. Gary liked the smell of it. He liked pushing against its current and negotiating its few rapids. Sometimes the river spawned tiny thunderstorms that followed only it, and these were Gary's private thunderstorms. He let them wet him good. At times he almost forgot what he was looking for, but he would stop and remind himself, and Moody's absence would return, surrounding everything on the river, and, like a child, Gary was overjoyed that it was still there every morning when he got up. He felt that Brenda, and Taft, could see, or at least somehow feel, everything he was doing.

Puss's crew didn't appreciate the help. When Gary passed them the first time, they threw rocks at his boat. One of them struck the side.

Puss gave a sign, however.

Stop it, boys, he said. He motioned for Gary to come alongside. They were all floating in formation in the middle of the channel. Their lines were down and the boats were moving up and down with the water, but the eyes of the squad men were glaring steadily at him. The heat was heavier, but cleaner, on the river. It reflected off the water and turned everything white. The whiteness slid up and down the blades of tall grass and changed positions on the surface of the river. It even found single strands of spiderweb and traced along them as if it were searching.

Come over here, said Puss through his megaphone.

Gary was afraid they might try to turn over his boat.

What? he shouted.

Come on over here. We aint going to hurt you.

Puss was in the bow of the lead boat and he had two men reach out and take hold of Gary's boat as he drifted up. They had a hard time holding it against the current, but they held on hard as if they were fighting and liked to be fighting. Puss had a long white roll of paper in one hand. Trembling, he extended it toward Gary and tapped him on the head with it.

Here, he said. You want to look. By God, look.

Gary peeled open the paper a little and it was a map. He nodded and dropped it in the boat. He had to pull the outboard coil nine times.

I reckon we're going to have to help him, said one of the squad men.

When he was alone on slow water behind a big island Gary unrolled the map. It named all the bends and the rapids, the islands and the bluffs. It even gave names to the creeks that mouthed into the river. From the map it was possible to see just how coiled up the river was. The boat began to wheel.

Gary traced his finger on the map. Sweat dripped off his forehead onto the paper, which was very thin. He was right here, he figured. It didn't give him much comfort. That was probably what Puss had wanted. Next time when he saw them he would pull up on the bank under the trees or skirt them on the far side of the river, out of reach of Puss's voice.

Gary didn't like going back into town either. Of course he had to go back when he worked, but something about the town repulsed him. He had begun sleeping on the river. He had bought a tent at the hardware store and he could recognize the time of evening when he needed to stop and pitch it on the bank. He would put up the tent before dark and his sleep was so black and deep it didn't seem like sleep at all but something very solid.

Gary went first to the side of the island where the campfire had been spotted. Three nights after Moody disappeared a man was hauling tobacco to the barn after dark and he saw the campfire on the broad side of the island. One of the men with him, who had better eyes, swore he saw the figure of a small man cut once in front of the firelight. Gary had to tie his boat on a grapevine that hung over the river and wade along the bank of the island until he found a way in through the brush. The island was full of poison ivy. The poison vine grew thicker than a man's arm and hairier far up the trunks of trees, and it came out with big branches and black fruit. Gary tried his best to avoid it. One of the rescue-squad searchers had already been put in the hospital with his eyes and nostrils swollen shut from poison. Gary couldn't help but think about Bid. It don't take on me, his father had said as he ripped the poison vine off the tree trunk.

The remains of the fire were on a sandy place. The sand was dark and full of tree roots. Gary looked around. He picked up some of the charred wood and it was cold. He found some pegs that had been whittled off and driven in the ground. In the sand toward the bank he found several footprints, one of which was from a bare foot. The foot was small, like a woman's or a child's. This was probably just a place where people came to party.

Gary also went to a sluice in the river where some people said they had seen a dead body, completely black, with its arms upraised, caught on a wide snag close to the middle. But the body with its arms up was a log. It was below Tampico Creek, where an old Chevrolet frame stood headlight deep. Gary saw the arms. One of them even had a wooden finger wrapped around with fishing line and a couple of lead sinkers. The log rode up and down with the current in a pattern and Gary watched it too long and got the boat sideways in a dip. It threw him down in the bottom and he busted his arm on the aluminum side. He sucked on his arm where it hurt, but he was glad the log had been a log and he could still continue. For the first time in his life, he felt as if what he was doing right now was what he had been meant to do, and at the time it was meant to be done.

On the next morning he found a good long pole to steer in the shallows. He had almost finished cutting the leaves off the pole when he saw the nest. It was a big beautiful one, the biggest he had ever seen. It hung on a limb over the water and hornets were coming and going from the nest hole at the rate of about one every second. Their wings sparkled in the light. Gary looked around for a landmark so he could remember where it was. Taft would have been fascinated with it. Gary would have to tell him. Maybe Gary could remember where it was and after frost they could come back and obtain it.

Bid had had some tremendous battles with bees in his time. Whenever he was ready to auction an old house that hadn't been occupied in a while he loved to search the eaves for wasp nests and eradicate any yellow jackets. He'd go up against bumblebees too, and even hornets, using mostly fire and diesel fuel. If a wasp were hovering in a window he could smack it so quickly with his bare hand that it could not sting him. Sometimes the nests were so bad he'd make Gary wait in the car with the windows rolled up, no matter how hot it was. Gary would always listen, though, hoping to hear the whoosh of flame and then maybe the anger of wings, like extra air being forced into the atmosphere, and many times he had seen Bid come running faster than a man should be able to run, sling open the door, and dive into the seat whooping and beating his own flesh as if the devil had possessed him. One time a swarm of yellow jackets from a cistern covered up the whole car, stinging its tires and the wiper blades and everything, and Gary still remembered the look on his father's face, as if this had confirmed the vast extent of hurtfulness in the world. Somehow a couple made it in through the air vents and one got Gary on the ankle. Bid, who always swore the stings didn't hurt, seemed amazed at Gary's pain. The stinger was still in his leg and Bid lifted it out with the blade of his pocketknife and said, Well, at least the son of a bitch is dead. They die, you know, when they get you. Here he is. Stomp him. And Gary stomped with abandon. Bid had other cures too. Piss was his big one. He would squeeze the flesh until it was blue and then tell Gary to catch some of his own piss and rub it on the sting. Piss was better than anything, he said.

The nest was built on a flimsy limb. In one place leaves stuck out from the side, and the limb had a fork in it, which Gary knew could be easily split. It hung out over a good deep pool of green water where the current swirled softly around. Squinting, Gary looked up at them. They were maybe twelve, fifteen feet above the surface of the water. Soon they would see the error of their ways. Gary could have taken his .357 and clipped the limb right off from a distance, leaving the nest to plunge into the water, but he didn't want to do that. The rescue-squad boys would ask what in the world he was shooting at, and he would look stupid. Anyway, he had a better idea. He'd break the limb with his guide pole, snap it right at the fork. Then, soon as the nest hit the water, he'd force it down with the pole and hold it on the bottom. Bid would have liked the plan. He would have approved.

The nest was higher than he had expected and the closer he got the more dangerous it seemed, but Gary liked it. Balancing in the boat, he leaned back as far as he could with the pole and brought it forward as hard as he could. The fork split right open, revealing the white inner wood, and the nest, which was even bigger than he had thought, made a hollow papery sound sailing through the air. He might have given it too much, though, because he lost the handle on his guide pole and it went flying, end over end, out into the river, and the nest hit the edge of the boat, where it settled for a second, and then rolled down against the front bench.

For an instant Gary was almost pleased, because he saw the full swell of it and the way the paper was beautifully marbled in different waves of gray. In the same instant the first ones hit him in the back like buckshot and he made vain motions to try to grasp his own back, and others got him in the arms. He never saw them. All he could do was hear. The sound of their wings was all over him. Gary gave a kind of shriek, which was half whimper, such as a dog might, and he jumped into the water. When he surfaced, blowing water out his nose, one got him atop the head in the center of his bald spot and he had to go back under without a good breath. Underwater it was as if he could still hear them, but his feet found the rocky bottom. The current was carrying him with it. He stayed down and swam out a little ways and when he came back up they had lost him.

They were all over the boat, stinging it a million times. Gary was trying to rip off his shirt because one was caught inside it but the shirt was wet and knotted and the hornet got him two more times before it died.

He floated and tried to look at his arms and chest. There were a couple of stingers still in the skin. They were pumping away like tiny evil hearts. Goddamn, Gary said. He tried to flip them off but they were stuck good. He wondered if others were in his back. The stings were not as bad as he had expected. Was that all they had? The water was very cold for August, but the boat hadn't gone far. It was hung on a snag about twenty feet out in the water. Gary got out on the bank and took off his clothes, ripping some of them, and tried to hang as many as possible on a limb in the sun. His motions were jerky. It was hard to breathe. Gnats were trying to get in his eyes. Gary stood there naked and looked out at the river and hoped that he wouldn't see the boat come floating past.

The stings started throbbing separately, but then they all got together and formed an orchestration of throbbing and burning. Each time his heart beat the pain doubled. Gary felt over his skull and the parts of his body he couldn't see and the swelling was coming up. Though it was hot, his teeth chattered and his body shook. He had never hurt like this in Vietnam. He had been shot at and it wasn't this bad.

He tried to calm down. There was nothing to do but wait for his clothes to dry. If he tried to throw the nest out of the boat, they would eat him up. Behind him it was woods. No telling how far the woods went before a road. Gary tried not to think of his situation, but parts of him were still swelling and couldn't feel, and it was as if he were still in the water even though he had climbed out. He could feel something like the weight of water all over him, holding back his breathing, and his heart took off flying on its own.

If he waited, the hornets would go back into their nest. The young were in there. There were different terms used for the phases the young went through, but Gary wasn't aware of them. Taft would have known the terms. He might have known about how long it would take for them to settle down too. Gary tried to watch some water striders skating on the surface of the water near the bank. But no matter what he looked at or concentrated on, he was still hurting and the only breaths he could get were little short ones.

Gary lay there for a long time. His mouth was dry but he was afraid to drink the river water and his head was pounding such that when he closed his eyes it was all blue. What he needed to do was piss. That would help the stings. Gary tried to piss and catch it in his palm, but he couldn't. The body didn't want to piss lying down. Even his dick was swollen up and it felt clogged. He thought they had stung it. About the middle of the afternoon, or what he thought was the middle, Gary couldn't stand it anymore. He left his clothes on the limb and walked into the water. It was even colder and more powerful than he remembered. It flowed against all the stings and they answered back with pain. Staying near the bank where the current wasn't as strong, he felt carefully ahead with his toes to avoid glass and turtles.

The boat bobbed innocently up and down on the snag. Gary got back at a good distance where he could see inside the boat.

The hornets had stopped stinging it. At least there were none on the outside of the hull. The nest still lay on the bench, but it was quiet. There was no cloud of hornets, but they came and went occasionally like glassy bullets in the sunlight. They had just gone back to their lives as they were before. He floated quietly over to the boat. He eased up and reached inside to unhook the chain on the metal gas can. It was rusted. Gary tried to fiddle with it. A hornet flew by, but it didn't bother him. He didn't think he could hurt a lot worse. A gnat made it into his eye. It was like that was gnat heaven, the eye. They all tried their damnedest to enter the gates of heaven. It burned and he had to work with one eye, but he got the chain loose. Then he got weaker all of a sudden from the effort and puked on the surface of the water. He tried to puke quietly but it was hard. The trees and the world sailed all around him for a minute and then he was through. He felt a little better. Gary half walked and half floated back to his place on the bank with the orange metal gas container.

On the bank, he cut a stick and tried to decide which article of clothing was most expendable. He took his underwear, which was almost dry, and wrapped it around the stick good and tied it with one bootlace and then soaked the cloth with gasoline. Then he got into his pockets and found Brenda's lighter. Gary tried it and the flame was a little weak. He took the lighter and put it in his mouth and held the stick in the air and reentered the water. A big striped water snake was coming downriver straight toward him, but it saw him and changed course. Something was wrong with Gary because he was glad to see the water snake. He wondered if he could latch onto it and it might pull him to safety. He shivered all over with every kind of muscle and his teeth chattered.

The boat had wheeled around but it was still stuck. Gary backed off and checked again. The nest was calm, except for what looked like a few guard hornets around the hole. It was quiet and almost pleasant when he reached it, but his heart was pounding. Gary lit his underwear with the lighter and raised the stick up over the side of the boat. He only had a second but he saw the guards come straight for his face, and the first one got him in the tender flesh below the right eye. Another got his ear. Gary hollered out a strange cry that he had never heard from a man before and stabbed the stick into the nest hole and jumped back down with his face in the water. He heard the nest crackle like a million legs on dry paper and then suck into flame. He swam out as far as he could underwater and when he surfaced a sour smoke was rising from the boat. Above his eye where the hornet had gotten him a black edge was forming. It grew larger and larger and Gary put his hand to the swollen place and it was covering his eye. His tongue was swelling up too. It swelled bigger and bigger until it filled his mouth and then his lungs. Gary hadn't thought the tongue was so big. He hadn't realized that hornets could sting the tongue.

What a funny way to die, he heard a voice say.

It was Bid's voice. Bid was standing on the bank and it was not the dying father Gary had found when he came back home but the strong young one. He was motioning Gary to the bank, but Gary couldn't make it. He was trying harder than he had ever tried at anything in his life, but the water was not just water but a greater heavier water.

Bid paced on the bank as if this were a sport. Come on, boy, he said. Come on.

THE NEXT THING he remembered with any kind of solidity was Brenda's purse. It was in the chair next to his bed in the little hospital, the same one where his father had died. He had other memories, but they were not as real. He had a memory of moving and the sky with tree limbs flowing along each side of it, and of voices, especially one that said, Who done this to you? again and again, and he thought he said, Bees. But the purse was the first thing. He knew it was hers. It had a strap that still held the curve of Brenda's shoulder. Gary went back to sleep or wherever it was he had been staying, and he was happy, because Brenda's purse was next to his bed. She knew why he had done it. The next time he woke up it was gone. Gary didn't realize he did, but he must have asked where Brenda was, because Puss said, They aint no Brenda here to speak of.

Gary looked up at Puss. Whiskery, unfanciful, he was standing over the bed, too close. Gary was afraid to move in the bed, because he had heard hornets can still sting even after death and they were all around him.

We saved an old boy one other time, said Puss. He was about drownded and we pulled him out. After that he joined up with us. Joined the squad. That boy will do anything I tell him to now, he will. How come you to be naked?

Gary thought. It seemed like a long time ago. Did you get the boat? he asked.

We got it, said Puss. I got my map back too. He sat down. I

ought to have knowed better, he said. But I'm too good, I reckon. That right there is the problem. Old Puss is too good.

He squeaked his little dolly over and sat and thought about this. Gary felt of his face. It was a mask of knots.

We thought you was Moody Myers, said Puss. I thought for sure you was, all swole up and everything.

He continued to stare at Gary.

But you aint, said Puss.

12

LET'S GET IN BED.

Tanya immediately turned around and disappeared up the carpeted steps. A black iron railing rattled. The house smelled like SpaghettiOs and socks. For a second Taft just stood inside the front door. He hadn't had a chance to say anything yet, but if he had, he wasn't sure what it would have been.

The house was bigger than Taft's. The first thing he noticed was a tall golden trophy on the console stereo that said SALES LEADER 1975. On top was a golden man carrying a briefcase. Taft made sure he closed the front door. Her mother might be home, for all he knew. The iron railing rattled when he went up the stairs. Between the kitchen and the hallway there were swinging doors like in a Wild West barroom. Large pieces of the household were missing. Hangers were left on the walls, and in the living room it was apparent where the sofa had been. Down the hallway, which was dark, one blue sock lay on the carpet. Perhaps there were other articles of clothing farther along. At the end of the hall the master bedroom was visible with its glass cabinet and an enormous bed, the biggest one Taft had ever seen. The door to Tanya's bedroom was closed. He knew it was hers because a sticker on it said TANYA'S ROOM. It was right below a yellow warning sign that said CAUTION: LOVERS AT WORK. The door had a hole knocked clean through it at about knee level. Taft decided to look through the hole before he tried to go inside, but when he did all he could see was the bottom of a pink bedspread, so he knocked on the door.

I said come in, said Tanya, in an exasperated tone.

She didn't look at him when he opened the door. He didn't really look at her either but he did long enough to see that she was sitting on the bed amid a pile of stuffed animals and pillows. Tanya was barefoot, but all her other clothes were on. Her toenails were painted blue. Taft was still standing in the doorway and looking around the room, which had writing and posters all over the walls. Everything was very neat. Tanya was patting the bed, so Taft went over and sat down on the edge of it.

That's not very good, said Tanya.

Why not?

If you don't know, I can't tell you.

What if somebody comes home?

Nobody comes home, said Tanya. I hate it here.

Why?

Lots of reasons. For one, it sucks. Can I show you something?

I guess, Taft said, but Tanya was already climbing past him. When she stirred up the air it smelled like powder. Tanya crawled across the floor like a baby and opened the bottom drawer of her chest of drawers, which was pink and white. Taft looked at the small of her back, which was visible between her jeans and the bottom of her T-shirt. The bottoms of her feet were softly wrinkled. The drawer was full of socks. From beneath them Tanya took out a big picture album. She made Taft look at every page. Some were of Tanya as a baby or a little girl. In some of them Taft's house was visible in the background. Her parents were in them, clowning around. There were other family members from other states. They stayed on the floor until Taft's legs were numb, but he was afraid to suggest moving back to the bed. Tanya closed the last page with a crackle. She looked at him, squinting a little in one blue eye.

Do you think you could get me pregnant?

Taft looked at her.

I think I could get pregnant. I could. The best time is right after your period. Right after your period is a good time for it. Tanya seemed to be thinking aloud. Taft couldn't help looking at her eyes. They were dead serious. He watched her lips too, and that tooth that overlapped the others.

It can't be that tough, Taft, she said.

Why would you want to be pregnant? Taft asked finally. It felt funny to use the word *pregnant* in front of her.

To have a baby, stupid.

You'd have to change its diapers.

I don't care. If I had a baby, I could stay here.

Stay here?

Tanya brought her face up close to Taft's.

I wish my parents were dead, she said.

Dead, said Taft.

If I was pregnant, I wouldn't have to go.

To school?

Away.

Away?

Are you dumb?

Tanya's breath smelled like cinnamon candy. He could feel her breathing, not just with her mouth or her nose, but her entire body.

You're moving away.

Tanya lay back on the floor and held her hair back in a ponytail with one hand and let it go.

I'm not, she said. *She* is.

Your mother. Where?

Birmingham, Alabama.

There's no for sale sign in the yard, said Taft. He thought he had a catch.

Tanya sighed. Just wait.

You're not going with her?

She thinks I am. I got other plans. She sat back up close to him again. Don't I?

You do, said Taft. He stood up and looked out the window. He had never looked at the world through Tanya's window before. Taft saw his own house and his mother's vegetable garden. His mother was gone to his grandmother's. The afternoon sunlight from the world was falling through Tanya's curtains. Tanya was rustling through some books.

Here, she said. Here are some pictures.

Taft turned around and Tanya had the *Life Book Encyclopedia* open to some fetal photos. They were in color. The same book had layers of clear pages that revealed the human anatomy on down to the skeleton.

This is just a zygote, she said. They start out as a zygote. This is eight weeks. But here it's sucking its thumb, said Tanya. Don't you think it's cute? I'm just afraid.

Of what?

Of my heart.

I thought it was better.

Tanya gave him a look he had never seen before. He remembered what her mother had said about a normal life span. Somehow he had thought that had changed. Tanya wasn't as skinny anymore. He had thought her heart was better.

What's the matter with your heart? he asked.

You know, she said.

No I don't.

It has a hole in it.

Where?

She shrugged. Tanya was still looking at the zygote.

How long are you going to live? he asked.

How long are *you* going to live, Taft?

Taft couldn't look at her. He looked at the zygote in the book instead. Somehow, he felt as if it were his and Tanya's. It felt as if they had conceived something, but that it might not live.

Your mom did it, didn't she, Tanya said.

She said she wouldn't recommend it to anybody.

They all say that.

She was a lot older.

Not that much. People are starting a lot younger now. We'll be fifteen next year.

Tanya popped the book shut. Well, if my parents were dead we wouldn't need a baby.

Taft was a little disappointed. He didn't much want a baby, but he wanted something.

No, he said.

They could die in a car wreck.

Things like that never happen, said Taft, when you want them to.

Tanya stood up and pushed him until he was on her bed. Taft resisted a little. She was strong. Then she lay down right beside him. They lay like this for a while. Taft's heart was pounding. He was afraid she might be able to hear it. Looking at Scott's books, Taft had imagined what it would be like to lie down on the bed with a woman. But it was entirely different. The women in Scott's books bore absolutely no resemblance to the real thing. It was like the difference in seeing a picture of a squirrel in a nature book and trying to catch one bare-handed. Perhaps it was true, Taft figured, that there was no pornography in life. That was why people had to make it.

Really, said Tanya, if my mother was killed everybody would think my dad did it.

Taft thought of Mr. Mayes crying facedown in the garden. He decided not to tell Tanya.

I wish she would just kill herself, she said. Or they would kill each other. Do you think your mother would let us live with her if I was an orphan?

Then you'd be my sister, said Taft.

She looked at him. Her eyes were hard to stand they were so large and colorful. Even the white part was colorful. It had all colors of glimmers on it like oil. Taft didn't know the white part of the eye could be so large in a human being. Eyes like that could not have been constructed by nature simply for vision.

I wish you were my brother, she said, and suddenly kissed him on the mouth. Her teeth clicked against his. It happened so quickly Taft had no memory of it later, except for the click of her teeth. They were very solid. Instead of saying anything, Tanya miraculously produced a tube of lip gloss and began to rub it back and forth on her lips. That was where the cinnamon came from.

Do you think it would be hard?

Taft hoped she was talking about their baby again. What? he said.

To kill somebody.

It probably is, said Taft.

Tanya propped her head on her elbow and started looking at the ends of her hair.

I could do it, she said. Then she added, If it was somebody I hated. That's why your fake dad killed himself. Because he was somebody he hated.

I don't know why he did it, said Taft.

She goes right to sleep, said Tanya. She rolled over on her

back. That would be the best time to kill her. Late at night would be the best, because she is so drunk and she goes straight to sleep. She always sleeps on her back. That's why she snores. You could be like Beowulf.

Beowulf?

He killed Grendel's mother.

But he killed Grendel first.

So skip the first part. Tanya had a calendar on her wall with rainbows and pictures of kittens. It was still September. Taft was surprised. He had thought it might be much later by now, Christmas, or maybe next winter. Tanya turned it over to October and circled October 9. It was a Friday.

Right here, she said. After everybody goes to bed, you meet me at the white rock. I can let you in and hide you in the closet. Then when the time is right, you come out and do it.

With what?

Don't worry. With a knife.

God, said Taft.

Chicken.

Taft didn't say anything. Tanya started clucking. She wrote October 9 on a slip of paper and folded it up and put it in his front pocket. She put it way down in there and the feeling of her fingers in his pocket burned all over him.

How come you hate your mother? he said. He didn't know what else to say.

Tanya was staring at the ceiling.

Because, she said. Because it was her fault.

What?

Tanya seemed angry. I don't have any idea, she said. But I don't want to be her daughter. She breathed out. I'm not, really.

I think a baby is better, said Taft.

Tanya was still mad. Easy for you to say, she said. Beowulf.

13

AT FIRST TAFT tried to study the little notebook inside his grandmother's house or on the porch, but eventually he had to take it out in the fields. He couldn't stand them watching him. If he looked up, either his mother or his grandmother would be staring at him, so he put Moody Myers's notebook in his pocket and walked up toward the woods.

Last night they had wanted him to sleep in Moody's room. Taft didn't want to. He said he would sleep on the couch and let his mother have the bed, but they wouldn't hear of it. Even his grandmother participated. Taft thought it was weird. He was already in a bad mood because staying at his grandmother's had messed up the routine of times when he could see Tanya.

Finally he went into Moody's room and closed the door. It was still daylight and the room had one window. The evening light was coming through it strong and the window had a fat writing spider in it and the leaves of a Virginia creeper. Moody's bed was made up neatly. It was a wooden spool bed. Taft remembered that Moody said the old beds slept better to him because they were more his size. The mirror of the dresser was angled up so that it showed the ceiling. The dresser had several things on it. There was a little chair carved out of cedar and a rock that had crystals in it. Next to it was the smallest sharpest white arrowhead he had ever seen, and some pieces of dried mud with patterns on them. The other side of the dresser had a little stack of change, but the coins were from other countries. Some of them were odd colors or they had holes through the center or images of men with beards.

Taft decided he could sleep on the floor. For about an hour he lay down on it but the floor was harder and more level than he had imagined. His neck and the lower part of his back began to hurt and when he turned over he could see all kinds of papers and boxes and even three large stones under the bed. Taft didn't look anymore. He got up on the bed, but didn't unmake it, and lay down on the edge. He didn't sleep. He did something else all night. He didn't dream about Moody as he had feared, though when he woke up in the morning he felt as if the light were looking in at him through the leaves and the writing spider, which had moved down to the center of its web.

Taft got up and stood on the floor barefoot. It felt as if no time had passed since last night. His mother and grandmother were moving around in the kitchen. He kneeled down and pulled out one great sheath of papers from beneath the bed. They were engineering plans Moody had drawn a long time ago for the mines. Thinking they would show what was underneath the whole county, Taft sifted through the big pages, but he couldn't make sense of it. He put down the papers and took out one low flat box that looked easy to put back. It contained some more rocks and what looked like a brick covered with dry moss. There was another taller box and he started to slide it out but it was top-heavy and spilled over. A skull rolled out and went across the floor over the rug and hit the hardwood where it started to bounce lightly like a basketball about to settle. Taft went after it. He was sure they had heard him. It was a human skull. It flashed through his mind that perhaps God rolled a skull out from under the bed of every human being who contemplated murder, because today was October 9. He still had the folded piece of paper, which he had never opened, in his pocket. He had carried it every day, not to remind himself but to feel the warmth of Tanya's fingers whenever he touched it.

When nobody was in the house he was going to call her and say he couldn't get back home tonight. They would have to postpone. Taft wondered if it was a conspiracy, that they had made him sleep in Moody's room to show him this. The skull had good teeth. Taft thought of how his teeth had clicked against Tanya's. He noticed notation numbers in pencil on the back of the skull down near the base. Did Moody have so many skulls he had to number them? He got a handkerchief off the dresser and picked it up by the eyehole and put it back in the box and slid everything back under the bed.

Taft had already read enough of the notebook to see that Moody spent most of his time searching. He searched for various things. One whole week he had looked for a spot on the river people called the galloping sluice. The galloping sluice, he wrote, was three successive rapids, each a little lower and quicker than the last. He also searched for the remains of Chinese work camps along the railroad. Taft thought Moody's disappearance had to be related to his search, which he always referred to in the notebook as his quest.

The notebook wasn't anything unusual. It was made of the same kind of denimlike cloth as Taft's notebook in third grade. As he read it on the hill above his grandmother's house, a grasshopper landed on the page. It had the face of a gazelle. Taft left it sitting there for a long time and read around it.

8 January 1977

Out this morning before dawn as usual, continuing my quest. Temperature 25 degrees, heavy frost. Ice frozen in the bottom of the boat. Searched all day to no avail. Where the books indicate canebrakes, now there is nothing. Just a few pitiful sprigs of cane remain. Still, when I see them I think of how they once stretched for miles and were home to canecutter rabbits and canebrake rattlesnakes and the buffalo.

Clouding over. Flurries by dusk.

Taft closed the notebook and listened to the grasshoppers. For a man who never seemed fully present even when he was here, Moody Myers had set off a cluster of reactions when he disappeared. The people at church had brought pound cakes and fried chicken even though no body had been found, and the *Plain Talk* counted the days since he had disappeared. Taft's mother tried hard to take care of her mother, but he didn't think she wanted to be taken care of. Gary checked himself out of the hospital though he could barely walk from the bee stings and went right back to searching the river. Even Scott had tried to mow the lawn at Taft's house until his spark plug went bad.

But Taft thought they were all doing the wrong things. He walked under some huge trees in the woods. It was fifty, maybe seventy-five feet to the first limb. He came out on the bluff way above the river. He could see up the bend and down the other way. A heron was flying upriver just a foot or so above the green surface. There was a little perch you could get to and sit and look out over the world, but Tony was already on it. Taft almost said his name, but he stopped. For an instant he was scared. It was like coming upon a bear or some other dangerous animal alone in the woods.

Plus, Tony had a rifle. It was a rifle with a black scope on top, and he had his eye to the scope and he was sighting with it up the river.

Goddamn, said Tony, rubbing the trigger with his finger. I wisht they could drag a river. My god, look at the fools.

The rescue-squad boats were coming back upriver, maybe ending for the day. He didn't really feel like Tony was going to shoot them. It was in the way he held the gun. He was just looking. Taft felt calm about it, but he had both fingers in his ears anyway. He looked down from the bluff. In the air below it, on their way down to the river, a few thin yellow leaves fell, flipping over and over. The place was too large for the voices of the rescue-squad men to be heard.

Where you been? said Tony.

At first Taft thought he was talking to the men in the boats again, perhaps to the one he was planning to shoot, but he said it again and then added, Are you deaf?

You're talking to me? said Taft. His voice sounded funny, like part of his body, with his fingers in his ears. He took them out.

Who else would I be talking to?

I don't know, said Taft.

Tony turned around on the bluff. He grinned a little and it had that goofy look from a dip of snuff. He looked a little rougher, Taft thought, which was unusual for Tony. He always looked like he had just taken a shower, but his hair was dirty and he had on an old pair of blue jeans with a stripe down them and a green T-shirt.

You ever been squirrel hunting? asked Tony.

No, said Taft.

I thought we'd go. Tony gestured toward another gun beside him. I brought you a shotgun.

Taft stared at him.

Don't worry, said Tony. Squirrel season is done started. I made sure of that. It started September 5. So right now it aint too early and it aint too late. You don't even have to have a license to hunt on your own land.

Taft went up closer and sure enough Tony handed him the shotgun. It was heavy.

Be careful, said Tony. Both barrels are loaded. It's a twelve-gauge.

Tony stood up and brushed off his pants for a long time. How do you like my pants? he asked.

The lighter stripe had ALEXANDER COUNTY DETENTION CENTER printed down the leg.

I was going to change, said Tony, but I decided not to. Not for the moment. I was going hunting. He got hold of Taft's gun. This right here is the safety, he said, clicking it forward. A red dot appeared. That means you're ready to go.

Taft clicked it back. The shotgun smelled like oil.

Always keep the safety on until you're ready, said Tony. These will both be yours someday.

They will?

Who else would I leave them to? He laughed. I aint got nobody else.

Below them in the rocks of the bluff crickets sang like whistles someone was blowing too softly.

This world is not arranged right, Tony said. He motioned toward the rescue squad. Give me one hour down there and I could show them something.

Taft shook his head, as if he too regretted the world. He looked down on it. Why don't you go? he asked.

Tony half closed his eyes. A lot of times when he spoke he half closed his eyes, and sometimes their lids trembled in thought. I'll show you why, he said. Later on I will.

They watched some more. From this height the river seemed still. It was luxurious and green. The boats moved together in a formation, and all their little men wriggled with life. The leaves kept falling, even though there was practically no wind, and the whole sky was timelessly blue. It was Friday too. Tony used the muzzle of his rifle to scratch inside his shoe. It didn't bother him. Taft held his as if it might explode any second. It was hard to hold it with the notebook under one arm.

Come on, Tony said.

They went back into the woods. Taft thought the two of them made too much noise in the leaves. Below the trees Tony and Taft were about the same height. As they walked, Taft began to feel glad that he had found him. It felt good to have the guns. Tony was running from the law, and Taft felt like running with him.

How long does the day seem to you? Tony asked.

It depends on which day it is, he said.

I guess that's true, said Tony. He looked at Taft for a minute, as if he expected him to finish.

Tony stopped and leaned against one of the biggest trees, thumped the bottom of his snuff can, and then opened the lid and took out a dip. He was scanning the top limbs.

Your granddad at one time squirrel hunted up here, he said. If he saw one it was dead.

Taft nodded.

You and me are alike, said Tony. I never did know my daddy either. He died when I was little.

It could have been worse, said Taft.

How?

He could have come back.

Tony stopped and looked surprised, but then he seemed to know what Taft was talking about.

Don't you like old Gary? said Tony.

Taft shrugged. I like him, he said. I don't really know what to think.

Tony thought for a minute. He'll be all right, he said. Both of you will.

They started down a steep path, stumbling over roots and flat rocks and sawbriars. Taft felt cockleburs on his socks. He wondered what Tony meant by being all right. He said it as if Taft were his now, but he realized he would have to give him over to Gary pretty soon. Taft didn't want to be given over. He had a new feeling inside. The new feeling was that he wanted to see it all destroyed, and he wanted to come out at the end with Tanya. Soon the path grew level and they were alongside the river. They followed a little branch up from the water and came to a pool back in the trees. Taft said he smelled mint.

That's what this is, said Tony.

What?

Mint Spring. People used to come down here of a night to fuck. He laughed. Mamas used to say, Girl, you come home minty and you might as well not come home. Tony crouched down and rubbed some on his hands and lifted them in front of Taft's face. Smell of that, he said.

I smell it, said Taft.

Tony went over close to the bank. The water was empty now of boats and it only had swallows whirling above it and kissing the surface as they went. Pull on that rope, he said.

There was a rope around a musclewood tree. Taft set his gun down and tried to pull it, but he wasn't strong enough and Tony had to stand up and help him. In a minute they had pulled a big rock or a wheel up out of the water. Slipping in the mud, they went down to look at it.

So what? said Taft.

Tony poked at the tire with a stick. It was covered with moss and strings of watery grass. Then Taft heard a hiss, as if the tire were still losing air, and a pop, and the crack of Tony's stick breaking.

Tony held up the broken end of his stick. The head's over here, he said.

Then the wheel, which Taft saw was all solid, began to shift itself around in the mud. It was so big he could feel it rise up and then slap back down, hissing, and it stank like stagnant water. Taft backed up, almost sliding down in the mud, and then moved closer.

Don't let him get hold of you, Tony said. He won't let go till it thunders.

God, said Taft, trying to get a better look. It was a huge turtle, an armored animal such as he thought did not exist anymore. It hissed and clawed holes in the mud. The shell, covered over with raised plates, had a jagged edge where the tail came out. If he got closer up, Taft could see faint red, almost cowardly eyes, and the end of a hooked beak.

How did you catch it? he asked.

With dead fish. I trapped him. This is a by god bull snapping turtle. Look at him. He's got fifty pounds of good white meat.

Tony squatted down just out of snapping range. He started talking to the turtle as if it were a dog. But nobody aint going to eat you are they, buddy? No sir. Nobody aint going to eat you if I can help it. Then he looked up at Taft. Taft wouldn't believe what you're going to do if he knew it, would he? I doubt he would. Yes. I seriously doubt it.

What are you going to do with him?

Tony stood up and started wiping off his hands. Find Moody, he said.

Find Moody?

The snapping turtle is the buzzard of the water, Tony said. He can take you right to a body.

Taft looked at him.

Tony let go of the rope, and the turtle slid back into the water. Underneath, it moved gracefully and it was quickly gone. Going back up the path through the mint Taft thought there could be hope for the world. If it had an animal like that in it, completely undiscovered, there could be. He hoped the things Tony was telling him weren't lies.

Tony stopped and took out his snuff can and thumped it and took another dip. He asked Taft if he wanted a dip. Taft put his fingers into the can, moist as dirt and warm from being in his pocket. Like this, said Tony. Taft put the snuff in his lip. It tasted like bitter oil. Specks of it got under his tongue, which began to numb. Taft felt as if he were being saturated by Tony, who began to laugh.

Tastes awful, don't it? said Tony.

No, said Taft.

Tony laughed again. Yes it does, he said.

Did you used to come out here? Taft said. His voice sounded funny and weak with the dip.

Tony looked surprised. Oh no, he said. That was a long time ago, what I was telling you about. Times have changed. People don't do nearly as much fucking at the river as they used to.

They did when I was little.

Tony straightened up for a second. Then he broke out laughing again. But after a minute, he seemed to be enjoying his own laughter too much.

It was my fault, said Taft. He was about to say he was sorry, but Tony didn't let him.

The hell it was, Tony said. The hell it was.

I'm the one that saw it.

Tony stopped laughing. No you weren't, he said.

Who else did?

Nobody had to. I already knew it.

Taft watched him spit on the ground. How? he said.

Tony pointed to his forehead. My light went out, he said. I was scaling and my light went out. You know what that means.

No.

Your woman's cheating. Tony started the same laugh again.

Did you believe that? Taft asked.

I do now.

It was quiet. Tony looked up into the trees, as if for squirrels. Only leaves were coming down.

Don't make a mistake, Taft, Tony said. Because when you do, it is a whole lot easier to keep making them.

Tony kicked at the ground. Taft, he said, aint you ever going to ask?

Ask what?

About me being here. Tony tapped his leg where it said ALEXANDER COUNTY DETENTION CENTER.

How did you do it?

Tony laughed. He was doing more laughing than Taft had ever seen him do. I just left.

Just left?

I'm going back.

Why in the hell would you go back?

Tony shrugged. After tonight I am. Tony picked up his rifle and started back.

But it aint tonight yet, is it, Taft?

CLARICE WAS IN the bathroom when they went inside the trailer. Tony hit the door once and said he was going to take a shower, but Clarice didn't answer. He took Taft into the bedroom and reached under the bed for his gun cases. On the nightstand Clarice had a tiny cedar chest with GREAT SMOKY MOUNTAINS and a red heart carved on the top. The bedroom was all neat and the bed was made up.

We ought to clean that shotgun, said Tony, sliding it into a long yellow sleeve. We will later on.

Clarice had come out of the bathroom and gone into the kitchen.

I'll be right back, said Tony. He went into the bathroom.

Taft didn't think Clarice even knew he was here. Stepping heavily, he walked to the living room, but she still didn't turn around. She had on a T-shirt that hung down almost to her knees, and her hair was pulled back in a tight ponytail.

Hey, Clarice, Taft said.

Clarice turned around with a look on her face Taft had never seen, but it didn't last. She went back to work and answered, Hey, Taft. The shower had started running. It was loud. Just about everything in the trailer was. Something was wrong. Clarice just kept taking down dishes.

Can you come over here a minute, Taft? she asked after a few minutes.

Taft went over and leaned on the little bar, which had high stools, between the kitchen and the living room.

I mean in here, honey, said Clarice.

As soon as he got close to her Clarice turned around and put her arm around him and pulled him over to her.

You just don't know, she whispered, as if she were about to cry or scream or both. Taft looked right in her eyes. Clarice looked like she was injured. The color of her face wasn't right and her eyes were thick. Taft nodded. Don't you go nowhere with him, Taft. You don't know what all, said Clarice, but she stopped. Then she went back to work. Taft could tell that she was used to working when she was upset. It only took her a few minutes to have tenderloin frying. Clarice shook some pepper on it and said, How is Tanya?

Taft didn't know what to say. No one had ever asked him about Tanya before, but Clarice had asked as if maybe he and Tanya had been established for a long time and asking about her was as common as asking about the weather.

Okay, he said.

What do you mean, okay?

She has to move, said Taft.

Clarice turned around and shook her head. Taft had surprised even himself by telling her, but she seemed mostly relieved.

I bet you hate to hear that, said Clarice. Where is she moving?

Alabama.

Clarice was mixing cornbread. Alabama is a long ways off, she said. Are you all upset about it?

Yeah, said Taft. Her parents are getting a divorce.

Clarice shook her head. It was strange that he felt good. Even though he was talking about something he didn't want to talk about or even think about, he felt better talking about it, especially to Clarice. Taft wished he could tell her everything, but he knew when you talked about these things you talked about the outer parts, not the mess inside. To him, it was as good as if he had told everything. He felt as if he and Clarice had talked a long time. He wanted to tell her about the skull under his bed too, but he didn't. That might have been expecting too much.

I want you to see, said Clarice.

See what? said Taft. He could see she had tears in her eyes and all of a sudden he was not comfortable anymore, but afraid.

To see what happens, she said. I have to take my jeans off, but don't pay no attention. You have seen a girl before, Taft?

Taft didn't say anything. Clarice lifted up her long T-shirt and unbuttoned her blue jeans and pulled them down almost to her knees. She let her T-shirt drop over her panties and kept it there with one hand. The other hand that held the waistband of her jeans was trembling. Clarice had a long piece of gauze taped to the outside of her thigh, but she untaped one side and peeled it back. The flesh had a long slender sore on it, all down her thigh. The sore was yellow and runny in the center and pink along its edges.

What happened? Taft said.

Clarice nodded with her chin toward the bathroom. One tear had gone down her cheek and run under the edge of her chin.

He burnt me, she said.

Burnt, said Taft.

He got me in the car, she said, so loud he was afraid Tony would hear. And drove around and burnt me with a lighter.

Why? said Taft.

Clarice shrugged. She had put the tape and the gauze back on and was pulling up her jeans. He was mad, she said.

Taft didn't know what to do. A few minutes ago, he had been ready to run off with Tony.

You eat with us, Taft, said Clarice, louder. I'm making some for you too.

Did you go to the doctor?

I don't need to, she said. I'm leaving.

I can take you to the doctor.

Clarice looked at him. You eat with me tonight, she said.

When Tony came out, Clarice didn't say another word. They sat down and ate. Tony had left his hair wet and he had put on another pair of jeans and a flannel shirt. He looked all cleaned up like he always did, but there was still something different about him, as if he had not been able to wash it off this time. Clarice had made cornbread with cheese in it and tenderloin and mashed potatoes and gravy. The potatoes were instant. Tony ate staring straight ahead, as if there were a television or a window on the wall where there was nothing except a tiny cuckoo clock. Clarice watched Taft. She ate very neatly and slowly. She was still eating when Tony got up suddenly and went outside and started the Corvette. Taft heard him rev the engine.

Clarice shook her head. You stay here, Taft, she said. Don't get in that car.

We're gone, said Tony when he came back in. The evening light entered with him.

Where are you going? Clarice said. It was the only thing she said to Tony.

To see a man about a dog, said Tony.

Taft had gotten up, but Clarice held on to his arm for a second before she let go.

I'm fine, said Taft, as if he didn't plan to leave. They went out on the porch. Tony had taken the top off the Corvette, which was idling in the grass. When Taft got in, it didn't even feel like he was inside anything. Instead, the world just started sweeping around them. They went flying up the lane with a dust trail behind them. At the road Tony paused and drove more leisurely.

We're going to the race, aint we? he said.

Taft started to answer, but he could tell Tony hadn't meant for him to. I thought you had to get back, he said.

Not me, said Tony. I'm on vacation.

14

LET GARY DRIVE, the sheriff said. I feel like talking.

He sat in the passenger's seat, tapping the folded warrant on his skinny knee. In green, STATE OF TENNESSEE was printed across the front. Nobody said anything over the radio. Even the other counties were quiet. The sun had thickened in the air, as it will between afternoon and evening, so that little bugs floated effortlessly within it. Bottoming out in the low places, the line of patrol cars made Gary think of a headlong funeral. He didn't want to be leading it. He didn't even have on his uniform or his gun. All he had done was stop by the sheriff's office to pick up his paycheck, and the sheriff said come on.

Gary, said the sheriff.

Sheriff.

Think the sun will hurt the rhubarb?

Gary kept his eyes on the road. I think it'll do it good, he said. That was what you always said when the sheriff asked about the rhubarb.

You know you're still swole up, said the sheriff. From the side you can see it. You can tell where every one of them stingers went in.

Gary felt of his face.

God, I hate bees and shit, the sheriff said. I can't hardly stand them. They react on me.

His gun, a little .25 caliber, was lying on the bench seat between them.

The sheriff was still thinking. I know why you're out there, he said.

Out where?

On the river.

Why? said Gary.

That girl.

Gary didn't say anything.

That's how come me to be like I am, said the sheriff. Women.

Behind them, Gunn, the chief deputy, flipped a cigarette out his window.

I guess we can all say that, said Gary.

The sheriff leaned back philosophically. That we can, he said. You been married once before, hadn't you?

For two days, Gary said.

The sheriff laughed. See. It was her then. She was the reason it didn't last. Aint that right? They is always a reason, Gary, for everything. Two days? That aint very long, is it?

No.

Why, that aint even long enough to see if she snores. I bet you couldn't have done it six or seven times. How many times did you all do it, Gary?

Gary laughed. None.

None? Well, shit, you wasn't ever married then. That's what I would have told them. You wasn't never married. How come you all never did do it?

It just didn't work out.

A lot of people has done it and it not work out.

We knew it was a mistake.

It's always a mistake.

South of the river the hollows narrowed. The car moved more freely in the cooler air. Gary thought the people, bent over in gardens or standing on porches, had no urgency in their bodies. The sheriff watched them all pass by. To each he made a small gesture, not a direct wave but more of a reflex, as if he were taking a private count, or giving a signal he doubted they all would recognize.

What did you do so bad, said the sheriff, that she won't have you?

I'm not sure, said Gary.

Yes you are. You always know. I always do.

Left, I guess. I wish I never had of left here.

Did you ask her? I mean, did you come right out and say?

I asked her, Gary said.

What did she say?

No.

Did she really say no, or did it just feel like she did? Sometimes it just feels like they do.

I think she said no.

My daughter, she never has married. See, she's like that. I asked her one time if she had ever thought about getting married, and she said nobody ever did ask her. I felt bad about that. So I thought maybe you didn't ask her.

I asked her.

A woman is a funny thing, Gary. They work on an entirely different system. Let a certain smell be in the air, or the light coming in a certain way, and everything can change all of a sudden. With them it can.

The sheriff stopped talking for a second and watched the houses pass. Supper's about over, he said. Reckon what they had. Beans and cornbread at that one I bet, and I hope tomatoes. I hope tomatoes. Probably they wouldn't be no greens just yet. That's something that makes me look for fall is greens. Let the frost touch them a little, that's when they are the very best.

The sheriff began to study his hands, as if he had run out of things to say.

Moody Myers, he said finally, was cut from my same cloth. There was topics, Gary, that me and him could talk about for hours. Ones nobody else could understand. Every so often, if the time was about right, you could get him to take a drink. Did you know that?

We won't ever find him, Gary said. Not at this rate we won't. Every day less boats go out.

The sheriff seemed not to comprehend. I've seen two dozen, he said. People brought all kinds of boats. I pulled a many out when I was coroner. The whole bank would be people. God, at the food we used to have. One thing I learnt from all that. You know what it is?

No.

You got to give up.

Give up.

The sheriff nodded. Give up. About the time you do, that's when he'll be right there under your nose. He'll pop right up out of that water.

I guess we ought to give up then, said Gary.

I would, said the sheriff, if I was you. Turn here.

Gary did. Every joint in his body was still sore from stings. They turned off the highway at Fielden Store Road, which cut back under English Mountain, and then went right again onto Muddy Creek Road.

Turn here, said the sheriff.

Gary shook his head, but he didn't say anything. He had been afraid he was right. Goddamn, he said.

I was afraid you wouldn't come if we told you, the sheriff said.

Gary was the first one to pull up in front of Tony's trailer. Then they all came in a boil of dust. Gunn said over the radio that they were all present, and the sheriff swung open his door, but didn't get out. He was looking at Clarice on the porch.

Yes sir, the sheriff said. I would give up.

15

THE AIR BECAME one sound, vibrating the metal snaps on Taft's blue jean jacket, sucking away the announcer's voice in a whirl of ground-up syllables. What I like, Tony had said, waiting for the race to begin, is when they all let go out of the pole. Talk about a goddamn noise.

Tony had been drinking beer all night. They had stopped at a little market on the road and he did a lot of cutting up with the man who worked there as he bought the beer, but out in the car Tony opened the first one and his hand was trembling. He drank it in a second and then looked at Taft.

Don't ever start, Taft, he said.

When they were back on the highway, Tony had reached down and gotten another beer for himself and handed one to Taft. Taft drank the beer. It tasted sour and warm. He had only taken a few sips before he started to feel what the beer was going to do to him. It loosened the wind around him even better. It gave him a vantage point from which he could stand to think about what he had done. What he had done was run off with Tony again. He had run out on his mother and his grandmother. He had run out on Clarice too, whom he loved for no reason the way his grandmother did. He was running with the very man who had hurt them both. Worst of all, Tanya would be looking for him tonight. It was the night she had circled on her calendar in her bedroom, and now Taft had run out on her too. Taft looked at Tony as he drove and sipped his beer. The one thing Taft had never wanted to be was someone who ran out, but there was something else he had not anticipated, something like a current or a tide that kept pulling him farther and farther away.

In the notebook, Taft had read about a dream Moody had. The dream was written up one margin and around the top of a page and then continued on the back.

I knew I was going to have the dream before I had it. I can't say exactly how I knew, but I did. So I stopped. I had been going through some Confederate pension records. I put it off for as long as I could, but then I just went on home to bed and had the dream.

In the stands at the Atomic Speedway Taft felt the notebook, containing Moody's dream, inside his pocket. He and Tony talked to several people. To all of them, Tony had pointed out number 14, Carl Vineyard, who was the one to watch. See, Tony said, he'll line up about eighth on the pole, but it won't take him long. As Vineyard sailed past each lap, Taft glimpsed him through the mesh of tape that served as a window, and there he was, working the steering wheel as if it were clay that might harden any second. Once you see his ass, said Tony, that's all she wrote.

After the race, far later, because Tony and Taft were among the last to leave their seats in the stands, once the dirt oval had fallen quiet, though its red dust kept settling and would keep settling without anyone's knowledge into the morning, Tony eased the Corvette out of the parking lot, which was only a field, its grass flattened and dewy. The grass was wet and pungent as the champagne they spewed on Carl Vineyard, hugging the girl in the swimsuit.

Goddamn, Tony had muttered, with a look of fulfillment, champagne.

Tony didn't let up on the gas when he shifted. He was driving like Carl Vineyard. The car seemed to lift off the ground with each new gear. At first the air stung, and then it was so fierce it wanted to shut Taft's eyelids and stop him from breathing. Tony, however, showed no pleasure. He leaned forward slightly as if he were reading a long, long sentence, and it was this way for miles with no hope of speaking, fence posts zipping past with a sound like shuffling cards. The smell of entering Alexander City was stronger tonight. They flew past the sign TRUCKS! TURN RIGHT 1,400 FEET. AGRICULTURAL LIMESTONE. FAST LOADING! and got to the zinc mines property, and Tony just turned in. It caught the men with strike signs by surprise. At first they just stood up, as if they had been asleep and were certain Tony would stop, but then they all hollered out and one threw a rock. It fell way short, but Taft still ducked. Tony ignored them.

Where are we going? Taft asked.

It seemed like the wrong question.

To work, said Tony.

Taft looked at Tony. Somehow, he wasn't surprised. At the race, the first thing Tony told everybody was that he had been on strike thirty-four days and that if it wasn't for a bunch of son of a bitches he would be going to work about now and he wouldn't be here to see this race. All evening Taft had felt that Tony was restless because he wanted to go to work. He had a beer between his legs but he seemed to have forgotten it. Taft wondered how many he had had. After a certain point with Tony it was like pouring them into a cloud.

Taft had never been inside the mine property before. To the left the bluffs of limestone loomed over them, bigger and steeper than natural hills, and there was iron machination all around, much of it rusted and old. Tony cut onto a narrow road and Taft saw that the sides of the road were lined with stacks of huge black tires which echoed the sound of Tony's engine. Sometimes he could see the tread of them and they were so big he could not imagine what kind of equipment they would fit.

They stopped at a big tin-covered barn with a row of windows in it. It was the changehouse. The windows were lit up and Taft could see rows of coveralls and hip boots still hanging inside. The mill, bigger than the changehouse, was lit up too, and so were all the wires and the steel that connected to the headrig tower. Up this close the sound of Moody's tower was loud. It was the same sound Taft heard in the air at night when he woke up, but fully realized. Tony was already out and trying to open the door to the changehouse but it was padlocked. He only beat on the door for a second and then he quit. Taft just watched him. People always said of Tony that he sure was a good worker. They said it as if they were trying to find something good to say about him despite his problems. Tony was always on time for work. He never missed a day. Tony's life, Taft saw, was like a machine. He knew exactly when to drink and how much to drink so that he could have his drinking and still be sober for work. He kept himself clean and he kept his hair cut to a certain short length. He knew exactly what it took to keep the machine running.

Lights were moving up the road, so he called out Tony's name, but Tony ignored him. After a minute he walked back to the car and stood over it, thinking.

Don't worry, Taft, he said. I know another way in.

He had found something that looked like a belt with a battery on it and a little lamp with a clip. Tony fiddled with it until it came on. The lamp was bright.

You don't have to go to work, Taft said. We're on vacation.

Tony got back in the car, which he had left running.

Vacation's over, he said. Taft could see that his face had turned red. Then they shot off again down a gravel road full of potholes. Tony tried to dodge them, but sometimes they would catch one and the car would bottom so fast Taft felt as if he might be thrown out. The gravel road went past the headframe, which hovered above them on huge iron legs, and they passed a square hole in the hillside from which steam was boiling, and went on into the piney woods. They drove a long ways, the road turning back on itself and twisting in and going almost straight up and though it was the woods it didn't feel like the woods. Tony shut off the engine and pulled the car over. Taft half expected to hear people behind them, but there was nothing, absolutely nothing, except the whir of Moody's tower, louder than ever. Taft saw that they were exactly at the base of the tower. It stood on huge metal legs too, like the headframe, but toward the top it was rounded like a metal rocket. Air gushed out of the top with enough force to vibrate the ground. All of a sudden the tower started clicking and went quiet.

Tony had his light on. He had strapped the belt around his waist and the light was clipped to his shoulder. His movements were frantic, as if bugs were crawling on him.

Come on, Taft, he said. I want to show you something.

What, said Taft. He didn't make it a question.

Come on, Taft, goddamn it.

A ladder went up the side of the tower and Tony was already ten feet off the ground. Taft looked up at him. Tony's light swept over the side of the tower, which was beaded with sparkly dew, and then rambled through the pines below him. It fixed on Taft.

Goddamn it, come on, Tony said. He was hollering.

Taft felt the way Moody had about his dream. He started up the ladder. Maybe he could talk Tony into coming down. The tower seemed to sway but maybe it was only the tops of the pines. They were moving in a wind that could not be detected from the ground. Taft realized he was trembling, but Tony would turn around every few seconds and his light would cover him.

Come on, said Tony. We got to get in before the fan starts up.

They reached a catwalk and the catwalk went around to an opening in the side of the tower. Another ladder came up over the lip. Taft gripped the railings so hard his hands hurt. Tony pointed his light down and it revealed a fan blade the likes of which Taft had never seen. There were three huge blades around a central knob the size of a car engine. Tony was already descending the ladder toward the fan. Taft went over and put his hand on the ladder, which was cold, and Tony looked up at him. His look was almost kind and encouraging.

You can come on, he said. Taft.

Taft was afraid. Tony's light was moving around in a tunnel about as wide as a creek, and that seemed to go down forever. It breathed up a rocky oily smell. Even though Tony was drunk, Taft didn't want him to know he was afraid. The hardest thing was getting turned around so he could go down the ladder. It felt like dropping his legs off the edge of the world. But it didn't take long to get to the fan, which sat in the tunnel like a giant metal spider. Tony had already gotten below it. One blade was close enough to touch, but Taft didn't touch it. He moved down the ladder so quickly he almost stepped on Tony's hands.

Whoa, Tony said. Hold on. He seemed happy now. We'll get there.

The hole was much wider than a well yet the deeper they went the narrower it felt. Tony laughed. It aint going to come on, he said. It makes a noise before it comes on. I've heard it a many a time. But then he added, That thing would cut a man in half.

Below the fan a big cartridge dangled on a chain.

That is the torpedo, said Tony.

The what?

You can ride up and down in it. If something happens, you can.

A cable dangled from the torpedo. As they moved down, a cowl slid over the circle of night sky at the top like an eclipse and then there was nothing except Tony's bubble of light and the rock sides and the metal ladder. Tony's mood was getting better and better. He got almost talkative.

I swear there is something about being underground that makes you crave it, he said. I mean, there is a lot about it to hate, but you get used to it.

As they went deeper the air began to feel colder to him, and the ladder was wetter and wetter and at times it was missing a rung. Usually Tony warned him. He would say a foot was missing, but sometimes he forgot and Taft's foot went down into nothing and it stung all through his body.

Hear that? said Tony.

What?

Tony stopped. Taft didn't want to stop. He wanted to get to the bottom and stand in a solid place. Listen, Tony said.

Taft listened. All he heard was Tony's voice still inside the narrow rock tunnel around them, so close it seemed as if it had come from inside him, but in a second he did hear another sound. It was water. Not a drip or even a small stream, but a huge pounding sound of water, soft because it was so distant.

That is the sump, said Tony, as if he couldn't believe it himself.

The sump? said Taft.

It's at the bottom of the mine. You never can hear it when you're working, because everything is so loud. But you can right now. Listen. It's peaceful enough to hear it.

How big is it? said Taft.

Big. Like a waterfall.

They went on. Taft wished he had never heard the sump. If it was big, like Tony said, it was very, very far away and they were very, very far from the bottom. Of course, the air shaft might stop in an upper portion of the mines. They might be coming close to the bottom of the ladder even now. But he didn't think so.

Tony stopped. Taft felt his weight shifting around.

Wait, he said.

Taft hung on. What is it? he said.

I aint got no feet.

No feet?

The ladder shifted.

Maybe we're at the bottom, Taft said hopefully.

We aint at no bottom, said Tony. You wait.

The metal handgrips gave a flip, a little like the ladder to the high dive at the city pool when somebody jumps off. In a second the ladder thumped again with a crash sound that made his heart sail higher in his chest than he had ever felt and Tony's light was gone. Taft gave something like a whimper and held on tighter. His face was against the metal. For a few seconds there was something, some old vision or stored up light, left in his eyes, but then it was dark. It wasn't just regular dark. It was dark that swallowed you whole instantly. It took away your body and your mind.

Tony was out of breath. Well, goddamn it, he said, mildly irritated. I must of busted my light.

Taft heard Tony fiddling with the light. The sounds were too loud, as if someone had turned the volume way up, and he felt himself freeze. A blazing numbness circulated through him like blood. For what seemed like whole minutes at a time, he thought he was falling, flying through the air toward the bottom of the mine. Not just the tunnel but the earth, the planet they were on in space, was tilting. Taft knew all he had to do was release, and the axis would suck him away. He began to feel as if maybe his mind had split off from his body, as it might just before a person died.

As he dangled, Moody began to speak to him through the notebook.

Release, Moody said. *Release, Taft.*

Taft felt the notebook vibrate a little on his thigh with Moody's voice.

I dreamed I was working. I was writing note cards for the whole collection. They were all new note cards and I was writing them in a new language. I was so proud of the new language because I had made it all up and it was the first language that was ever true and accurate. I wrote as quickly as the shadows of clouds move over the mountains, but I wrote so quickly I began not to understand. I began not to know what I had just written and then I failed to know even what I had written before that or what I had written at the very first. And then I realized the language was not mine but that of the objects and they all began to move around me and torment me in their language. I knew then what was in the way, what was in the way all along. I knew what I had to do with myself.

Any second his hands might do what Moody wanted. They might release their grip. Tony was still messing with his light. It flickered and the flicker was stronger than lightning.

16

TONY CARTER, the sheriff said. He here?

Gone, said Clarice. You just missed him.

Just missed him, the sheriff said. Then he stood up slowly. Gary kept looking straight ahead. He still had his hands on the wheel.

Clarice had been burning trash. In the corner of the yard a little smoke, only the color of heat, still rose from the rusty metal barrel. The sheriff handed Gunn the warrant and he unfolded it at the porch steps and revealed its contents to Clarice as if he were giving her the instructions for a new appliance. The sheriff never went inside. He just motioned for them to come around him and enter even as he was talking to Clarice. Gary saw him reach into his pocket and take out a red-and-white peppermint and hold it out to her. She looked at Gary and he shook his head slowly, as if everything were out of his control, but she didn't seem to notice.

It was fifteen or maybe thirty minutes later when she ran inside the trailer. They were already searching good. She made it inside and was headed toward Gunn, but Bill Strange caught her arms from behind. One kick hit Gunn in the inside of the thigh, maybe a foot from its mark, but it was solid and he bent over. Her legs kept going full force while Strange, grinning, carried her back outside to the porch. The sheriff had been talking to her the whole time in the same tone of voice, and it didn't even change. The sheriff sent three men in a pickup truck up the hill toward the bluff. They had big machetes and one rode in the back of the truck. The others started searching the trailer. It was so small everybody was crowded together. Gary tried to stand out of the way or look at something somebody had already looked at. It started to get dark and they had to turn the lights on.

The trailer smelled like supper. On the table there were still three plates. Gary figured it was Tony and somebody else. The sheriff let Clarice come inside for a drink of water. Everybody treated her very politely. She went to the kitchen and took out a glass and ran water in it and drank. They hadn't found anything, and already the tension had gone out of the searchers, as it does from fishermen when nothing is biting. There was laughter.

Tell Gary to come over here, said Gunn, hunched over something on the floor.

Gary came in from the hall. Somebody had tried to stretch a pair of green panties over Strange's head, and they were all laughing. Gunn had put on his half reading glasses.

Do you think this is what we're looking for, Detective Solomon? Gunn gave one of his looking-over-the-glasses grins.

Everybody crowded around. It was a set of color photographs, each one of the same woman. It was Clarice. She was naked in all of them. In the first one she sat on the bedspread upright, in the same room they were in, and she was looking out in a way that distorted her face. In another picture she reclined on a pillow. Others had her standing, and in one she looked at herself in the mirror. One was a close-up of her crotch, but it was out of focus. Some of the pictures had pink dots in her eyes. It must have been summer, because she had white patches in the good places. It must not have been this summer, because her hair was different.

See that, Detective Solomon, said Gunn, pointing to the crotch picture. That is what got you in trouble.

They were all laughing and socking Gary in the back and the shoulder. Gary tried to grin, but he couldn't.

Gunn dropped the pictures in his shirt pocket and tapped them twice. I collect pictures, he said. All over the walls in his office were pictures of broken stills and marijuana patches and stolen guns rowed up and people wearing handcuffs, all escorted by Gunn and the sheriff. There were pictures of walking horses too and one of Gunn's second wife. One picture showed a belly with six bullet holes. Nobody had been hired who didn't stop by Gunn's office only for him to be in a philosophical mood. He would take out a black-and-white picture that seemed to show a charcoal face and say, It must be hell to burn to death.

It was disturbing to think of Clarice naked in Gunn's desk

with the charcoal man. Gary moved back toward the porch to see her with her clothes on. She was holding herself and leaning over as if she might vomit. The sheriff himself stood on the threshold of the door. He was smoking and blowing the smoke outside, where the porch light had a whirl of moths in it.

The pickup's headlights had been moving down through the field and now it pulled into the lane. When it got into the headlights Gary saw the bed was full of big marijuana plants, so tall they hung off the back.

We got his patch, Jackie Northern was saying. I smelled it. We got up there on that bluff and I smelled it. They is a lot more, sheriff.

We'll get it tomorrow, the sheriff said. He picked up one of the stalks and it was big as a dogwood trunk. That is a big one right there, he said.

As they were all getting ready to leave Gary went up to the sheriff and said, I quit.

Quit what, Gary? the sheriff said.

I quit.

The sheriff shook his head.

Don't you want to think about it? he said.

No, Gary said.

The sheriff just shut his car door and they all took off up the lane and it was quiet.

Gary started walking up the lane, but he stopped. It was pitch dark but he thought he could see the ridges. One window was lit at Brenda's mother's. He went right up to the house. They must have known what was going on tonight, but they had stayed inside. Gary stood there for a long time, so long the river became louder and he began to see a little in the dark. Then he turned around and started walking back toward Tony's.

Clarice wouldn't answer the door for a long time. It seemed busy inside. Gary heard things moving around and a television set going very loudly with what sounded like the news. Finally he saw her look out a window and the porch light came on.

Clarice let him inside without saying anything. Most of the lights were on. Clarice had been straightening everything up, but she had been crying too. Even after Gary was inside, she just kept on straightening things up. Finally she said, Do you want something to eat?

No, said Gary.

He had sat down on the couch.

They didn't find him, did they? Clarice asked.

No, said Gary.

Clarice seemed relieved. I hope they do, she said.

How come?

Clarice shrugged.

For at least an hour and a half, she worked. Gary watched the television or watched her. He stayed on the couch. Johnny Carson ended and a late movie came on. Several times Gary calculated whether it was too late to go to Brenda's and finally he knew it was. He had let it get too late on purpose. Clarice had made him a glass of iced tea and opened some potato chips. Once she went in the bathroom and he knew by the length of time she was there that she was crying, but when she came out she seemed happier. Sometimes with women crying made them feel better, he thought.

They looked through everything, Clarice said. I didn't think it would be that bad.

Gary didn't say anything. Clarice had the trailer back the way it had been. When she stopped working she sat down on the couch right against Gary and he put his arm around her shoulders. It didn't feel odd. It felt like they both deserved something. She kissed him first, on the neck. The kiss felt less like a kiss than something you might do to take your mind off something else. They kissed several times and the kissing was mainly to see what it felt like. Clarice turned toward him and straddled his right leg and they kissed while the movie continued. It went into a commercial about how children should not smoke cigarettes. Clarice stood up and took off her jeans and panties at the same time and left them on the carpet.

I hurt my leg, she said, turning her thigh so Gary could see the bandage.

Gary pretended to look at the bandage and not at Clarice.

How did you hurt it? he said.

Clarice shook her head. Be careful, she said. It hurts.

Clarice didn't take off her shirt, but Gary reached up under it and pushed her bra up over her breasts. She was so warm inside that it didn't last very long at all, but she still seemed happy. They lay so close together they could not see one another and the television went to static. Over the smell of her body, he could smell the bandage and something strangely sweet. Gary was careful not to touch her thigh.

He began to feel trembly and heartsick. He had been feeling this way since he got into the hornets. Gary had noticed that people will cry at nothing after they've come close to dying. He felt like crying right now, but he didn't. You are supposed to learn something, he thought, when you come close to dying. But Gary didn't know what he had learned.

He and Clarice took turns going to the bathroom. While she was gone Gary looked at the inside of her jeans lying on the floor. He had intended to stop, but when she took off her jeans and her panties at once something changed. Gary turned off the television. He wanted to stay here, but he wanted to run. He wanted to run as far as he could, but he knew it would not be far enough.

When she came out, Clarice said, Taft was here. She sat down on the couch and put her panties back on. She pulled them up carefully over the bandage.

Taft? he said.

He went off with Tony, she said. She had pulled her feet up under her. Then she said, I don't do like this. It just happened, didn't it? Didn't it, Gary? I was showing you where I hurt my leg.

You were, Gary said.

I know he's yours. Taft is. Of course, I've known it for years. That was why I was glad when I heard you was back, because I was glad for Taft.

Gary tried to smile. I haven't helped anything, he said. He said it strongly.

Yes you have. Clarice lay down and put her head in Gary's lap and looked up at him. I can't have babies, she said.

Gary tried not to look pleased, but he thought she saw him. She was watching. You can't, he said.

I always wanted me a family. Sometimes though I feel like Taft is my baby. He belongs to all of us, don't he?

Yeah, said Gary.

He's the only one we got.

It's too late, said Gary. It's too late for me to do anything.

No it aint, said Clarice. Didn't you know about him?

I did. I mean, I knew she was pregnant. But I guess I always thought I would come back here and he would still be a baby.

That's a man for you, said Clarice, but she said it as if she were happy about it. But he is, Gary. He is still a baby.

Gary remembered what the sheriff had said about Brenda's being the cause of everything in his life. Surely she was not the cause of this.

How come you to come down here? Clarice asked. She said it sweetly as if she wanted to hear a sweet answer.

Gary remembered the pictures Gunn had taken for his desk. I don't know, he said. I quit my job.

Clarice looked surprised. How come?

I don't know, said Gary. I was just tired of it.

I know, Clarice said.

What did you do to your leg?

Clarice started to cry. She didn't make any noise. She just looked straight ahead and the tears began to come, not just a few but an almost comical number. For a long time, they dripped off her chin and the end of her nose, but she never looked at Gary. Finally she said, Tony. After she said it, she stopped crying. Her face was still wet, but she stopped crying. I was the one that called, she said. I was the one that called the sheriff.

You did?

I told him not to tell nobody. There wasn't nothing else for me to do.

I have to go, Gary said. The second he said it he wanted to take it back. He didn't know how he was going to go, anyway. He didn't have a car. Gary wished he had his tent and he had pitched it somewhere on the river.

I know, Clarice said. I know you do.

17

TAFT UNLOCKED ONE FIST from the ladder rail and reached into his pocket and took out Moody's notebook. He wanted rid of it. Moody Myers was the reason Taft and Tony were hanging on a steel ladder with nothing between them and the bottomless dark. Taft stuck his arm out as far as he could and let the notebook go. It fluttered for an instant like the wings of a bird.

What was that? Tony asked.

His voice sounded hollowed out and booming at the same time.

I bet it was a damn bat, said Tony.

It was Moody's notebook, Taft said weakly.

Moody's what?

His notebook. I dropped it.

Tony started to say something, but his light blinked on. It

was blinding. Tony called out, loud as if the light were sound, Squint for a minute and you'll get used to it. At least that was what Taft thought he said, because as he said it the fan kicked on. There was a sound, a kind of whirring buzz, and then there was the sound of the blades beginning to turn, less like the propeller of an airplane than the wheels of a locomotive. Air, deep oily violent air, shot up the tunnel as if a dam had been opened. Taft was shouting and screaming and he thought Tony was too but he couldn't hear either of them, and now he was less afraid of falling than he was of being lifted by the air and hurled through the blades of the fan. The current of air went up his pants legs and his shirt and through the eyelets of his tennis shoes and up his nostrils and over his eyes and sealed over him tightly like water.

The air was Moody Myers. This was his tower. He had designed it and the air was not his spirit but something powerful and violent he had opened up and set running and that would go on running even now that he was gone, that would suck Taft and Tony and everybody else away with it. Taft thought Moody regretted it. He thought he regretted building his tower so the mines could get bigger and bigger. Taft had first seen it in Moody's handwriting next to the Two Articles of Human Suffering and now he sensed it in the little notebook too, the way he searched around for everything that was lost. By the time the fan went off, slurred down and then quit altogether, Taft figured he was dead. If not for Tanya, he would have hoped he was.

You can come on, Tony was saying.

At first he couldn't speak, but then Taft said, I thought the steps were gone.

Hold on to the rails and stick your feet in the rock, said Tony. I'm going on down.

The light jiggled and turned down and the ladder started moving again, shaking loose its grit and dust.

Come on, Taft, Tony said. He shook the ladder some and Taft gripped it closer.

Taft, said Tony, I'm down here. I can stop you if anything happens.

You're drunk, Taft said.

Taft heard some noises that told him Tony was taking out a dip. He was hanging in the air five hundred, maybe a thousand feet up a ladder in a dark hole and he was taking out a dip. Danger did the same thing to him that drinking did, Taft thought. He needed it.

Do you not trust me, Taft? he said. You can trust me. Then he said, Don't you want to see the sump? We can walk on down to the sump.

Tony swung a little on the ladder as he said it. The world swung too. Taft heard Tony spit into the nothingness.

Please, Taft, said Tony.

Tony talked like this at other times, always right before he did something to somebody. In a second Taft felt Tony's hand on his ankle, and the hand pulled his foot off the ladder.

Taft put it right back on. Tony took it off again and Taft returned it. Tony didn't do it with much force, as if he were testing the parts of a machine to see how they worked. Then Tony gripped both of Taft's ankles in his hands and pulled a little. Taft gripped the steel rung even harder. Without his thinking about it, his mouth opened and he bit down like an animal on the rung that was next to his face.

Let go, goddamn it, Taft said, through his teeth. His voice shook.

Tony didn't let go. Listen at that, he said, as if he had stirred up some kind of nest. Listen at that.

Taft felt the tears come up in his eyes and they ran down his face more freely than he had expected.

Look at me, Tony said, but Taft wouldn't look down.

Look at me.

Tony laughed. Taft tried to figure out what kind of laugh it was. He thought he knew, but he hoped he was wrong. But he knew he wasn't. His ankles felt like twigs in Tony's hands, even when he turned them loose.

Go on up, Tony said. He had to say it several times, each time slower than the last, before Taft moved. It was as if his hands had stuck into the metal. They climbed up for a long time and neither of them said anything. They went on for so long that Taft thought several times that he saw the stars above them but each time it was water drops or something, because the sky never seemed to come. His wrists were trembling and his ankles hurt. Each time the arch of his foot found a new rung it felt as if the bone would break across it. At each missing rung his hand grabbed into the air for nothing and hit rock, and it sent a shock through him like striking metal.

They did not so much find the top as feel it. It felt like a weight lifted off his back, and it smelled like the openness of the world, yet when Taft looked up he still couldn't see it.

We're almost there, said Tony. He was still calm.

Taft saw the stars, but he didn't feel the way he had expected to feel. He was sorry. He felt as if he had left something down in the air shaft, but he wasn't sure what it was. He still wished that he and Tony could have climbed to the bottom, that they were standing at the base of the sump right now, and it was like a great waterfall somewhere deep in the wilderness. But instead, when Taft made it to the top and started to climb down the outside of the tower he saw the sheriff below, leaning against the steel siding. He was smoking a cigarette.

Hi, the sheriff said.

Tony just came down and stood and stretched as if he did not see the sheriff standing there.

You aint going to run, are you? said the sheriff. It sounded like a threat.

No, said Tony.

How did you get out?

Tony ignored him.

The sheriff flipped away his cigarette and walked over and opened the back door of his car and said, Let's go.

What about my car? said Tony.

It aint going nowhere, said the sheriff. He turned on his flashlight and pointed it at the Corvette. The tires were slashed and flat, and somebody had scratched all up and down the sides. On the driver's door was etched the word *scab.*

Well, goddamn, said Tony, mildly.

You can ride in the front with me, the sheriff told Taft, but Taft got in the back with Tony instead.

The sheriff took them to the jail. Taft hoped he was under arrest too. If he got a phone call, he was going to call Tanya. He thought of how Tanya's voice might sound if she were awakened in the middle of the night. He could tell her that the reason he hadn't been available tonight to murder her mother was because he was in jail. Taft glanced at Tony once and Tony raised his eyebrows and smiled as if everything were still okay. He took the keys to his car out and handed them to Taft, but he didn't say anything.

The sheriff seemed to take great pleasure in driving. Each curve he took them around, each time he tapped the brakes or accelerated up a hill seemed to bring him extensive calm. When they finally came through Shelton and reached the jail the sheriff eased the car up as if he were docking a boat.

Inside the jail, which was very quiet, a baldheaded jailer yelled out, Well, lookie who's here. Even the radio woman, who was leaned over her radios with a bowl of cereal, looked up and grinned. Taft wanted to say something to Tony but they were all looking at him as if they wondered who in the world he was. He looked over at Tony while he was sitting in the booking chair and said, I'm sorry.

Shut up, Taft, said Tony.

The sheriff took Taft home. He volunteered to. Taft had to wait a long time in the front seat of the sheriff's car while he went back inside the jail. The sheriff's gun was stuck between the seats. It was a little gun in a leather holster. Taft thought about taking the gun and shooting up the place. When he went through it in his mind it ended with him opening Tony's cell, but Tony wouldn't even come out. I shot my way in here, Taft told him, and you won't even come out. But Tony just grinned.

Instead, Taft put his fingers around Tony's keys in his pocket and felt their Tanyatic potentiality. He made the sheriff stop at the lane instead of letting him drive down to the house.

You like old Tony, don't you? the sheriff said.

Taft looked at him.

I like him too. They aint a thing wrong with him. The sheriff turned back to the windshield. You better go where you're supposed to, he said, but he said it too strongly, as if he didn't really care. Taft shut the door and started walking, but in a second the sheriff's car turned around and came back and slid up next to him. The window went down.

Is this yours? the sheriff said. He was holding Moody's notebook out the window.

Taft took it.

It landed right next to me, the sheriff said. Like somebody dropped it out of the sky.

He drove away.

Taft went on down the lane. It must have been almost dawn, but there was no evidence of light anywhere. It was plain cold. The crickets had slowed down to their lowest point. Taft had made it down almost to the houses when he saw the porch light come on at Tony's trailer. The door closed and the figure of a man walked down the porch steps and up into the lane and Taft saw from the way he walked that it was Gary Solomon.

18

OF COURSE HE KNEW. But Taft acted as if it were nothing unusual to meet up with Gary at four o'clock in the morning, and Gary acted the same way, which made it worse. Gary kept glancing back toward Clarice's trailer, as if to measure the distance, and then looking back to Taft. This was when Taft began to hate him. Hadn't Taft always hated Gary, even when he didn't have a name, when he was only his maker? But Taft hated hating Gary too. It was like hating a part of himself.

So he talked too much. Gary seemed very interested. When Taft told him about the big snapping turtle, his face, or what of it was visible, brightened.

I hadn't thought of that, Gary said.

Taft told him about Mint Spring too.

Gary was still saying, I hadn't thought of that.

Bastard, Taft said when he told Tanya. But he didn't know if he meant Gary or himself. Taft still thought of the bastard as a part of himself he didn't want to part with yet. Even Tanya had begun to look at him with a new suspicion since he failed to show up October 9. She ended her sentences with things like If you actually do anything or If it really happens. The real estate sign had been in her front yard for two weeks when they decided they had to go ahead. Only the wet basement had delayed it this long. At least one customer, a man who lived with his mother, would have made an offer had it not been for the basement. The agent told them it was the zinc mines, that when the workers went on strike it left the mines to flood, and the water table all over Alexander County rose. But Tanya, who happened to be standing nearby, pointed out that the strike was over.

Taft had told her that. It had ended two days after Tony went back to jail. Thank you, young lady, said the real estate agent, who added that surely now the water table would be lowering itself.

A Friday night would have been too obvious anyway, Tanya said. This time they settled on a Thursday night. Taft set his clock radio for two in the morning, and sure enough, she was there. Standing atop the white rock, softer in the light of the stars, she was still in existence. She was still alive, like the rarest insect that unbelievably still lived in his jar and had even eaten of the leaves.

The night was cold for October. Far off, Moody's tower sang like the sound of the stars themselves. Every so often, the earth gave a little tremor, as if a new small space had opened up within it, because the zinc mines were blasting extra to make up for lost time. The grass atop it all was dewy cold. Tanya didn't speak at first. She was all dressed up. She had on a dress made out of a velvetlike material, which he thought was blue, and had a matching band of velvet around her neck. Her hair was pulled up so that he could see the outlines of her ears. Taft thought she was the most strange and beautiful thing he had ever witnessed. He thought she was chewing gum or eating something.

You, said Tanya, stepping off the rock, are late.

Is she drunk? Taft asked.

Do birds fly?

She took him by the hand and her hand was cold. Tanya was cold-natured. Every time her fingers curled around him and they were cool, Taft felt a stab of terror because he was afraid her heart wasn't working right. People didn't realize how irrevocably someone like Tanya could just slip away, like an endangered species. They crossed the yard and headed toward the Mayes's basement. Tanya shut the door very quietly, even though it was warped, and they were in a deep, damp place stacked all around with gleaming silver cookware and burglar alarm boxes. They found the wooden steps and Tanya went up first and Taft followed.

The velvet dress had some kind of horizontal pleats up the back of it. Tanya opened the door at the top and a faint light fell over them and the whole house was more quiet than Taft had imagined. Tanya pulled him in front of her and put her hands on each side of his rib cage to guide him down the hall. She was breathing on his neck. The door to the hall closet was open and Tanya put him in and and pressed down on his shoulders to make him sit down. Then she closed the door as softly as his mother used to when she put him to bed. Taft heard Tanya start to go. However, the door opened again and only Tanya's head entered, level with his, and she kissed him. The kiss was a little loud because she flinched when it was over, but Tanya closed the door and this time she didn't come back. She tasted like toothpaste.

Tanya planned to wait in the backseat of the station wagon so she wouldn't have to hear everything. Her stuff for school was already in there. Taft felt around for the flashlight she had promised and after a few minutes found the handle of it, he thought. The closet smelled like coats and carpet and people's hats and shoes. He was afraid to turn on the flashlight, because he didn't want to see the knife yet. Taft felt for it, but all he could find was a long metal tube. He traced along it and came to the gloves. They were the ones Mrs. Mayes wore when she worked in the yard. She didn't work in the yard very much. Taft held them up to his face and they smelled of burlap. Encysted in the walls of the Mayes's house, Taft stayed as still as he could, monitoring his breathing and the little movements he made to keep from going numb.

He was strangely happy in the dark closet beneath the coats. It was far better than lying in his own bed, because even if Tanya was not here, he was still in conspiracy with her, and that was where he wanted to be forever. He tried not to think about his life before Tanya, and he especially did not want to think about her life before him. These belonged to another era, an ice age, perhaps, or a climatic span dominated by giant ferns.

The idea of killing her mother had given him some pause, however. But maybe it wasn't unusual. Probably all girls secretly wanted to kill their mothers. Tanya just had the guts to plan it out. She was that way in every area. Why not in the area of her mother? Mrs. Mayes wasn't doing a great job handling things. It might have been better to poison her, though, or cut the brake lines on her car. Taft wasn't sure which ones were the brake lines. Or he could have steered Tanya more toward the pregnancy idea. Taft imagined the look on Scott's face when he found out Tanya was pregnant and what honor surely would have been lauded upon him by the only other member of the Tittie Society. But Tanya was stubborn, and when you struck upon a topic about which she was stubborn, she gleefully sailed into a rage that could last for several days. Remember, Scott had pronounced, it aint what them titties can do for you, son. It's what you can do for them. Anyway, the idea of pregnancy gave Taft a weight in his own stomach. People didn't understand that. Murder they understood. How hard could it be? He'd done the fetal pig at school. But even if nobody ever found out who did it, as Tanya was certain they would not, what if Taft still had to hear a heart beating for the rest of his life, like that guy in the story by Edgar Allan Poe?

Taft kept seeing Gary step off the porch at Clarice's again and again. He would rewind it in his head and look to see if maybe there might have been time for him to hide. It was dark. He could have hidden in the bushes beside the lane and Gary would never have seen him.

When he thought it was time to come out of the closet Taft came out. He hadn't fallen asleep, but he had gone into some other state below wakefulness where people go when they cannot sleep for some important reason. It took him at least twenty minutes to open the door because he did it so slowly. In the hallway there was enough light from the moon, or something, to see that Tanya had not left him a knife. It was a sword. The sword was in an ornate silver sheath, and it had a big metal handle encrusted with jewels.

God, Taft thought.

The sword must have belonged to Tanya's father. Probably he would have appreciated the idea of sticking it through his wife. If he'd done it, Taft would not have had to be here. But if their parents had done anything right, he wouldn't have been here. Taking a step and then waiting what felt like five minutes before taking another, Taft went down the hall to Mrs. Mayes's bedroom. He clamped the sword under his arm as he put on the gardening gloves. Taft wondered if fingers left fingerprints in the fingers of gloves. The door was open, but there was a note on the floor in the doorway. It had a large *T* on it.

Taft opened the note quietly and it was written in big thick Magic Marker letters so it could be seen with only a little light.

It said, *When you do it, close your eyes and think of me.*

Taft unsheathed the sword and crept into the bedroom. Mrs. Mayes lay on the bed as if she had been thrown there. Her head wasn't even on the pillow. She wasn't covered up. She had on a dark gown and Taft immediately saw that it had gotten turned around and one of her breasts had fallen onto display. Each breath was half breath and half snore, and they were spread so raggedly apart that Taft knew she was far down in sleep. The breast moved up with each breath. He got up closer. Taft looked at the breast. It didn't look like the breasts in magazines but more like something else, simply a utilitarian part of the body.

It was malformed somewhat by the position in which she lay. Taft wondered if Mrs. Mayes had fine hair on her stomach like Tanya, but he reproached himself for wondering. How could he kill it if he became too familiar with the body?

Taft stood over her. He didn't want his breathing to mesh with hers but once or twice it did. The best place was probably just above her breast. That was where the heart was. A little mole marked the spot as if God had put it there. At the bottom of her neck there was a little vein going up and down with each heartbeat. It made Taft angry that Mrs. Mayes's heart worked just fine and nobody gave a damn about her while he loved Tanya and her heart had a hole in it. Taft was about to raise his sword when her eyes opened. They didn't squint or even blink but opened all of a sudden as wide as they went. They opened so widely that Taft almost assumed that he had already done it and they were opening in fright as she died, but he hadn't even raised the sword. Her eyes were brown. Taft would always remember the brown eyes, which had smeared black makeup still on them. She was quick too. Before Taft could get a grip on the sword she jumped up and got him by one arm and he gave a little cry and tried to dodge but was too late. She had pulled him down on the bed and the sword went rolling across the carpet. Taft started trying to wrestle his way out but she had both arms around him. An immense flush of heat, greater than he had ever imagined the body could produce, great enough, he thought, to produce spontaneous combustion, had gone the whole radius of his body beginning at the heart, which was pumping so wildly it hurt. Then she giggled. Taft didn't know why he quit wrestling, but he did. He stopped and she stopped too. He must have passed out from fear for a second. When the world came back he was lying on his side. Her arms were around his stomach and her chin was jammed into the bottom of his neck, right on the spine, and she had one leg completely over his leg such that he could feel what he thought was her crotch plastered around his thigh. Taft's hands were cramped under him and burning hot in her gloves.

Boy, had he fucked up now. That was what Taft thought. In his mind it was spoken in the voice of Scott Woody. It didn't seem funny either. He was afraid to move, in bed with Tanya's naked mother on top of him. She was drunk. Not just her body, but the whole room, smelled of whiskey and corn chips and some other scent he could not name. Only moving his eyes, Taft looked around. She had a night-light that made the room so bright he couldn't see how she could sleep. Clothes were all over the floor. A faucet in her bathroom was dripping fairly briskly. The nightstand had a bottle of whiskey and a glass that still had some in it. The corn chips had spilled out of a bag next to the bed. They were all over the carpet. The awful thing was that when his blood calmed down and her breathing had gone back to where it started Taft began to have an erection. He tried to feel with his back where her breasts were. He could tell that her gown, which was made of silky material, had gotten up over her hips in the struggle and he thought he could feel the whole front of her crotch against his leg, even through his jeans. He thought he could hear the hair rub softly against the material when her breathing got stronger, and of course the air from her nostrils was coasting down his neck into his shirt. She was heavy. He knew that. He wondered if he could turn over and they would do it. Taft didn't want to think these things. It felt like cheating on Tanya, who was lying outside in the backseat of the station wagon she hated. To Taft being with a woman other than Tanya, or even thinking about it, was a crime against nature. But Mrs. Mayes was drunk and she was all messed up from a divorce so maybe none of it would be remembered and it would be okay.

It turned out that Taft was flattering himself because then she coughed and spit on his neck and turned over the other way and went back to sleep. Taft didn't move. He was afraid he had gone to sleep. Waiting in the closet all that time had made him sleepier than he could ever remember. Yet what he had just had was not really sleep but something blacker and sharper around the edges, but he didn't know how long it had lasted. Taft felt as if he had done it with Tanya's mother. After all, did he not lie in the bed way longer than he had to after she had gotten off him? How could he be sure what he had really done?

Taft got down on the floor in the corn chips and picked up the sword and crawled out of the room.

Defaro, said Scott's voice, you are now not only a bastard but a motherfucker too. Attempted.

19

MINT SPRING. Gary asked Sylvia the dispatcher, who always said she had the entire county on a map in her mind, but she just widened her eyes and said she was surprised at him. He drove over the roads he knew that came anywhere close to the river. Some of them didn't seem to have been traveled lately, because they were covered with dry leaves and the black-and-brown woolly bears of fall were crossing at will.

He still had the sheriff's pickup with the empty boat rattling behind him on its trailer. Gary knew he would have to take them back now that he had quit his job, but he was afraid to. If he didn't have his job or his boat, he wouldn't have anything. He passed a little store and hands went up from all the people on its porch. At another place three young women were lying on a quilt in their bikinis, and one of them got up and took several steps toward him when she saw the truck. She stopped, however, when she saw Gary and forlornly watched the truck pass. She had a magazine in one hand. Dogs came out from other houses and chased the pickup. In the middle of the afternoon Gary found an old man leaning on his hoe.

Mint Spring? said the old man, shifting his chew of tobacco to the other cheek. You got a woman in there with you? I don't see her. He laughed as if it were the punch line to an old joke.

Gary saw others stand up from the garden behind a line of dried pole beans and start toward him. One was a woman, carrying a pumpkin, and one was a teenaged girl. They all talked with him for a while.

We thought you was the sheriff, said the woman. That gave her a funny look in the eye.

What have you got in the back of this truck?

Nothing, said Gary.

The woman had started to pick up the canvas, but she looked afraid to after Gary spoke. He ignored her. He was looking out at their fields.

This, thought Gary, is what I wish my fields looked like. It discouraged him to realize that there was no proof he had even been here a whole year. It was supposed to be autumn, and what was he hauling in from the fields?

You look awful, said the woman. You look like you need to rest.

The woman offered to give him the pumpkin. She said for him to save the seed.

Mint Spring, said the old man. Why, I can remember. He breathed in a long soggy breath.

I surely aint never been, said the woman with the pumpkin.

You surely have too, the old man said disdainfully. Gary saw that he was younger than he had first appeared. He had thought the man to be the woman's father, but now he perceived that they must be married.

You take this punkin, she said. We got them everywhere. Just look.

Oh Lord, Mint Spring, the man said, growing younger still. Lord have mercy.

As Gary drove slowly away the man followed him on foot. Finally Gary stopped. The man came up to the window.

I'll tell you where it's at, he said.

THE TURTLE WAS the biggest one Gary had ever seen in his life. When he went to pull the turtle in toward the bank he was amazed at how heavy it was and how smooth and powerful it seemed while it was underwater. He could release his grip for a minute and it would wheel and start back out into the middle. Gary didn't mess with it. He knew better than that. He would like to have pulled it up on the bank to see how hard it could snap, but he refrained. He couldn't figure how Tony had ever gotten a chain around it.

Plenty of afternoon remained. Gary crouched for a minute at Mint Spring. It was a little clear pool in a flat alongside the river. He hunted up a few flat rocks and skipped them at the water striders on the surface of the pool. Gary was trying to make sure they were still unsinkable, the way they had always been when he was a boy. They were. He couldn't sink a one of them. He tossed his rocks, even some fairly big ones, and the water striders just rode the waves with each foot on a little dimple of water. He laughed.

When all his rocks were gone, Gary uncoiled the chain from its tree and fastened it around the front bench of the boat. He didn't crank the motor. Instead he let the boat drift out a little and then down along the bank, which was rooted with sycamores and dotted with muskrat holes. But the turtle headed straight for the middle of the river, and Gary poled behind it. The boat passed from the shade of the bank into the yellow light, through a mist of gnats. The water felt so much more free and clean than the land. He saw the turtle rise, farther out than he would have thought, and float with only its bony nostrils above the surface. It stayed that way for a while and then submerged with the softest boil on the green water.

He came to the fish traps, big Vs made of rocks set in the river by the Indians. The water had to be a certain level, and the light, and they would show up clearly. Gary had been stopping here because of the graves. There were about seven on the bank below a fringe of trees. The clay had been removed down to the bones, and the skeletons were all curled up in their graves. When he first found them they were covered with canvas cloths. There were tools around the graves, little silver dentistry tools. Gary had gotten down in one grave and looked at the hands. He knew Moody had been here.

The skeletons had little shells, periwinkles, scattered all around them. The dirt had been neatly removed from each periwinkle. One of the skeletons was much smaller. It was probably a child. Gary wondered if that was probably all that was left of James now—bones. He remembered that his mother had worried that James had never been baptized. At Taft's baptism Gary sat down in the back of the church and Taft came down into the baptistry in a white robe and the preacher laid him back into the water.

Gary let the boat go with the current beyond the fish traps. The boat would turn so that the October sun seemed to slant in from different directions. Sharp-winged swallows skimmed the surface of the river like boomerangs. He went over shoals where suddenly waving grass appeared and the mouths of creeks where cattle stood, watching him pass without expression. A heron stayed just ahead of him, flying from rock to rock on wings so large they needed only to dab at the air. Gary wasn't sure where he was when the chain went taut. It made the boat wheel and he realized the turtle was behind him. Gary tried to pole back toward it but the current was too strong and he had to start the outboard.

He saw the head and the arm first. The boat labored against the water and moved up and down such that he could only see it in glimpses. Soon as he reached the little gravel bar not twenty feet from the bank, he jumped out of the boat but the sand began to suck away so quickly he had to climb back in. Gary held on to a broken tree limb that stuck up out of the water and looked for a long time. He had expected a drowned man to be all watery flesh, but Moody Myers was a polished black, almost like coal, and his neck and head and limbs had assumed a slender graceful form. He still had Moody's teeth. The whole body, resting on its gravel bar, seemed to be in the act of rising. Gary held to the tree limb. He was filled with loss. He couldn't stop here. Inside he wanted to push off from the gravel bar and search on until night. He wanted to search on until he himself had disappeared.

20

SHE DIDN'T EVEN ASK. In the moist hour before dawn, Taft had tried to see through the windows of Tanya's station wagon, but they were all covered with dew. Tanya had warned him not to get his fingerprints on the metal or glass, but he went around to each side and tried to see through without touching it. Finally he gave up and went home, but he didn't sleep at all.

When they got to school in the morning Taft was going down the hall toward biology, and she came up from behind and pushed him into a corner in the cinderblock wall and just looked directly in his eyes for a long time as if that would answer for her and then smiled. She got closer as if she were smelling him.

You did it, she said. I can tell.

Taft looked at her.

I can smell it, she said.

The rest of the day she stared at him as if he had opened up for her the most secret pleasure. The older the day became, the less available the truth became, the less true it became, the less possible it became to give up. On the bus in the afternoon on the highway an ambulance passed with lights and siren going, and Tanya looked at Taft as if she would die of ecstasy.

You can tell me later, she said. Everything.

Tanya kept talking, but Taft was unaware of all she was saying. The bus was noisy, and he was unaware of what passed outside except that it was a blur of orange and red, blue, and brown, and all the air was pouring in through the windows and his heart dipped each time she punched at Scott or allowed him to touch her on the shoulder or to grab at her hair as it flapped in the pouring air and separated into tiny strands that caught across the bridge of her nose and in the folds of her eyelids and on her ears and chin and neck. She was in the middle. Her shoulder pressed against his and he felt her movements, and when she lifted her right hand to put back a strand of hair he felt it, and the side of her leg, her thigh, and the bone of her ankle against his. She had led them directly to the backseat, the back-most, wheel-bouncing seat, where the smokers and numchuk carriers resided.

Drive on, driver, Tanya had shouted, laughing, as the bus rolled away from the high school. We are free.

This seemed to give Scott great pleasure and amusement, even though he didn't know what she was talking about. Everything Tanya did seemed to give him great pleasure and amusement. She knew that. Still, Taft thought she stayed closer to him on the seat most of the time, leaning more heavily into him on the curves, nudging him harder on the bumps. And she reserved for Taft only a new long glance of admiration and absolute melting love which appeared both too often and not often enough. When it came, and Taft was under it, he could not look into her eyes for very long, and he wished it would end because it was almost like a sickness and because, when she couldn't see, Scott was looking at him too and flipping his eyelids with a bastard version of the same look.

Scott was his big mistake. All Taft had done was show him the key, the one to Tony's Corvette, and Scott grabbed it. His fist closed round it, and he started walking in a march down the hallway, where lockers banged and there was the hum of combination locks. Though it was steel, the key seemed vulnerable in his palm.

Hot damn, Taft heard him say. Tanya still had on the velvet dress, which did turn out to be blue, and now some kind of hat. Scott held the key up in front of her eyes. They grew larger and more colorful yet didn't register anything.

I'm going with you, said Scott. Or I'll have to report a car theft.

Tanya shook her head at Taft, as if she were sorry he was such a coward but was too happy to care.

Good, she said. We can kill you when we're finished.

But on the bus she quit glaring at him and started to laugh. Taft had never imagined that Scott could make her laugh. It was because she was so overjoyed at having her mother dead, he figured. But he hoped she would remember who did it.

Nice place, Taft, she said, standing in the exact center of the road next to his grandmother's lane. Tanya got out a menthol cigarette and Scott lit it for her. The bus was already gone around the curve, backfiring. All Tanya had was a small velvet purse. She put her cigarettes back inside it. Are we here for some reason?

Yeah, said Scott. He had picked up a handful of gravel to throw. The car, he said, popping one off Taft's arm.

Leave Taft alone, said Tanya. He's going to show us. Right, Taft?

Taft wasn't sure if she was protecting him or just liked to scold people. He wondered if he could kill Scott. Maybe once you have killed your first person, or at least come close, it is easier to kill the next. Taft started down the gravel lane. Behind him a rock smacked the mailbox.

Drop the rocks, said Tanya. Please.

One whizzed overhead.

The feeling in Taft's stomach was like hunger, the kind of desperate lightness and hunger that must come from being lost in the woods for weeks. He liked the way Tanya walked beside him. Her walk had a glide to it, unlike a girl's, more like a cat's, independent and balanced, with smoothed-over caution. She was letting them hear her giggle. It only came out when she was content. It was a kind of deep giggle, which seemed to keep on pouring out like water through a very small leak, and she smelled like clothes detergent and menthol cigarettes and a little of the halls at school. Everything about her seemed so permanent in his life that he could not believe it could ever be otherwise. It was difficult, however, to take pleasure in any of this with the gravel flying overhead and the possibility that his grandmother or Clarice or even his mother might not only be home but outside.

Hot damn.

They heard Scott's gravels drop. There she is. They had just topped the hill, with the river below them, its trees leaning out over it from each side. The Corvette sat astraddle the lane in front of the trailer.

Son of a bitch, said Scott.

Clarice was mowing the yard. The white river rocks had been moved from around the birdbath and piled up. Clarice had on jeans and a white T-shirt instead of the bikini she usually wore when she mowed the yard.

Tanya rearranged the purse strap on her shoulder. She said, There's got to be something we can do till dark. Think, Taft.

Taft thought.

They cut through the woods behind his grandmother's house. Tanya managed to keep her hat on, even with low limbs. When they reached the clearing along the river, the air suddenly grew cool and damp beneath the great strands of ivy closer to Mint Spring. Scott had found a headknocker weed, and he had been knocking them both from behind, but when they emerged from the woods he threw it as far as he could and started picking his beggarlice off, but Tanya didn't. Taft was itchy all over, but Tanya didn't seem to itch or even notice. Taft wondered if women didn't feel the same things as men. Tanya surveyed the whole place with her colorful eyes and then sat down next to the spring pool, crossed her legs, and said, Let's talk.

Taft watched her take out a vial of lip gloss and start rubbing it on. He felt ready to kill Scott. It was a lot easier to kill somebody when you hated him. Taft wished he could shake the sycamore, where Scott, smelling of sweat and aftershave, had already climbed up to the first limb, and fling him off onto a rock. Or knock him out and then dump him in the river, where the green water would escort him away forever. Instead, he sat down on the soft grass a good distance away from her.

Some place, Taft, she said, shutting her eyes for a second. It smells good.

This is Mint Spring, said Taft. He was looking around for the chain and the big turtle, but they were both gone.

Let's climb the bluff, Scott called from his limb. Let's go to the very top.

Let's not, answered Tanya. She was smelling a sprig of mint she had picked.

There was a thud and then a rolling sound in the leaves as Scott obediently struck the ground.

Tanya opened her compact and took out a wrinkled cigarette with twisted ends. She lit it with Scott's lighter and held in the smoke for a few seconds and then coughed it out. Then, as if he had asked, she handed it over to Taft, and he dropped it on the grass. Without speaking, or even smiling, she picked it up again, flicked open the flame of the lighter, and this time she held his wrist steady with her other hand, as carefully as she might hold a baby's. Taft lifted it to his mouth, and the paper was sticky from her lip gloss, and he sucked in the smoke.

It didn't do anything.

Taft looked out at the river, which continued to flow at the same speed, and then at Tanya, who was taking another draw. She leaned back and let the smoke come out of her throat on its own.

I like to get stoned so much more than drunk, said Tanya, handing him the joint again.

Taft looked at the glowing end for a second. He smelled the smoke, and it smelled less official and more like wilderness than tobacco smoke.

Not me, said Scott, who had kneeled down right next to Tanya. Aint nothing on God's green earth better than a cold beer. He looked up through the trees, which were releasing yellow and brown leaves. Pardon me, God, he said. Hurry up, Taft.

Taft held the smoke down in his lungs the way Tanya had, and then Scott grabbed the joint out of his fingers. When it grew too small to hold, Tanya took out a little alligator clip and they held it with that. This went on for a long span of time, longer than the whole day, probably the whole week, had lasted. Taft noticed that Tanya was smiling and that she had a new filling between two of her upper teeth, and he was smiling back, not with his lips and his teeth but with his entire body.

Scott asked Tanya where this came from. Her hat was askew.

It grew, she said.

Taft smiled.

Taft's mother grew it.

She did not.

Did so.

Where?

Tanya grew serious. In her garden. I planted it for her.

Taft laughed. The laugh continued for several minutes.

Let's take the Vette to the ball game, said Scott.

Right, said Tanya, losing her good humor. I want to watch

a bunch of faggots pile all over each other. I got other plans. So does Taft. Right, Taft?

Uhuh, said Taft.

Scott lay back on the grass. Like what?

Like you'll see what. Tanya looked straight at Taft for a long, long time. She seemed to be looking for something but had trouble finding it. What about it? she said.

Taft didn't answer.

I hated her, said Tanya. I mean, I don't really hate her. It's just the way things are. If things were different. But things are different. Aren't they, Taft?

They are, said Taft.

Goddamn if they aint, said Scott. He was staring perplexedly toward the river.

Tanya crawled over on her knees and gave Taft a kiss. It was so light he couldn't feel it. Then she licked in his ear with her tongue, muting the sound of the river and the whole afternoon, and she lay back on the grass and said, Be quiet. After a while Taft lay backward too. His mouth burned and there was electricity all over him, but it was relaxed electricity. He began to hear the river whispering and he felt the air moving across it and cooling, not saying anything, just breathing.

Do you know about the mines? said Taft.

Sure, said Tanya.

Some of the rooms are taller than that tree, said Taft. There are rivers like this one.

Really. Who told you that?

I was down there.

When?

A little while ago. With Tony.

The one that's in jail?

He was out. He escaped. But they got him back.

Don't lie to us, Taft, said Scott.

It's true, Taft said.

Are you about ready? Tanya said, sitting up with a sound that seemed to flow down his spine.

Ready for what?

To tell us about it. It was a long time before Taft comprehended the words, because they were only objects at first, and he had to wring out their meaning, as if he were in first grade. Tanya started looking hard into Taft's face. From certain angles she seemed ready to cry. Tell us, she said.

Taft started talking. The words came out exactly as Tanya's had, as things, and he completely lost the idea of what they were saying. However, he noticed that Tanya and Scott still watched him closely, nodding every few seconds, and their eyes kept twitching and widening and narrowing, as if they understood. After a while Taft realized he was speaking from Moody's notebook. Total darkness, he said, the most total, perfect darkness imaginable, in which it is absolutely impossible to see. At the end Taft told them about the skull that had rolled out from under his bed. He didn't mention that it left an odor on his fingers like that of old coins.

Later, Taft saw that he had finished, because Tanya was staring at him not as if she were looking for something anymore but as if she had found it.

You bastard, she said.

Taft thought she was joking.

Scott shook his fist at the sun, which was still over the trees. Go down, damn it, he shouted. Get dark.

I know you didn't do it, Tanya said. I know.

Taft thought she might be testing him. All of a sudden he went numb all over and she was glaring at him with a fury he had only seen in animals. Then she jumped to her feet and her hat fell off and she was waving her arms and calling him a bastard again. Tanya ran off toward the water. She was crying and screaming.

She is goddamn nuts, said Scott, smiling. I like that.

Taft didn't know what to do. He followed Tanya a little ways, but she had gone down a skinny path toward the riverbank. The path was full of tree roots and she had disappeared. Taft was afraid she was in the water. But when the path made a turn he found her lying on the ground with mud all over her velvet dress. It was even in her hair. Taft went to try to pick her up, but she struck him hard in the mouth and one of her fingernails cut his lip. He reached for her again because she was trembling and crying but she hit him harder so he backed off. She was screaming for him to get the hell away from her and smacking her fists in the mud. Taft turned around and went back up the path and she still kept screaming. They were sharp lingering screams that seemed to come out of her guts. He tried to get farther away and the farther he got her cries slowed down a little. Taft went back up to the spring and Scott was still sitting in the leaves smiling.

What are you doing to her? he asked.

Nothing, Taft said.

It don't sound like nothing. Your lip is busted.

Taft touched it. There was a little blood on his fingers.

I guess it is harder to get some than you ever thought, said Scott. I was wondering when you were going to see that.

They sat down next to Tanya's pocketbook to wait for her to come back, but a long time passed and there was no sound except the river and the leaves falling and some small birds. Finally Scott started scouting around and found a stick and then climbed onto a shelf of rock next to the sycamore tree. In a second he was motioning for Taft.

What?

He motioned some more.

Taft climbed up the rock and they could see down the river and the end of the skinny path, and Tanya was standing about thigh deep in the water. She didn't have anything on but her bra and panties and she was wringing water out of her velvet dress. She laid it out on a rock in the sun and started smoothing it down. Scott, arms folded over his chest and head laid to one side with a squint in his eye, showed absolutely no emotion. Taft didn't really feel surprised either. He wanted to, but he didn't.

Too bad she didn't get her panties dirty, said Scott.

They watched her for a while, in the way a person watches directions to a complicated place or the way parts of a machine go together. They watched her until they were almost tired of watching her and Taft began to feel the one single emotion for her he did not want to feel. Here was Tanya Mayes, the same one of fifteen minutes ago, on the riverbank in her panties, which were no color but white. Light from the water, he imagined, was sometimes visible between her legs. But she had been crying and screaming because Taft had not killed her mother, and Taft felt sorry for her. He didn't want to feel that way, but he did. Taft was suddenly afraid that all his love was pity. In a second he turned aside and pushed Scott, who went careening backward with a shocked look in his eyes, much farther than Taft had expected. Instead of jumping up to attack him, Scott lay wheezing on the ground until Taft had decided he was injured. Gradually he saw that it was a laugh, one so heavy, or so mild, that it barely made a sound. He kept on laughing that way, no matter what Taft said, and he was still laughing when Tanya came out of the weeds.

Taft looked at her and then he looked away at the river. She still didn't have her clothes on. He had only looked at her long enough to see that she had washed her face in the river, because the ends of her hair were wet with it. Out of the corner of his eye, he could see that even Scott was also unable to look at her. He was still lying on his back and staring straight up into the sky, as if that were perfectly natural.

Hey, Scott, said Tanya.

Hey, said Scott.

What are you looking at?

Nothing.

Look at me.

You aint got no clothes on, said Scott.

I do, said Tanya. Did you not ever see a girl?

Plenty of them, said Scott.

Then look. She had grabbed him by the arm and was trying to drag him up but he was still trying to look away. See, she said. What do you see? All girls look alike.

They do not, said Scott. Not all of them have got hair on their belly.

Shut up, said Tanya. Make him keep his head turned.

Who?

You know who.

Keep your head turned, Taft.

Taft didn't say anything.

This aint for him, she said. I need you a minute. For a second Taft thought she meant him, but she didn't.

Ah God, said Scott, with great distraction. Can you not see I'm busy? But in a second he jumped up and trudged off with her. Taft still had not looked, but he turned just in time to see them disappear down the path, Tanya all white all over and Scott like a big dog just let out. You know that water is nasty, he was saying. Taft's granddaddy is in it.

So is yours, said Tanya.

Taft couldn't hear anything else they said but he could hear their voices. They stayed gone awhile. At first Taft wanted to run. He wanted to run as far as he could, but he didn't move. He wished a tree would fall and kill him or the rocks would shift. But Taft's problem was that he couldn't give up. He never could. When they finally came back out of the weeds Tanya had her dress on again, though it was still wet, and she was thanking Scott and Scott was motioning for Taft. They went through the trees again. It was much easier to look at Tanya now that her clothes were on, but she wouldn't look back. Spiderwebs hung between all the trees, sometimes simply in the air itself, and she acted afraid of them, grabbing Scott's arm with a fierceness that seemed to scare him too. Sometimes by accident Taft was close enough to smell Tanya and she smelled like the river.

It's not even close to dark, said Tanya, keeping her arms folded and watching the ground under her shoes. Scott put his arm around Taft and pointed at the two houses. I don't care, he said. He started running, or trotting really, and Taft felt stupid following him, but he still did. Tanya never quickened her pace. When they reached the Corvette she had not even crossed the last gate.

What the hell is this? Scott was saying.

The Corvette's tires were flat and it still had the word *scab* scratched on it in scraggly letters.

What in the hell happened? said Scott.

Taft looked at the car. It was as if he had forgotten what happened or as if he had expected it to heal the way a body might have. Taft felt naked as Tanya with the water going over her feet. Scott still took out the key and opened the driver's door, which gave up its smell of oil and metal.

21

SCOTT WAS STILL trying to start the car when Taft went to the porch. With each twist of the key he would stomp the floorboard and hurl forward his entire body, yet it registered only the same strange empty click from the engine, followed by a continuation of field crickets. Tanya stayed in the passenger's seat, where she still had hold of herself with both arms, as if without warning the Corvette would shoot away like a rocket across the lane and the pastures and even the ridge in the distance, despite four flat tires. Clarice's yard was not large, and the grass was newly mown and damp, but the trip across it seemed to last long and the smell of the mown grass was sickening. Where in hell do you think you're going, Taft? demanded a whisper so coarse and hard he couldn't tell if it was Scott's or Tanya's. Where in hell do you think you're going? What in hell. Then

Clarice's door began to open, and their bodies flew out of the car like birds. Scott thudded down behind the car and stayed down, but Tanya just stood in the lane, balancing on one leg as if suddenly surrounded by water.

Clarice looked at Taft for at least fifteen seconds. Her hair was behind her ears again. Taft? she said. The television was on behind her, and the trailer smelled of perfume and cigarette smoke.

Taft stepped back a little, hoping she would see Tanya in the front yard. Scott's voice was hissing, *Tan*ya, Tan*ya,* from his place in the grass, but she ignored it and walked toward the porch instead, with both hands in her pockets. She had a mud streak, or maybe a grease streak from the Corvette engine, on one side of her forehead. Clarice, standing so the door blocked her body, as if she wasn't decent, saw her. She whispered, Is that your girlfriend?

Taft shook his head. He felt as if all that had happened had somehow changed him physically, and Clarice could tell.

Is that Tanya? said Clarice. She's cute.

Taft wondered what it might have felt like to be proud of her. Clarice opened the door but hurried back into the bedroom. Taft went inside first and a few seconds later Tanya followed, stooping down as if the ceiling were even lower. She was still mostly damp. She looked at herself in the mirror that hung over the television, cleaned the mud off her face, and then went to the pictures of Tony and Clarice. They were stacked up on the coffee table. Some of them had been taken out of their frames. The kitchen was full of boxes. Tanya didn't say anything.

In a minute Clarice came out wearing jeans and a flannel shirt. She was brushing her hair, and the brush crackled with static. Aint you going to introduce us, Taft? she said.

Taft had sat down on the couch. Beside it was a high school annual, opened to a page that said JUNIORS above the first row of black-and-white pictures. He was suddenly aware of the stinging burned places on his fingers. The cut on his lip had dried.

This is my aunt Clarice, said Taft.

Tanya smiled, but she didn't seem to want to talk.

That aunt stuff sounds too old, said Clarice. I like your hat.

I'm his aunt Tanya, said Tanya.

Clarice looked at her a long time as if it were true. She had been making little jerking movements Taft had never seen and had also developed a new habit of holding her lower lip between two knuckles. Taft thought it made her look confused. Oh, she said. She didn't ask any questions. Clarice went to the kitchen and got out bologna and bread and milk. She cleared them both places at the table. While Clarice's back was turned, Tanya went over every square inch of her several times, and then looked at Taft to show him she was still as angry as ever. Even after Clarice had the table set Tanya wouldn't sit down.

Sit down, Tanya, said Clarice.

I can't, said Tanya. I'm wet.

Clarice looked at Taft, who had not started his sandwich. She's wet? she said.

She fell in the river, said Taft.

Taft, Clarice said. You all ought to stay away from that river. It's dangerous. It don't matter, Tanya. You can sit down.

No, said Tanya.

You won't hurt nothing. Sit down. Clarice got her by the shoulders and made her sit. You *are* wet, she said. You are going to get sick. She seemed to size Tanya up. They would be too big, but I got some clothes you could wear.

It's all right, said Tanya.

In a minute we'll check, said Clarice. You're just a little thing, aint you? I used to be just like that. She sat down with them too, not eating, but watching them closely. Taft ate. He wished that they could sit here and eat and talk until winter and let Scott run away or die of exposure. Maybe it would all be over now that they were with Clarice. Maybe she could talk to Tanya. Clarice was easy to love. Taft didn't hate Clarice for sleeping with Gary. In a way, he was glad she had. It had pointed something out. Taft just wished his mother could see it. He wished it wasn't trapped with him. Clarice's bologna was delicious. He ate three sandwiches.

God, Taft, said Clarice on the third one. How do you stay so skinny? But she seemed glad because while she watched them eat she didn't know what to do with herself. She crossed her legs one way and the other and looked around. Finally Clarice trembled a little and stopped herself and said, I'm going to miss you, Taft.

Miss me?

I thought you knowed I was leaving.

Taft looked at her. No, he said.

Clarice nodded. Can't you tell? She motioned at the boxes

and then glanced at Tanya. Men don't notice nothing, do they, Tanya?

No, said Tanya. She stopped chewing and stared at Clarice, as if she would like to discuss it but couldn't. Then she started chewing again. She didn't eat the crust.

I'm going to get me another job, said Clarice. I'm tired of this one. I used to work in a nursing home. I think that's what I'd like to do.

Taft was trying to figure out something to say. He didn't want to say something a boy would say. He wanted to say something that had meaning, but he didn't know what. He felt as if he were losing everybody. But he guessed that was how it was. You did lose everybody. His mother had lost her father and she'd lost her husband. Now they had lost Moody, and other things, even Tanya and Gary, were coming apart too. Taft wished something could be done to stop it or at least slow it down, but it was the natural motion of the world. Taft could have said that to Clarice, but it wouldn't tell her what he wanted to tell her. The time for him to say something slipped by and it was gone. Clarice stood up to get them oatmeal cakes, and Tanya said Clarice's name as if she were trying out a foreign phrase.

Yes? said Clarice.

Tanya stared at her for a minute. Taft could still smell her. She smelled like algae and mustard with a dose of smoke. It reminded Taft of the snapping turtle. He could see that Tanya wanted to say something, but she was too mad and too hurt to say it, so she said, Is that your annual on the table?

Clarice changed. She laughed and looked away, but her laugh

was inviting. She seemed embarrassed and happy too. The annual had a thick red cover on it with silver letters. Before she could pick it up, Tanya asked her, Are you in there?

I am, said Clarice. But a lot different.

Show us, said Taft, but Tanya glanced at him as if he had gone too far. Show *me,* she said.

Is Taft's mother in there? Tanya asked, touching the pages, which had been written and drawn on.

Law no, said Clarice. She graduated way before me.

They both giggled. Tanya began to turn the pages of the annual, and Clarice began to comment on each.

Taft's mother was fairest of the fair, Tanya said.

How did you know that? Clarice asked.

Research, said Tanya. For a book I decided not to write.

Taft got up and looked out the window. He wondered if Scott, somewhere hunkered down in the weeds, could see him. But it was little pleasure. Clarice was still holding her yearbook. How come you all to come over here? she asked. I can't believe how you got all the way out here. I was feeling just kind of lackadaisy before you come. But I guess you done it because of Tony and all that. Aint that why, Taft? You didn't come out here just to see me, I mean.

Taft wanted to say that he did, but he could only shake his head.

You and Tony was real close. I knew that from day one. He looks like you in here. Look at it. He does, in the eyes.

Taft looked over their shoulders. Tony's ears were large with youth in the picture, but the rest of his face seemed far older.

Everyone, in all the rows of photographs, looked older than high school age. His mother had told him it was because people got older quicker then. Tony had on a white shirt with an enormous collar. It was evident that he had refused to smile. Instead, he seemed surprised, as if the photographer had cursed him back.

Hey, Tanya, said Clarice. Don't you think he looks like Taft?

God yes, she said, but Taft didn't think she looked at the right picture. Where is he right now?

He got in trouble, said Clarice.

Is that why you're leaving?

Sort of, Clarice said. I can't stay here no more.

They had both slid off the couch onto the shag carpet. Taft knew that when women got on the floor with pictures, it could be lengthy.

What did you say your last name was, Tanya? Clarice asked.

Mayes, Tanya said, as if it hurt.

Mayes. I don't think I graduated with no Mayes. What was your mother's name before she married?

She's dead, Tanya said. She looked straight at Taft.

Oh, said Clarice. I'm sorry.

What could we do tonight? said Tanya.

Do you want to do something, Taft? Clarice said.

I guess, said Taft.

Tonight is the fair, said Tanya. She laughed. Taft wanted to go.

Did you, Taft? I wisht we could go. We could go riding around. I used to go riding around. I can't though.

You can too, said Tanya.

I keep thinking I have to stay here, but I don't.

Let's go riding around, said Tanya, touching her on the arm.

Can you go, Taft? said Clarice.

Taft gave a shrug.

Let's go, Tanya. Let's go riding around.

In what? Tanya's face had wizened so that it looked especially cruel and beautiful, as if this was exactly what she wanted to hear.

In my car. Clarice put her hand on Tanya and drew back. You need dry clothes, she said. I forgot about you being wet. Why didn't you say something? She took Tanya into the bedroom and they started hunting for clothes. Taft heard their voices. You are so tiny, Clarice said. I used to be just like that. Then she said, Don't you come back here, Taft, and they giggled. In a few minutes she came back without Tanya.

She's cute, Clarice said.

Tanya came out with Clarice's clothes on. They were too big for her. It was strange to see her dressed up like Clarice. Clarice was already checking the stove to make sure it was off, and then she left the porch light on so they could see. It was going toward dusk. Before they got off the porch Clarice screamed and jumped back. Scott was standing on the stepping-stones about five feet away. He was hugging himself and shivering.

Look at what the cat drug in, said Tanya.

Ha ha ha, said Scott.

We're going riding around, Tanya said. You going with us?

Clarice still had Taft's arm in a death grip, but a giggly one that made her seem disturbed. Do you know him? she said.

No, said Taft, and she gripped harder.

He's all right, said Tanya. He can't help it if he's got behavioral problems. She wrapped one arm around him. Can we take him with us? Can we take him please?

22

GARY TOOK OFF his shirt and tied it around his face. He rammed the boat against the gravel bar as hard as he could and got out, shifted the body to one side, and laid a blue tarp from the boat down under it. Dozens of black beetles ran out. Then he went to the other side and pushed it over on the blanket. Other beetles ran out. Gary took hold of the corners of the tarp and carried it over and laid it in the bow of the boat. As he lifted it up higher over the edge of the boat and set it down, it creaked and shifted within. He could not believe how weightless the body was.

Gary stood on the gravel bar, which had already sucked his boots down far enough to fill them with water, and tried to figure it out. There was no way to know. Moody's boat had been found maybe three miles downriver. He looked all around for some reason but all he saw were the trees arching out from the banks on both sides and the thousands of tiny movements that made up the water. A tall yellow light filled the open space above its surface.

When he climbed back into the boat Gary became worried about the turtle. He had only unfastened the chain from the boat and thrown it into the water. Now it occurred to him that it could tangle her up and she would die, so he got back out on the gravel bar and hunted for the chain. It was a couple of feet underwater, but he reached it and pulled until he could see the turtle. The chain was wrapped around her middle several times, but he could see a piece of rope he figured was knotted on the underside. He took out his knife and unfolded it and put the handle in his teeth. He got down on his knees and pulled the turtle up on the gravel bar and it spun around in the sand and started digging in with its claws. He tried to hold the chain with one hand and grab the edge of its jagged shell with the other to turn it over, but one of the back legs got him in the wrist. Gary knew immediately that it was going to bleed good, because he saw the open white places and they turned pink, and then red, immediately, but he still flipped the turtle over. It looked like an alligator underneath with only a little cap of shell and big white muscles working furiously. He was sawing on the rope when it started to piss. The piss, which was very hot for a cold-blooded animal, struck him in the chest and the neck, but he kept sawing. The turtle was popping its jaws and hissing and the urine burned in his cuts and stank, but he got the chain loose. There, goddamn you, Gary said, flipping it over with a sound like a metal drum, and the turtle glided away beneath the water.

Gary looked at Moody. Who would have thought a turtle could piss like a horse? he said.

He took his shirt and wrapped it around his arm where the turtle had gotten him. He was wet from the waist down and the turtle piss clung to his bare skin like sap. For a while, Gary steered the boat around with Moody in the stern. Moody rode up and down with the current as one piece, instead of the many pieces of a living man. He still had a yellow pencil in one pocket, except the pocket had become part of him. They crossed the shoal of the fish traps, so shallow the boat scraped bottom for a second, and Gary saw the waving grass below him and the shadow of the boat on the sand with a school of fish squirting away. They rode around this way and the river began to look different with Moody in the boat. Gary began to see places he thought he would have liked to search, if Moody hadn't already been found. A form of gnat, millions of its individuals, emanated from his body. They were on Gary too and in spiraling cones in the light on the river.

As they rode, Gary thought for a long time about what to do with Moody. He didn't want to turn him over to Puss and his crew. Then Moody Myers would belong to them in a way. But he had to give him up. He didn't want to be like Bid, hiding James's grave for all those years. As the afternoon grew later he became more worried and frantic. He wanted to do the right thing.

He headed the boat up toward the Shelton bridge. On the way, he didn't pass anybody. As he came around each bend, he kept to the bank, in case he needed to duck into the trees.

But when he came to Mint Spring he saw a person standing

in the water. It was too late to hide. Gary decided to keep going and act natural. As he came closer he saw that it was a girl standing in the river. She had seen him, he could tell. She was standing about thigh deep in the water and she was almost naked except for her bra and panties. She was a kid. Gary didn't say anything but just stared straight ahead as he passed and she looked at him as if the river had created him. She never moved. Even after he was far away from her, she stayed still, looking at him and Moody, but Gary just plowed on.

He beached the boat under the Shelton bridge and got Moody rolled up the best he could in the blue tarp. He gave some thought to how he would prefer to be seen carrying the body if it came to that. It would be best to hold it like a baby instead of throwing it across his back. Gary climbed the bank up from the river and started down the road. Shelton was empty. It was always empty the minute the courthouse closed. Shirtless and covered with turtle piss and mud, trotting until he was winded, Gary headed down the sidewalk with Moody Myers in his arms. Not a single car passed. Above the town the chimney swifts were beginning their crazy evening flight.

Gary was out of breath when he got to the courthouse, but the front door was open. When he entered, creaking and popping across the floorboards, he could hear some kind of meeting going on in the courtroom, but it was a small meeting.

He had a sudden pang of fear, as if he were doing the wrong thing, but he didn't know what else to do. He set the body of Moody Myers down on the creaking floor in front of the glass cases. It was between a giant stump chewed by beavers and a stuffed redheaded woodpecker emerging from a log. Gary unrolled him from the tarp. The black beetles scattered again but quickly relodged. He wondered if he should say something or write it on a card. He thought for a long time and finally he said, We were part of the same family, and went back out of the courthouse into the dusk toward his boat.

23

THEY ALL HAD TO SIT in the front seat of Clarice's station wagon, because Tony had removed the back one to make a bench for his garage. From the right it was Taft, then Tanya, then Scott, and Clarice driving. Somebody could have gotten in the very back, where there was one or maybe a couple more bench seats, but that seemed too far away. There was plenty of room up front, Clarice had said. She was right. They weren't even crowded together. Taft wondered why Clarice had a station wagon. She didn't have a family. The dashboard before them was so large and so deep that Scott had propped his legs up on it and he was eating a bologna sandwich and drinking a Coke.

They hadn't even gotten out of the lane before they met another car. Tanya pushed Scott into the floorboard, spilling his Coke, and Taft got down too.

Oh my God, said Clarice.

The other car passed, but they stayed down.

Who was it? Taft asked.

Who do you think? said Clarice. Her face had turned reddish white. Brenda.

Tanya had gotten back up on the seat, as if she were not afraid. Are you turning around? she asked mildly.

After a minute Clarice said, No.

On the way to town, Tanya and Clarice did all the talking. Tanya had already told Clarice about her parents' divorce and her mother's drinking. Clarice listened without any change, as if she didn't remember that Tanya had said her mother was dead. At certain points in their conversation either Clarice or Tanya or both of them together would break out laughing, as if it were the funniest thing in the world, but Taft never could understand exactly what was so funny. He noticed that Clarice put on her brakes way, way before the curves and she steered as if the car might go off one of them at any unexpected moment.

I feel like doing something awful tonight, said Tanya.

Me too, said Clarice. She giggled.

Scott belched. He was staring up through the huge windshield and chewing his sandwich, but his eyes were fixed, as if seized by good fortune. He was unable to do more than nod.

The fair was visible from a long ways off. Taft remembered it. Even coming from Shelton there were places where the land dipped just right and the spoked circles and shapes of neon appeared as if a new and colorful city had just been erected in the country. Alexander County didn't have much of a fair. It was little, but it gave off a certain feeling of possibility.

That is so sad, said Clarice, looking at Moody's tower.

What, said Scott.

How Moody Myers is gone.

He's not gone, said Tanya.

How do *you* know? said Scott.

I saw him, said Tanya.

Where?

In the river. While I was standing in the river. He was in a boat.

I bet, said Scott, that you saw a lot of things.

Out on the new highway, closer to the neon, cars were lining up but not for the fair. The Maloy Drive-In was playing *As You Lick It,* and *The Tailblazers, A Frontier Story.*

I love Shakespeare, said Tanya. Don't you, Clarice?

Clarice laughed. Not really, she said.

I like that second one, said Scott.

Rescue-squad men with orange flashlights were helping people park in a big field for the fairgrounds. Taft knew they were the same men who had searched for Moody Myers for so long. They were the ones Tony had said didn't know how to drag a river. The grass was all mashed down. One man threaded among the cars with a huge green panda bear riding his shoulders. The panda's head flopped a little with each step. Clarice had to pay their way in. It embarrassed Taft because her money reminded him that he didn't have any, and what had they thought they would ever do without money? Tanya and Scott didn't seem to mind. They didn't even say thank you, and the way they walked in, almost running, was even more like children.

Tanya stopped for a minute and let Clarice catch up.

Taft's mother was fairest of the fair, she said.

I know it, said Clarice.

Do you remember it?

I remember.

What did she look like?

She was real pretty, said Clarice.

Taft has been here before, said Tanya.

Clarice turned to look at him. He has? You should have said something, Taft. We could have went somewhere else.

I love you, Clarice, Tanya said.

I love you too, honey, said Clarice. She pushed Tanya's hair back out of her eyes.

The fair had an exhibit barn and the rides. There was a dirt field where they had demolition derbies. Taft remembered what Tanya had said this spring about how she loved the smell of the fair and he kept watching her nostrils to see if he could sense any pleasure. Mainly the smell was of the crowd, its cigarettes and perfume, the food it carried and its clothing and hair and feet, but in places was the smell of animals, of their urine and dung and fried onions, of cotton candy, grease, engines, the smell of wood shavings and milk both sour and sweet, and surrounding it all a greater atmosphere of the ground on a fall night and the penetration of the ground into the air itself as if all were one entire substance. They entered the exhibit barn in the softness of sawdust and they saw the beehive under glass and the array of colored jellies and the samples of pole beans and pickled okra and subtle gradations of eggs. They witnessed the best hands of tobacco, its finest ground leaves, the long red, and in one corner the biggest pumpkins grown this year in Alexander County. The pumpkins were warty and distended with size. Clarice had taken to holding Taft and Tanya by the hands. At first her hand had felt good, but the longer it clung to him the more confining it became.

They took to riding the rides. At first Taft rode too. He rode the Ferris Wheel with Clarice and it lifted them up above the whole dark country with the people milling around below them. Look it, Taft, said Clarice. She pointed at the moon, which had come up above the horizon as yellow as an old tooth. Then Tanya had to ride the Tilt-A-Whirl over and over, so long that a look of pacified bliss came on her face as if she were asleep, but it was an excited sleep. Taft couldn't figure it out. She had said she wanted to do something awful tonight. Was this the best she could do? Finally he let her get separated from him in the line and she went on again as if she hadn't noticed he was gone.

Scott grabbed him by the shoulder.

Piss break, Taft. Piss break.

They went over toward the rest rooms, which were in a little cinderblock building. There was a line. I got to piss like a racehorse, said Scott, hopping in place. They ran around to the back of the building. Behind a little grassy strip beneath the slotted back windows, through which light came and the sounds of men talking and coughing and shuffling and flushing, the wilderness began. The wilderness owned by the mines circled the town. Scott went to one place and Taft to another. Another cinderblock house a short distance away held the women. It had a longer line.

Taft was poking around waiting for Scott when he noticed the path. It cut back under a big hackberry tree. He went a little ways down it and came back. It reminded him of finding the old road with Gary.

There's a path over here, he told Scott.

To where?

I don't know, said Taft.

Scott came over, zipping his pants with great effort. They went on a ways and the path just got better and better. It was a little thin at first through some sedge grass, but it widened up and got to where it had a packed dirt surface. Even when they got almost out of range of the light of the fair it was easy to stay on the path. They went through some woods and then it opened up into a field and the path curved among some big rocky sinkholes and kept going.

Well, goddamn, said Scott. Wonder where we're at?

I don't know, said Taft.

They stood for a second and listened to the music of the fair and looked for its glow. Taft was glad to be out here. He was afraid Scott might decide to go back. He thought of Tanya on the ride. She was like an animal in the zoo when it does the same motion over and over in the cage. When he was with her, and everything she was doing was unpredictable, he felt distant, but when he was away from her, and he could go over the things she had done, he felt near again. The field they were standing in and even the black dome of the sky seemed to speak of her.

Listen, said Scott.

They listened. Gradually Taft began to hear a sound like water. They went on down the path and the sound seemed to grow louder. Then the path lowered into a marshy place and there were dewberry sawbriars and animals that scampered away from them. Taft saw the trees ahead had light in them, something like the light of the fair, and at first he was sure the path had simply doubled back on the fairgrounds from a different angle, but when they came up through the trees they were in a broad open place full of a kind of shifty light.

The first thing Taft saw was a penis. The penis was taller than a silo. Then the light changed, and with it came the sound of skin sliding together.

Goddamn, said Scott. It's the Maloy.

The field before them was dotted with cars beneath the big screen, which seemed to angle toward them, and the beam of movie light was emerging from a white building off to one side. The skin was sliding together. It was a lapping sound like water, issuing softly all around from the speakers on the cars. Taft and Scott didn't say much else. They were like wilderness explorers, like Lewis and Clark when they reached the Pacific. The light colored, then sank, and then rose again. Scott's eyes had black shadows under them so that it seemed almost as if he were wearing a woman's makeup. He could have been watching a fistfight or a race. His whole body began to quiver, urging the people on.

Seeing the naked bodies in action was different from seeing them in one of Scott's books. No pose lasted very long and there was no dignity of stillness. Taft regretted that there were men too. Fortunately, they were only naked briefly, if at all. Part of the time they did not even take off their clothing, and sometimes it was just two or three women together, under the clever guise of teaching one another about the ways of love. The movie had bluegrass music. A man and woman were in the woods. Except it was not really the woods, but a picture of trees and vines with some turf on the floor. The man was wearing a fringed shirt and coonskin cap, and the woman had on a long dress. Huge shadows changed across the field as scenes changed on the screen. In seconds they were fucking away again. It just took seconds. Taft tried to walk out a ways into the field where he would be alone with it, and now it began to seem more realistic and less comical.

Hey, buddy, said a man's voice only a few yards away. You'd make a hell of a door.

But not much of a window, said another.

The field was full of people. They were visible during the brighter scenes of the movie, sometimes even their eyes. Some sat on buckets or some just in the weeds. A few cigarettes glowed. Some of the shadows were really shadows and not people, but it was hard to tell. Taft tried to crouch down in some briars. Scott had crouched also, frozen in the ready position, but neither of them ran. Giggles rippled across the field like wind, but the people were too far away for Taft to tell what they were laughing at.

Taft stood back up on his achy knees. Afterward, he always wondered what had made him stand up. It was almost as if something lifted him up, not something physical, but maybe a feeling or a spirit. Taft knew early, perhaps before anyone, that he had to run. He just didn't know which way. What was remarkable was not the sound, because there was no sound. Like that moment when a person gasps in the midst of his talking, just before he begins to laugh or cry or shout, the movie and all the speakers and everyone in the cars fell silent. There was only the hum of the vent shaft at the mines. At first it seemed like part of the movie. But its picture began to totter forward, creasing in the middle, and then jerked backward as if pulled and completely disappeared in a flume of something like cool vapors, all iridescent with movie light. For an instant the vast colorful image of a naked couple, twisting rhythmically together, was projected onto a thicket of cedar trees across the highway, and then the image was obscured by coils of red dust, blowing over everyone as if from a great door shutting.

The silence was followed by one scream and then a mass of screams. It seemed to open up something in Taft's heart too. His first thought was that he wished Moody were here to observe this. He was elated to think that he had witnessed such a thing himself. Then a lightness began in his feet and fled straight up his legs into his groin and the knots of his intestines even as he tried to run. It was all the kind of running done in dreams, the hopeless kind. He started out toward the highway, which seemed safer than the woods, and he thought he heard Scott going the opposite way, but he kept on. Then something split open like a great ripping cloth, and the snack bar dropped front first in a smattering of sparks and Taft clearly heard someone say, Well, it was good while it lasted, and in its spot there was an open place, not a fall or a crash, but only an open place more terrible than any sound.

For a short time, which lasted long, Taft didn't have much of anything except his thoughts. He assumed he was falling as the screen and the snack bar had, but he didn't know because his eyes had closed with a stinging crust. He had his hearing, but it seemed to be filling up grain by grain with a quietude. When everything stopped moving he was left only with the smell of rocks broken open, which was a violent smell, exactly like the one deep in Moody's tunnel, and Taft wanted to leap up and shout and tell Moody what had happened and that he understood. He understood the language Moody had found in his dream.

But he must not have been very deep. He must not have been deep enough, because he forgot. He forgot the language. It had seemed deep to him, but it must not have been. Presently he began to hear car engines revving, revving and roaring and softly spinning their tires, and as he forgot, in his mind he fastened the sound together with forgetting. The sound grew stronger and nearer with his forgetting, and he listened to the wheels of the cars as a sick person might in falling asleep.

It was not until they uncovered his face, and someone put smelling salts under his nose and the scent went through him like an electric shock, that Taft realized he had been buried. Someone had hold of his head and was trying to jerk him out, saying, Lookie, lookiehere what I got. But he wouldn't budge, and somebody else was cautioning the first man not to pull too hard or something might pull off.

Its nose is broke, said the first man. Lookie how its nose is broke. And another one said, You busted it with the shovel, smartass. They were still pulling. They pulled harder and harder, closer and closer together, and at last they gave one big heave that seemed to come not from above but from beneath him instead and Taft spilled out in a splash of dirt and little gravels. They were sticking sticks in his nose to get out the dirt and somebody reached into his mouth and Taft felt the fingers on his tongue, pulling out dirt, and he tried to breathe and spit.

A man's voice said, I bet he's paralyzed, or worse. Taft, however, wasn't afraid. He knew there was something he had to tell all these people. The biggest fireman lifted him by the arms and shook him a little and set him on his feet. Taft was wobbly but he stood. He could walk fine except for some soreness. He felt like he had been busted in the face with a basketball.

You'll feel worse tomorrow, said the fireman who had picked him up. He seemed disappointed.

He tried to answer them, but he had too much dirt in his mouth for them to understand at first. The dirt was sweet and gritty. It was in his eyes too. Taft looked around him at the new world. He was near the bottom of a great hole. He couldn't see the top or the stars for the red dust. He saw now that the hole wasn't as deep as he had hoped. It was just barely deep enough for the movie screen to stand in, but the screen wasn't standing, and was folded in on itself like a book instead. There were, however, smooth boulders and steep sides, and one small steamy geyser shooting out in a corner where it was dark. Spotlights were shining down from the rim, and Taft could see them hoisting people to the top on ropes. Several cars tried to drive up the sides of the hole, but they kept sliding back down.

One fireman had a long, metal rod. Taft heard him say, That there is the only one we found buried. He was the only buried boy.

Taft went over to examine the geyser and he found that it was coming from the radiator of a Pontiac that had landed on its roof. The windows had all been smashed out. This corner smelled of sassafras roots and disturbed soil. Taft went all around the hole picking his way through the people and cars. Way up top the firemen were dropping down ropes to hoist people up.

Taft looked at his rope a long time before he grabbed it. A sudden fear came over him, and he had to touch each part of his body to make certain he still felt it. He had thought his nose was running, but when he touched it it was blood. Otherwise he couldn't feel his face. He closed his eyes as they pulled him up smoothly, closer and closer to the enormous red halo of dust and light, and he was surprised that the top still smelled of popcorn and grass. He looked back down at the broken ground, spilling down the sides in rivulets and noticed that his tennis shoes were missing, and his pockets, even his shirt pocket and his jacket pockets, were completely filled with dirt.

Tanya came up and carefully got some of the blood from his face on the ends of her fingers as if testing it for thickness.

We thought you were *dead,* she said rapturously.

As if he didn't know that, said Scott.

Clarice looked as if she would cry. Taft, she said. Oh God, Taft.

Taft had thought something had busted his eardrums, but when Clarice grabbed him against her dirt came out of his ears and he could hear well again.

We heard it, said Tanya. It was like the end of the world. She had her arms outstretched. Just a big cloud of dust.

That's what he gets, said Scott, for looking at a movie like that.

Clarice panicked. She made Taft get in the back of the station wagon, which she had parked on the side of the highway. He's mine, she told the firemen. As they drove, she kept saying, Oh God. He's mine. Oh God, Taft. Tanya told her that she thought he would live, as if that were too bad. I got some of his blood, she said. I got some of his blood right here. Are you still alive, Taft?

Taft said that he was. Most of all he wanted to talk to Moody Myers. He wanted to pick up his notebook and read the whole thing, because now he would understand it. How bad is my nose busted? Taft asked.

Scott turned around and hung over the seat.

Awful damn bad, he said.

It's not that bad, said Tanya. You might look better. Hey, Taft, the entire town burned to the ground. We watched it. Everybody is dead.

Now that *is* true, Scott said. I seen it myself.

Sure enough, there was nothing to be seen outside the headlight beams. Not one house, if houses still existed, had a single light burning, except an infrequent flashlight or a lantern someone was carrying. The air all over town stank of smoke, but there didn't seem to be any fire. Taft thought of Mr. James telling about Washington, D.C., and the missiles coming out of holes that opened in the ground. We're bringing it all on ourselves, he had said.

I reckon, said Scott, that was a act of God if I ever seen one.

It's a wonder, said Clarice. It's a thousand wonders.

We just forgot how powerful God is, is what we done, said Scott.

Man is the problem, Scott, said Tanya.

No it aint done it, said Scott. It's woman.

Tanya tried to spit on him, but he acted like he wanted her to, so she quit.

You all hush, said Clarice. You don't realize. Driving slowly, it took her forever to reach the Shelton bridge. All the lights were on at the courthouse, and a crowd had gathered, but Clarice drove past them to the river.

Pull over, said Tanya. Pull over right here. Wash him off.

Clarice pulled over as if she were incapable of thinking for herself. Where? she said. Where?

Right down here, said Tanya. We can wash him off. We can wash him off before we take him home.

Clarice stopped the car in a gravel spot next to the river and ran around to the back tailgate and tried to swing it open, but it was locked. Taft watched her frantic face through the glass. Unlock it, Taft, she said. Unlock it!

He didn't want to. Taft didn't want to be washed off. He wanted to stay just like this. He wanted it to stay dark too, because he was afraid to see his face. He wanted it to stay just like this forever, but Tanya had climbed over the seats into the back with him and they were swinging open the tailgate. He heard cars above them, passing over the bridge. Clarice was giving instructions to Scott, whom she had by the collar.

Make him get in the water, she said, and Scott started leading him toward the bank. He got ready to shove Taft into the shallow water, but they heard Clarice call, No, make him take his clothes off first.

And you bring them to us, said Tanya.

Taft heard Tanya giggle, and then Clarice did too. Taft heard the water too and felt cold whirls of air lifting up from it. He was happy to be on top of the ground with all the sounds. But he was afraid. A pressure was building up inside his head, and it was so cool it seemed to be made of ice. He was hurt worse than they thought.

He said he aint taking nothing off until you do, Scott called back. Taft laughed and he felt blood start down his nose again. It tasted sweet and metallic. I did not, he said.

Shut the fucking hell up, said Scott.

Tanya's voice answered, Okay, and they were both laughing again.

Taft remembered how freely she had taken off her velvet dress in the daylight. All he could see were the lights of cars passing over the river bridge. The damp night, nearly empty of insects, made him shiver. I aint taking your clothes off, big boy, said Scott. Then they both heard the weeds moving near them, and giggling again, and Tanya said, Okay, again, from a little distance out in the water.

Goddamn, said Scott.

Tanya was laughing as if she could see. They heard her say something to Clarice, who was evidently still on the bank, and then she threatened, I'm coming back, and Taft felt then as if he absolutely did not want that to happen, and evidently Clarice felt the same way because he heard her make a sound that human beings only make when they step into cold running water. Clarice's voice, the shriek she made when the water touched her, before she could bury herself inside it, did not seem to belong to her. Taft was afraid it had something to do with the burn on her leg. He was afraid the river would infect it.

I see two chickens, said Tanya, and she started making noises like a chicken and flapping her arms in the water.

Scott had gone around to a different spot to try and see better. Taft hesitated, and just as he pulled his shirt off both of the girls laughed. If he could just get into the water. Taft was afraid he would get hard, the way he had under Tanya's mother. Knocking his toes on the rocks, Taft felt his shins turn to iron before he got into the water over his waist. The water seemed to suck in his breath for him and then it was up to his neck and his body went light, so light and cold he didn't seem to have a body at all. The water brushed all over him, and it seemed to be carrying tiny electric shocks. Tanya and Clarice were splashing. He noticed they stayed a ways away.

Are you washing the dirt off, Taft? said Tanya, and she threw something at him.

Directly they heard a big splash that could only have been Scott, but he didn't answer when they called.

Taft tried his best to see Clarice and Tanya, but all he could make out were two forms. They were far enough out to float and move with the current, which was bringing them gradually nearer.

I hope this is finally the end of the world, said Tanya. She was near enough to Taft for him to see her face.

Tanya, said Clarice.

He can't see anything, she answered. Can you, Taft? The water is the same thing as clothes. It's even more than clothes. See? She was close enough for Taft to feel her breath, which smelled of some kind of candy from the fair. Tanya put her arms around Taft and then he thought she put even her legs around him and he was holding her against the current. See? she said.

Tanya, said Clarice.

Tell us, Taft, said Tanya, what it's like to be buried.

Were you scared? said Clarice.

Taft's teeth chattered. He reached out and put his arms around Tanya and his finger, he thought, fit right into her rib cage, and he felt the water pulling at her. No, he said. Were you?

I was, said Clarice. God, I still am.

Not me, said Tanya. I figured if he's gone, he's gone. That's the law of nature.

But wouldn't you be sad?

It wouldn't mean anything if I was.

Yes it would, said Clarice.

Tanya was kissing over Taft's face. He wished he could feel it, but he was still numb. She was probably getting blood in her mouth, but she kept kissing, more gently than he had ever thought she could kiss. The ice in Taft's head had solidified, and now it was threatening to crack his skull. The stars were sailing around. This all seemed to have happened a long time ago, and he was straining to bring back the memory. Tanya climbed slowly out on the bank and lay down in the mud. Taft came out too. His body was the heaviest it had ever been in his life. It was as if gravity pushed him down with her in the mud.

We have to go to our other plan, Taft, she said, kissing him on his face again, and Taft wished so much that he could feel this.

24

BRENDA SAID SHE just wanted to ride in a boat. That was all. She had walked down through her mama's field to the river and she was standing on the bank waiting when Gary came past. He had put his shirt back on, but it had streaks of blood across the front.

Am I interrupting something, Gary? she said.

Gary tried to position the boat so she wouldn't get wet climbing in. Brenda was saying that she wanted to feel how boats feel, the way they stick solid yet slip around slipperier than air, but Gary thought she was lying. He tried to clean off the front bench for her. He was afraid there could be black flakes of flesh or sour gnats, and he wished the hull of the boat wasn't full of rotten leaves.

No, he said.

No what?

No, you're not interrupting me. He was attempting to smile.

Brenda wouldn't let him help her into the boat. She climbed in over the front and perched like a bird. She held on and Gary gave a hard push and the gravel scraped beneath the boat. Once they were out on the water he saw she was scared. She was craning her neck and scanning both banks.

I know where Taft is, she said.

Where is he?

I saw him. Her body eased when she said that. I saw him a little while ago.

What was he doing?

I don't have to know everything, she said. I don't. It's okay.

You don't, Gary said.

But Brenda's hands were trembling. Gary stared at her in the front of the boat. He couldn't believe she was there. About a thousand times while he was out searching he had imagined it and some of the time he had talked to her as if she were present. Brenda's hair had gotten longer and she had it pulled back in a ponytail. From her face and her eyes he could see that she loved the boat. She loved feeling the banks pass and the barns turn slowly with the trees and the place they had started from growing smaller and smaller. The water beneath them had its smooth spots and its tough humps of current. Brenda held on to the sides of the boat.

He's going to find out, she said.

Find out what?

A lot of things. There are a lot of things he is going to find out. What can we do about that?

Not a thing, Gary said.

Brenda let herself slump back farther in the boat. She began to smile. Where are we going? she asked.

Gary stopped poling and sat down. The boat started to wheel in slow broad circles. It was beyond dusk, but the sky still had its color. It seemed as if the river were headed toward it, a big wing of red orange behind the black trees. Then the boat would wheel slowly around and the other, darker side of the sky took over. Gary hoped Brenda couldn't see how dirty he was. He had gotten some mud out of one ear. Finally he said, Nowhere.

Brenda looked at him. I mean what were you going to do?

Before I saw you?

Before you saw me.

I was going to go on down a ways and stop for the night.

Where?

I got a place fixed.

There was one blue star out. The side of the sky without the sunset came around again, and now the moon was rising, a big one. It had just gotten above the trees.

Then do that, she said. Brenda was letting one finger trail in the water. I want to see it.

When they got to the island the end of Brenda's ponytail was wet. It had little leaves, the kind from the willows, in it too. Gary got wet up to the thighs getting out. It was deeper than he remembered. Brenda laughed. When he got the boat beached she stepped out in the silt and looked at his tent and the big trees behind it. She was holding on to a grapevine.

I don't forgive you, she said.

Gary walked up the bank away from her a little. He picked

up a flat rock and skipped it out into the river. It was nearly dark, but he thought he heard it skip six or seven times.

I don't, Brenda said.

She had one foot on the front of Gary's boat, and she gave it a push, tender at first, and then harder, until it went free. Gary started to walk toward her, but he stopped. The boat wobbled and began to turn, as if it were surprised at its own joyful lightness. It had gone a long ways before Brenda turned around.

I will always be grateful to the National Endowment for the Arts for generous support of this book. Without Paul Cody, Michael Koch, and Kathy Pories, it would never have been published. Without my father, my mother, my sister, and my wife, Eugenia, it would never have been written.